*To my parents. Without them, nothing.*

# Table of Contents

# A Diet of Worms

# Supreme Commander

When we were little kids, we kept our toys in a corner of my sister's room. She mostly played in a dollhouse, with figurines. I played in it, too. With GI Joe's.

There were hinges on the dollhouse and a snap. It opened like a suitcase. There was furniture inside, little wooden cupboards, and bookshelves with tiny books. There were rugs on the floor and pictures on the walls. It was a nicer house than we lived in.

My sister bounced the figurines around. Her and her friend Alexis, they bounced them down the dollhouse halls. They were always on their way to a party, the figurines. A Movie Award, or something. One'd ask, "How do I look?" And the other said, "Super cute!" My sister and Alexis discussed what the dolls would do and then made them do it.

I played war.

I had a paper bag full of soldiers and I put snipers in the top-floor windows, infantry at the front door, all the rifles pointing out, waiting. I didn't have enemy soldiers, like Taliban dolls. My soldiers spent a lot of time on guard. "Snipers, keep your eyes on the closet door. Infantry, get ready to chuck grenades under the bed and don't shoot until the enemy's in the open." I snapped the house shut and left it on top of the dresser. The longer I waited the more I felt the soldiers getting nervous, squeezing their fists. I watched them through the little windows, the tips of their guns poking out the way insects poke their feelers from cracks in the wall and it's almost like they're touching you. Who gave a shit about Checkers! My men were mine. They were *me* in there. It sort of drove me nuts looking at the house and waiting. I flexed and twitched until finally I had to jump up and scream, "They're coming they're coming!" I punched the pillow because it was an enemy and when he rolled me off my sister's bed and got on top of me I yelled *Shoot!* and my soldiers lit him up.

My mother was down the hall singing in the kitchen. She'd have just come back from Diaconia, which is bible study for serious Christians.

This is the day that the Lord has made
You should rejoice and be glad in it
This is the day, this is the day
This is the day that the Lord has made

I used my dad's soldering iron to cook off infantrymen's arms. My sister's nail polish was blood pouring from the stumps.

When my mother was a kid a vein broke inside her skull. A scar from the surgery, all fat and pale, runs from her temple into her dark, curly hair. Now she can't smell. When I burned off the soldiers' arms my mother couldn't smell it if the whole house was creamy with smoke. I cooked off arms and legs and got nail polish out of my sister's drawer. There were five bottles, all the same blood color.

The cap was glued shut. I put the bottle between my knees and turned with both hands. It wouldn't open. I practically tore all the skin off my fingers. I knocked the cap against the dresser. "Larry, what are you doing?" My mother can't smell but she can damn sure hear.

"Nothing, ma. Playing."

"Don't touch your sister's stuff."

"I'm not. Just sing and leave me alone."

Finally, the bottle opened. I was next to the dollhouse and the red polish splattered against one of the walls and onto the floor. My mom heard it like a bat. She could *see* what happened. She stomped down the hall.

"Your sister's going to kill you. You destroyed her stuff! What's all this smoke? Is that your father's tool? Good lord! It's burn black what on earth is all over it?"

Mom's alright. She never hit me. She didn't even yell. When I did something I wasn't supposed to, like splash nail polish on my sister's dollhouse, she sat me down to talk. She'd tell me she's disappointed and ask me questions, like didn't I know I shouldn't do that, or why'm I so angry all the time.

My dad did both, screamed and hit. He was a fireman, he cursed. He screamed like his voice hurt to come out. Like it was gas or something. I was only better behaved around my dad because I didn't feel like doing anything. He made me nauseous.

After I spilled the nail polish I wasn't allowed in the dollhouse anymore. I didn't care too much. But it was a good fort for my guys.

There was a Barbie doll in the toy corner, too. Sometimes I pulled her clothes off and looked at her tits. There was nothing between her legs, just smooth plastic. I licked her.

See? I didn't play with girls' toys the way girls do. That's the difference. It matters *how* you play with things. Like the first time I dressed up. I did it because of a boner. You'll see.

I went through the chemistry set and board games and crap nobody cares about. I do the same at the fridge, even when I'm not hungry, just stand at the open door staring at salad dressing and slimy meet. One time I went in my sister's room and knelt down by the toys and found Barbie. I took her clothes off and started sucking the bumps on her chest.

"What're you doing in here, stupid? Get out!" That's how my sister talked to me. She took after my dad and I took after my mother. Alexis was with her. "What're you holding? God Alexis, you're lucky you don't have a fartknocker brother."

"Hey Le Perv. Why're you in here with the lights off? Huh, weirdo?" Alexis's hair was brown like new deck wood. It was long and curled and always moving. She brushed away ribbons of hair from her cheek.

Alexis lived around the corner. Our back yards were connected. She was a real bitch. Eleven years old and she was already hot. Grown men liked her. My dad's friends, even. "You're gonna be a heartbreaker," they said. Or, "If I was twenty years younger, my god." Everyone said things like that. So she started acting bitchy. I had a crush on her. I called her

Sexy Lexy. I was only seven. I didn't understand the feelings she gave me in my guts. Like tapping a wet tambourine. I got a hard-on looking at her. I couldn't help it. It was embarrassing as hell. I tucked my pin behind my leg. I walked around hunched over like I was carrying a cannon ball. Even now, it points to the right from getting stuck behind my leg for ten years. It's grown like a root around a fence post. Lexy watched out for it when I hung around. "Le perv," she called me.

"I have to pee," I lied if it showed through my pants. I get a hard on when I have to pee.

Lexy's boobs stuck out like pickle tops, hard and shiny, like Barbie's, I imagined. I got sick when I saw her. I didn't know about whacking off. Kids should be taught how to whack off instead of forcing them to tuck their hard-ons away, so when they figure it out, the correct grip, the right speed and angle to yank it, it won't be one-more-thing to be embarrassed about.

"Look at his curly blonde hair. His eyelashes are long like wings," said Lexy.

"I wish I had his nose," my sister complained. "All small. And eyes big like a baby's." My sister had a honker, oily and covered with black heads. You didn't notice the pimples too much because there were four thousand freckles on her face. Her face always looked dirty.

I hid the doll down my pants.

"Let's pull his hair back," Sexy Lexy said. "It's long enough for a French braid."

"I'll get Bobbie pins. Or would barrettes look better," my sister circled around back of me. I shoved Barbie all the way down my jeans, into my crotch.

"Definitely barrettes."

They went in like teeth, the barrettes, pinning down fistfuls of twisted hair. My scalp was on fire. I fidgeted like hell.

"Okay. Let's put a dress on. Or do we want him in a skirt?"

"I won't wear a skirt," I said.

"I'll give you a hug," Sexy Lexy said. "If you wear the skirt for an hour I'll give you a hug for one minute."

An hour is a long time to wear a skirt. But I thought carefully about it. I'd be in my house. I could watch TV. I didn't even have to look at myself. It was only cloth on my skin and powders and colors on my face. Who cares! Now think about a minute. Like if you're at a red light. Or when you stick your hand in a cooler full of ice and water digging for the last can of Coke. A minute is a long time. Sixty seconds hugging Sexy Lexy. Her hair falling over my face. Her pickle tops pressing against me.

My pin started climbing up my jeans.

I put my arms out. My hug would be paid up front! "And I get to count," I added. But Lexy took a close look and a light broke inside her.

"Le Perv! You dirty freaking pig!"

"It's not that," I cried. "It isn't me! Look." I pulled Barbie from my pants.

"God Larry, you're *nasty*," my sister said. "She's naked! What's *wrong* with you, ugh!" She snatched Barbie from my hands and chucked her into the toy corner. She landed upside down, legs apart.

Barbie smiled like she was in on it, planning her assault on the General of the GI Joe's. Supreme Commander of Fort Dollhouse. "That'll teach you to suck toy tits!"

They put purple powder on my cheeks and brown powder on my eyebrows and black grease on my lashes. Lexy had a tube of lipstick in her handbag. She twisted her hands. A red cone poked out. She swiped it across her lips. "Kiss," she said, and puckered. Lexy smeared my lips red. Her spit was mixed in with the lipstick. I could feel it wet-cold and when she finished smearing me I had a real boner.

"Put the skirt on, Le Perv."

I went to my room to change and to be left alone with my pin. I let it snap back from behind my leg. I touched myself for a while. It wasn't whacking off. It was more like the way you rub a cramp.

"Hurry up. It doesn't take that long to change."

They showed me to my mother. She thought I was adorable. "You'd make such a pretty girl, Larry. Such a lovely girl. Larraine! Yes? That's what we'll call you."

When my mother started saying *lovely* and calling me Larraine I felt worse than before. I guess I'm sensitive, like my dad said after he joked around and called me names and I got mad. I could go from feeling happy and safe to feeling angry and sad pretty quickly.

"Your father's coming home any minute," my mother said later. "You better get him out of that get-up."

"Can we keep the barrettes in at least," my sister asked. "He's got such soft curly cue's."

"Okay. But get everything else off him. Wash your face, Larry. Don't let your father see anything."

Nothing good comes from dressing up. I'm telling you. It only causes problems. You'll see. Even if you're doing it for a good reason. You'll see.

# The Tourniquet and the Tea Cup

Things happen and it's not always your decision, like every perfect asshole says. My guidance counselor at Huntington High School tells me all the time, "It's your decision, Larry. You can achieve anything. You can be whatever you want to be." I tell him I don't want to be anything. Like not a doctor or a politician or someone. I'll be a house painter, or a clammer in the Long Island Sound, or a fireman at Huntington Manor.

"That's fine. There's nothing wrong with that," he says. "You can be anything. The president if you want. You can be a billionaire. It's up to you," as if I'm Luke Skywalker and making decisions was magic. You have to want to be a president or a billionaire. I wasn't born like that. I'm a low life, or something.

Not everything is your decision. You could drive down a street on your way to the Fireman's Fair and a guy could blow a stop sign and smack into your car. And your mom's pregnant. Your father jumps out of the car and beats the guys face in. That happens to people. Nobody decides. Not even god. I won't start talking about him. I can go for hours. Everybody can talk about god for hours.

I want to tell you about my best friend a few years ago, Joey Nailati. His family moved to my neighborhood when we were in elementary school. But we didn't become best friends until the summer before eighth grade. It's weird to tell about how it happened but I'm going to anyway. I'm going to talk about everything.

I wasn't allowed to play video games at home. My father was sick and he was always watching TV, just lying on the couch and watching. Also, we didn't turn on the air conditioner because my dad wasn't working. It was only my mother working and we couldn't pay the bills. We kept a fan pointing at him while he was on the couch all day.

I went to Joey's to stay cool. It was summertime. And I went to play video games. We'd been through seventh grade together. We sort of got close from the hazing in Junior High. That's something that'll make people better friends, going through things like that. My mother has a friend she met in church. They're real tight because both their babies died. Getting hazed isn't as bad, but still.

In Junior High you're supposed to meet new people, kids from other schools and other parts of town you'd never been to. It's part of your education to become socialized. But you end up keeping the same friends from elementary school. That's how it was for us, at least. We stuck together out of fear, like zebra.

Mostly Joey and I stayed inside playing video games. Nobody made us go out and play. Both his parents worked and didn't get sick. Joey had an older brother but he wasn't around, he drove their father to the train station in the morning then went to the old neighborhood, to the private beach and all his friends, where they used to live.

All summer we had the house to ourselves.

When we went outside it was to hang out in the garage at the end of Joey's driveway. It was filled with old furniture, bike frames, junk I can't even name, crap left over from the people who lived there before: old cassettes, beach chairs, a rake, spider webs. Nobody'd been in the garage for about twenty years besides me and Joey. There was a loft above the garage.

If you wanted to get into the loft you had to climb onto a cobwebby tool bench covered in dust. From there, Joey made a ladder.

Joey was pretty smart. Not smart, tricky. He had all these tricks that took imagination. Stuff I wouldn't think of. Like the ladder he made from shims. Shims are splintery wood wedges that prop up shingles, or hold studs in place while you hammer them. They're junk wood, if you don't know. Joey stapled them together and tied string all around them. It wasn't meant to be a real ladder, more like a hand getting through the door in the loft's floor. If you were dumb enough to put all your weight on it, good luck, you'd fall and break your ankle. He poured rubber cement around the fort's door and stuck glass from broken wine bottles in it. If you didn't know where to put your hands, the glass mutilated your fingers.

It was only 150 degrees when you climbed inside. The air was peppery. Dust rolled in the sunlight slanting through a tiny window. There was a light bulb hanging on a hook in the I-beam, and a little fan stirred the heat. The place smelled like horseshit. Dark places smell like horseshit for some reason. I was once on the subway in New York City. My mother went to see a specialist after a guy crashed his car into us. She was pregnant. I don't know which subway it was but this one we were in, the station smelled like horseshit. I went with her while my dad was working. This was before he got sick.

"It stinks down here." I kept telling my mother the subway stunk. She was all nervous and looking at a map in the center of the platform with a red circle on it showing where you were. She put one finger on the circle then followed a blue vein along the map. She put her finger on another subway station we were going to. I hadn't even seen the city yet because the Long Island Rail Road dives under the river between Long Island, where I lived, and New York City, where the specialist was, and shoots through a tunnel into a giant bunker. That's Penn Station. You walk to a subway, get on a smaller train, get off at a new station to wait for one more train and *that* station smells like horseshit. Meanwhile, you haven't even seen any skyscrapers.

"God, ma. It stinks. When's the train gonna come?" She wouldn't answer me. She walked over to the tracks and looked both ways but there was only a black hole where the train should be. Then she looked at the map again. The thing about that black hole is the longer you look at it, your eyes adjust, and it gets brighter. You think a train is coming so you keep staring like a moron, just standing still and listening. When the train finally comes everybody gets excited because they've been staring so long and going crazy and they push you out of the way even if you're pregnant or just a kid.

"It smells like horse shit," I said. I wasn't allowed to curse. This was a long time ago when I was much younger. I'd never cursed in front of her before. My dad had a fireman's mouth and I cursed as much as he did when I was around people my age. I said *horseshit,* I guess, so she'd talk to me and not keep checking the map.

She smiled but she had this fat tear ready to drop from her eye. She said, "No Larry, I can't smell."

It's called anosmia. I'd forgotten about that, her not smelling anything. And it wasn't an insignificant fact, like a birthday or something. She had a *disability*! We joked about it all the time. Like if the cat pissed the rug and the den stunk like ammonium. We'd go, oh man, you're lucky you can't smell. We kidded her ten times a week, dad and me. I felt so horrible about forgetting her anosmia I almost started crying. If you think that was a decision I made you're crazy.

Why we'd go up in the loft in the hot middle of the afternoon when you could bake chicken in there is Joey found a stack of *Hustler* magazines. He'd covered the walls with the pages, real dirty pictures. They were everywhere, like fleshtone wallpaper. "Meet my sluts," Joey said.

And, oh boy, did I meet them! I moved slowly across the wall, straining in the darkness to fill my eyes with bulging tits and pink pussies spread open, shimmering like the flayed fish my dad pulled from Huntington Harbor and gutted on the kitchen counter.

"Holy shit," I said over and over.

"You ain't even seen the good ones yet," Joey said. I slipped a hand down my jeans and tucked my boner behind my leg. Joey pushed the bulb towards the other side of the fort. "Check this out."

On the other wall there were men in the pictures, too, pushing their veiny dicks into folded women. Sometimes all you saw was up close pictures of wrinkled skin and slimy red goo that looked more like a coupon for meat than two people fucking.

"Gross, man. What's that shoe lacy crap on her mouth," I asked.

"What'a you mean gross! Don't you wanna shoot your batch in some girls face?"

I didn't reply. But Lexy surged through my head.

"I'm about to shoot mine like that. You won't tell, right?"

"Tell what?"

"If I shoot now. I gotta do it because I been staring so long."

"I won't tell anyone."

"You do it, too."

"…"

"I won't say shit, bro. I swear," Joey said.

"I don't shoot batches like that," I told him.

"Don't you whack off?"

"Yeah, like I rub it and everything but nothing like *that* comes out."

"You're not doing it right. How many fingers do you use? I use my thumb and pointer. I make an 'O' and do it like that. You don't need lotion or anything. Which I don't like cos it's messy."

"I just rub it like this," I showed him on my forearm.

"Nah, man, that's wrong. I'll show you. No fag stuff. I don't want to touch your shit. You gotta do it right, though. I'm telling you, the first time you shoot your batch! Bro! You'll do it every day. My brother taught me. I got tissues right there."

It was Joey's idea to go back to back. We sat on buckets and faced opposite walls. We had different grips. Joey used his pointer and thumb, that's it. I watched for like two seconds. He practically choked the thing to death. It got all purple. I tried that at first. It didn't work for me. My way was three fingers and a thumb with my pinky pointed out. Before, I was always rubbing on it when it got hard. Like the way you rub a leg cramp.

Joey kept telling me, "You gotta go faster. You're going too slow." He could see my arm moving. His arm was going a hundred miles an hour.

He got all quiet, holding his breath, and you heard a sound like two cats sneaking through the walls. When he was done he went to the back of the fort and stuffed his tissue into the rafters and said, "Don't tell anybody."

"I won't."

"Go faster, bro."

"It's fine like this," I told him. He should have shut up but he was all proud he'd taught me to do it and was acting coachy.

"Go downstairs a minute," I told him.

"Dude, you gotta go faster, I'm telling you."

"Just go downstairs."

"Make sure you catch it. Don't squirt on the floor."

"Go downstairs, man!" He wouldn't leave me the hell alone. Finally he went down the ladder. I could hear him moving things around on the work bench, but I felt better up there alone. My pin ached and the skin burned. I started making these stupid faces. I tried not to make the faces but something was pulling at the corners of my mouth and my eyebrows twitched all over the place. A tissue spread over my hand like a wimpy catcher's mitt. The tip of my pin got all drooly. I pointed it at the tissue. I didn't know what would happen but something was *forming* inside and I knew it was getting close. My whole body was collapsing, moving towards my pin like it was the center of gravity.

It didn't shoot, my batch. Not like in the pictures on the wall. Like Joey'd told me. It sort of spilled into a clumpy pool on the tissue.

"You done yet? Shit, bro."

I balled up the tissue and stuffed it in a corner. I felt embarrassed. I wanted to go home. Instead we went and played video games.

We named our grips. His was The Tourniquet and mine was called The Tea Cup. It's not like we watched each other or any faggy thing. We just told each other about it. That's how I learned to whack off.

If it wasn't too hot we'd ride Joey's bike to the train tracks that run along Mill Road half a mile then slip behind the cement foundry. Across the street is Fat City, the car graveyard. There's a chain link fence around it, twelve feet high and crowned with gunky razor wire. The fence bulged in spots, and in a thousand places the chain's links are crimped. Guard dogs, well fed, muscular, long thick fangs, patrolled the stacks of pancaked cars and generally hung out by the gate, drooling and losing their minds any time you passed. When Joey and me cruised past Fat City they rattled the fence and dug at the asphalt. An old man humped over with a rolled newspaper, smacked it against his palm and yelled at the dogs when he saw it was a couple of kids on bikes. The sound of the newspaper drove the dogs wild. The old man swatted their noses while they bit the fence, their teeth turning red with blood. After about a week showing up at the tracks and the old man smacking them, they got used to us. They'd get our scent, piss on something, then sit around staring at us. No other animals came around, not a stray dog, not a squirrel. You didn't even hear birds in the trees over there. Even the flies left.

Other than Fat City there was nothing, no houses, no people really, unless they were dumping furniture or broken bricks on the track bank, or brush they'd cleared from their yards. There was all kinds of crap lying around, even a boat, a small one with no motor or anything, leaning on its side. We put things on the tracks and watched them explode under the train's wheels. Whenever the train passed, Fat City's dogs went berserk.

That's where we were when we became best friends, on the tracks behind the foundry with a thousand little stones. The stones popped when the train wheels hit them and exploded into dust. You had to have the right stones, really white and salty looking.

"I can't wait for school to start," Joey told me.

"What for? That's crazy." I hated school.

"We're in eighth grade. Girls start fucking."

"…"

"What's the look," he asked.

"What? I didn't..."

"You don't think we can beat some pussy up this year? Alicia Miller promised me." Joey had hair on his calves and forearms. And a sweater between his legs. I wasn't hairy yet. I was shy about it. I mean I had pubic hair, plenty of it, but it was soft and not curly. I had long straight pubic hairs, sort of reddish. I'm not even redheaded. I'm a dirty blonde like my dad was. The hair on my head is curly like my mom's. Now my pubes are perfect, like all coarse and brown. I like them now but, man, back then I had a complex about it.

"A girl's first fuck is someone cons them into it. And so then they like it and they let someone else beat it up. That's the best time to get in." We made sacks with our shirt fronts and were carrying stones in them. Joey bent over to pick up a stone and some of the stones in his shirt fell out.

"After that they get a reputation. They get a number attached to'm and they won't fuck anyone new. You gotta be one of the first to beat that or forget it. There's Springkill at the end of the year. That's peak time." He was real excited about fucking. Not excited, anxious.

"I know we can this year," I said.

"What? What's the fucking look for?" Joey had a small forehead, or his hair grew low on it or something. He didn't look very intelligent but I'm telling you, he was smart. He knew a lot about girls from his brother and the rest he figured out by reading magazines.

Sometimes I need someone to help me tell a story. The one I wanted to tell Joey would sound like I was bragging or not telling the truth. One thing about me is, I always tell the truth when I'm telling a story. I lie all the time, I'm not saying that, but if I'm telling a specific story it's true. Seriously.

I'm pretty good at remembering how things happened. In school, when they give you a story to read for ten minutes then take it away and give you a test, what were the characters names and how many apples were in the basket and all that, I always score high. I was in a program called S.E.A.R.C.H. in elementary school. There were only ten of us, all supposed to be gifted but this kid Mason Leech was in the group and he'd pick his nose and hide the boogers in his ear. So I didn't think it was so special. We stayed in from recess on Thursdays to take tests and you got extra homework. I quit after a month.

"Remember that girl? I think her name was Amanda Voyage, right," I said.

"Yeah, the girl that went to jail-school in Massachusetts or someshit. Her? She was blowing guys in the woods behind the football field."

"I mean, I don't know. Yeah everybody talked about that," I said.

This girl, Amanda, she was the perfect *looking* girl. Her eyes were the size of apples and penny colored, sort of cartoony. She was on the dance team. Whenever there was a talent show she'd dance in a body suit. She was practically the only reason anybody went to those things.

"You know James Peck, right," I asked Joey.

"Yeah I know'm. We sat next to each other in Mr. Brush's class."

"James Peck's sister used to mess with Amanda. She hazed her all the time. I don't know what she did."

"So what?"

"So one time me and James went to 7-Eleven after school. James wanted a cigarette. You know how strict they are. Can't even smoke *near* the school. They'll suspend you. Even if you're all the way in the 7-Eleven parking lot. They got spies every-friggin-where."

"Yeah, so?"

"Well and so James hid behind a dumpster. I was the lookout and I see Amanda coming. I don't think she's a spy or whatever. But I tell James anyway and he stubs it out. Amanda walks up and she's like, 'You're James Peck. You're Jackie's brother, right?'"

James's sister's name was Jackie and he had two brothers, Jayce and Jesse. I don't know what his parents were thinking. Their own names don't start with J. They drink all the time and they're always calling James one of the brothers' names.

"James gets all nervous. Actually, his parents are smokers. They're alcoholics, too, so he…"

"Go on, man. Fuck. What happened with Amanda?"

"Amanda smells the smoke and asks James for a cigarette. She says we can go to her house and smoke and it's all good. She lives about two feet from the school. I think it was a Tuesday."

"Who cares what fucking day it was?"

I mean she really *looked* perfect. She was wearing faded jeans with stringy holes in the knees, a tank top made from thick, blue cotton, and she had on a zippery black leather jacket. She sparkled in the sun, especially her big eyes. The thing I didn't like about her was that her hair was the same as my sister's, the same color and length. They both had this blonde streak coming off the fringe near their right ear. That must have been a style thing, like some actress wore her hair that way.

I picked up rocks while I told Joey the story. He stood with one foot on the track-rail and stared off.

"So what happened, man? She blow one of you? Don't tell me James Peck beat that. Holy shit, no way!"

That's what I mean about telling people a story. A person only wants to hear if you beat that or something. Most stories are boring without some fucking or violence in it.

"Listen. We went to Amanda's house and were smoking cigarettes in the back yard," I told Joey. "They were. I wasn't. Amanda kept coughing. I saw her. She only inhaled half the time. She turned green and pale. She was being really nice. She made us iced tea even though it was autumn time and there was practically no leaves left and it was about to rain. All a sudden she wants to go for a ride in her father's car. She knows where he keeps the spare key in a hall closet, hanging from a nail. I don't know where her parents even were.

"There was this old yellow Cadillac in the garage. It barely fit. Amanda had to back it out before we could open the passenger door. We didn't go far or anything. Just around the block, a little more than that maybe. It didn't feel like we were doing anything wrong. Just driving. But she drove so slow and cautious it was boring. What was the point, y'know? It wasn't even worth sneaking the car out if we didn't speed. That sort of made me sick in a way. James asked if he could drive. Amanda said yes, at first. Then she said, 'Wait till we get closer to the house.' But when we got near the house she changed her mind and said no. She was out of breath and her face was red. I was sitting up front with her on this long bench seat. We were getting close to her house going down a hill. And there was a truck coming up at us, a big ass Ford gunning uphill. I think Amanda meant to stomp on the breaks but missed because all a sudden the Caddy jumps. I'm sliding around on the seat. All you see are trees swooshing in the windows and one whole side of the car turns shadow. Brooong, that big truck passes and the world sorta wobbles, but then everything gets still and straight again. We're going fast and you know what Amanda does?"

"I don't know, man. You're telling me."

"She lets go of the friggin wheel! Brings her knees up to her chest and everything. So, I slid across the seat and body checked her against the door."

"Why, what happened?"

"A squirrel'd run across the road. It shot from the bushes when the truck passed and Amanda was scared she'd smoosh it."

"Bro, I'd'a ran right over that fucking squirrel!"

"Yeah well. I steered us to like the side of the road and smashed the breaks. James came flying over the seat. Amanda starts screaming that he left a footprint on the dashboard."

"Holy shit."

"And then. Then she couldn't park the car, even though they had a tennis ball hanging from the ceiling in just the right place so when it touched the windshield you knew the car was all the way in. James had to park it for her."

Joey waved his hand and said, "Okay, come on, and then," with this impatient look on his face. He's an anxious guy, Joey.

"Alright, so when we got back in the house she was strange. Like she turned on a little television on the counter next to the stove. We were sitting in the kitchen. She asked me to tell her a joke. I started telling a joke and she got up to switch the channel on the T.V. She came back and said, 'Okay, start again.' So I started the joke again and she went and turned the volume down. She couldn't keep still. James wanted a smoke.

"'Outside,' she yells. Loud. 'You can't smoke in here,' even though he wasn't going to smoke in the house.

"While James was outside she told me about his sister, Jackie, and how Jackie used to haze her, Amanda. She wouldn't tell me what Jackie did to her, though. She kept repeating how funny the whole thing was and she only went along with the hazing because it amused her. She said, 'It amuses me the way people treat each other.' I told her how that asshole Brian Stipple hazed me on the bus one time but she cut me off. 'God, it's stupid to the point it's amusing.'"

She wasn't any good to help tell a story.

"She's doing all this crazy shit and you don't believe the stories about'r? She's twisted. I bet she loves to swallow the batch," Joey said.

"Listen. Amanda asked if I want a drink. I thought she meant more iced tea so I said yeah. It was real iced tea her mom brewed with honey. But Amanda, she went to the cabinets. The kitchen was made of wood cabinets. Even the fridge had wood cabinet doors. It's supposed to be impressive, I guess. She pulled this clear alcohol jug from the ugly cabinets. Clanged it against other bottles like church bells."

Joey balanced more rocks on the track's rail and scratched. He got a mosquito bite about two days before. He's the type that scratches until he bleeds, and his mosquito bite was bleeding down his hairy leg.

"I didn't drink it. I *pretended* to, like I put my lips on the bottle and blew air into it so it looked like alcohol was gurgling out. I took big fake breaths, and made faces. Then, listen to this, I slid the bottle over to Amanda and she did the same friggin thing! I knew the trick. She wasn't as smooth as me. She stuck her two lips inside the bottle.

"See," I told him.

"See fuckin what?"

"She's a poser. I don't believe the rumors. She probably started them herself."

The dogs across the street, in the car graveyard, barked and charged the fence. We sneaked up and checked if someone was around. We were alone but a train was coming finally and we rushed to get more rocks on the tracks.

"So then she asked about our girlfriends. James was going out with Maria Pawling. Amanda didn't know who that was. James described her over and over and Amanda's saying, 'She sounds pretty,' with a tone a person uses to apologize."

The lights at the intersection down the road blinked but it was too far to hear the bells. The red and white striped crossing arms came down.

"I didn't have a girlfriend but I told her about one girl I met at Adventure Land two summers ago. We used to call each other and talk. I only ever saw her that one day I met her. But I told Amanda we saw each other every weekend. Amanda asked me, 'Do you do it with her?'

"'We used to,' I told her."

"You told her you used to? Are you retarded," Joey said. He put the last rock down.

"Yeah, well, like I felt like the whole time we'd been at Amanda's she was running a circus. I don't want to be a clown in someone else's circus, so I kept lying. I don't know. She must'a known because she said, 'You probably only think you did it. Some boys think they did it but they didn't.' And I said to her, 'I'd know if I did it or not.' I said, 'I bet *you'd* know if I did it to you.' She went and changed the channel on the television and said, 'I bet I wouldn't know if you did it to me.' Then she started dancing. She was a dancer, remember?"

"Yeah, I re-fuckin-member. And then? Where's the turbo slut part?"

"She danced a minute and then she goes again, she's like, 'I bet I wouldn't even know,' looking at the floor and rolling her shoulders.

"'So let's go,' I said. Almost like it was a fight. She stopped dancing. It didn't even register what we were saying. Like it was a TV show and we were rehearsing."

The train swelled through the crossing and gave three horn blasts that hung in the sky awhile. A minute later here she comes sliding down the tracks with a hum you feel inside your chest. Joey and me backed into the weeds and watched. You could see the passengers' faces, heads bowed forward, about ten feet up in the windows, and below, our eye level, the shiny train's wheels hit the rocks, popping them into white grainy poofs squirting from the steel, and when the dozen cars passed there was nothing left, not a speck of dust on the hot rails smooth as mirrors.

"So g'head, man. Finish telling me."

"Aright, well, like we went to her parent's room," I said. "Got on the bed. She was in her panties and tank top. She started making excuses, like saying there was something underneath her. She'd push me off and sit up to check what she was lying on. I went along with it. I helped her look twenty times. We kept saying it was weird when we didn't find anything and then we'd lie down and kiss and I'd feel her up and she'd go, 'What'm I lying on? It's so annoying,' and we'd look around the sheets again."

I didn't want to do it, to be honest. I would've if I weren't too embarrassed about my pubic hair. Seriously. It was really long and straight and soft. Plus she was a little too much like my sister. The way she wore her hair. I didn't like that.

Joey's sensitive about things like being a virgin if you're not a virgin. He's really competitive. He didn't say he was *glad* I didn't beat that, but I could tell.

"You still got that cut on your finger," he asked. I had a cut from a piece of glass in the fort's door.

"Yeah," I told him.

"Can you make it bleed?"

"Probably, if I suck on it and squeeze."

Joey went and sat on the track rail. I sat next to him. The rail was hot as a branding iron from the sun. It made my ass cheeks itch. We pressed our blood together. Mine was from my finger and his was from a mosquito bite. That's all you had to do to be best friends.

# I'm Here To Pomp You Op

You're supposed to get messed up for life when your dad dies and you're only thirteen. I never got along with my dad. He didn't like me either. That always happens in movies and stories so I know it's normal. It's not like I *want*ed him to die. We just didn't get along. He didn't hit me often. The way he talked to me though, it was worse than cursing at a stubbed toe. I guess I hated him.

One night I was joking around after my bedtime. I always did that, acted out shows for my mother to make her laugh. I get so hyper at night I can't sleep. I have to *do* something. In the morning I'm a friggin zombie.

What I did this one night was an old Saturday Night Live skit. My mother was crazy about old Saturday Night Live skits, like "Best Of" stuff old people watch that bores the hell out of kids. There was one I liked though. They make fun of Arnold Schwarzenegger. I like the old Schwarzenegger movies. We got them on DVD. He's better than fake superheroes, like Spiderman and especially Superman. He's a real person, you know, punching guys in the mouth or shooting guns. I hate it when a movie expects you to believe a guy can fly around or pick up cars. Some movies, you have to do all the work believing everything because some computer in Hollywood made it look real. You always hear people saying that after a dumb movie, "It looked so real!" Looking real doesn't make it good.

In the skit, two guys act like Arnold Schwarzenegger. They're in sweat suits and headbands. They stuffed their shirts and pants so they looked muscly. They did some gay ass exercises that cracked up my mother. What made me laugh was the part where they said, "I'm here to pomp," and then they clapped and pointed, "you op!" I copied it for my mother. She laughed her ass off. Even my dad called me a pisser. He was alright, sometimes.

I should probably tell you first, my mother worked at night. Her office was in the garage at her boss's house. His name was Don something. Spelter, I think. My mother and the Fire Chief's wife, Elsa Lundgren, worked together. Don's business was making parts for electronics, like the start button on machines that make knives and forks, or the little clips that hold wires inside air conditioners. Stuff you didn't know even has to *get* made. They worked nights because the parts came from China or somewhere on the other side of the planet where it's always tomorrow morning. My dad teased my mom about it all the time, he said Don had a sweatshop in the basement. "He's got six-year-old Nips making firecrackers. Prolly missing fingers. Chains'm to the furnace at night."

"You don't have to like him, Otis, but he's my boss and he pays our bills," mom sort of sings.

"I don't have to like him? No shit, Fran. Twerpy bastid, sweating and breathing like he's got a cock in his throat. He's an itch up my asshole." They only talked in the kitchen. "I went and got his ticket like I told you I would."

"Are you kidding, Otis? You did not."

"Yeah I fuckin did. He won't give you two crinkled dollars to play them numbers? Has'ta put them in your paycheck! Bet that's how he makes his customers pay for it, right? Fuckin Jew."

"That was *my* idea, so I wouldn't have to ask him for it. I hate to *ask* for two dollars."

"I got'm now! 2, 28, 19, 33…"

"Just please stop."

"You *write'm* on the calendar. Every Tuesday. Or Friday whatever the fuck. You got Luke 25 this, Alexander 30 that…"

"There's no Alexander."

"…all the numbers in the bible memorized but you gotta *write* his lotto down. Where I can *see* the motherfuckers. And you play it for'm. He won't even make it an office pool. He's gotta keep it all. Well, I play his numbers, too. Till he wins I'll play'm and he's gonna haf'ta split it with *me*. Jackpot this, cock sucker."

I didn't like Don either, for what he did to Noogie. I don't know what kind of dog Noogie was. He was orange and had a big foldy face. There were no kids my age at the barbecue, so I played with Noogie, mostly. Whenever I stopped messing around with him, like to drink a can of Coke or something, he jumped all over everybody and licked sweat off their faces. He raked his claws over your skin and gave you pink welts that look like strands of bubble gum on your legs. Don kept saying, "Noog likes ya. Why don't you take him over to the soccer field to play?" He tried to stick me with him.

When the food was ready you loaded a paper plate with chicken and burgers and macaroni. The plates bent and Noogie followed you to the table waiting for a chunk of tomato to slide off your salad. He ate everything that fell. He'd crawl under the table and plop his face in your lap. Women kept shouting, "Ew ew ew," and reaching for napkins to wipe off their shorts.

Don got a leash. Noogie saw it and whimpered and put his chin on the floor.

There was an above-ground pool in the back yard with chunks of mud and grass clippings stuck to it. There were a million leaves in the pool, floating or sunk black and rotten on the bottom. It was in the shade of an oak tree all day long. Nobody could swim in the pool. It was cold as hose water. I put one toe in and my balls clung to my ass, like a lion's. Noogie tugged on the leash, his paws dug into the ground, the grass tore with a sound like a comb through knotty hair. Don dragged him behind the pool.

You couldn't see what happened exactly. Don's head was barely higher than the pool's lip, but it looked like he was *stepping* on old Noogie, holding the pool side for balance and squashing him on the ground. Everybody mumbled it was about time he *did* something. "If I got scratched by that mutt one more time I was gonna stamp on its paw, I swear to god. You gotta train your dogs. My dog don't do that." Don's neck wobbled under his sweaty chin and his pink-rimmed eyes bulged all over the place.

So then they came around the pool, both of them breathing heavy. Don's bald head shined with sweat and zigzagged with strands of black hair. Noogie followed, sort of hiding behind him, crawling to the back door, his belly practically dragging on the ground. He begged to go inside, looking back at us, whimpering and scratching at the door. He looked embarrassed.

"You got to show them your Alpha side," Don said. He kept laughing about that alpha comment. "Sometimes we get Alpha, don't we," he'd brag to other men at the party. He acted like a hot shot the rest of the day. Anytime a man gets into an argument with someone, like at the grocery store, or he beats his dog or something, he'll act like a hot shot the rest of the day.

I was having a hard time falling asleep. Like I said, I'm a real night owl. I get up to pee about a hundred times. Lying in bed I pushed on my bladder, checking if I had to pee. I get fixated on things. I checked every two minutes, pushed my fingers into my bladder, felt like I needed to pee, and then went to the bathroom. Not much came out, just a trickle. Each time I went to the bathroom my father grumbled, "Again!" from the couch. I knew he was shaking his head as if I was pissing in his cereal. "How many times you gonna go to the bathroom? Hah? You don't need to flush. Jesus fucking Christ."

"Otis!"

My mother only got mad if he used the Lord's name in vain. He could call me a *fucking slob* for spilling a molecule of milk on the countertop and she wouldn't sniff. But say *Jesus* when someone needs to pee and she'll bite your head off. "Don't take his name…"

"Oh, Jesus Christ, Fran. Why don't you leave me the hell alone, hah? Go to work already. Goddamn nagging bitch."

"I'm trying, Otis, believe me, to get OUT of here! Where's my bag! I can't find my bag!"

"If it was up your ass you'd know where it was."

My mother clomped her heals around the house. Normally she waited to put her shoes on, to be quiet while me and my sister were trying to sleep, until just before she walked out the door. When she got mad she put her shoes on and stomped all over the place. Nobody was allowed to wear shoes in the house but she sounded like a friggin horse when she got angry. She could wear shoes if she wanted because she cleaned the floors.

I put on my sweat suit, the one I wore in gym class. It was grey and loose. I stuffed the sleeves with balled-up socks and put pillows down the legs to look pumped-up. Then I went out to the den. My dad was sitting on the couch watching television.

"My name's Hans," I said with a real stupid accent. "And om here to pomp," then I clapped and pointed, "you op!"

"Bed," my father pointed over my shoulder. "No pissing, no flushing the toilet. Bed."

My mom though, she had a smile on her face. She was looking through her bag and sort of giggling. As long as she was smiling I knew I was safe, kind of.

"Hey Otis. Watts za motta? You feeling tie-yud? You little girly mon? Hey, somebody eez feeling crabby. I theenk you need to change yaw diet. I think you need me to pomp you op." I could be a performer sometimes. Seriously. I could've probably been in a movie. My parents never thought of showing me to a studio or whatever, to an agent. Things like that didn't cross their minds. All they wanted me to do was get good grades and stay out of trouble. Once I asked my mother why I needed grades. She told me so I could get a good job. Like what kind'a job, I asked. You know what she told me?

"Whatever job you want."

What a load of shit!

My friend Ben Croton. He knows exactly what job he's going to have. He's going to be an entrepreneur, which is a guy who starts a business, like a bar, or a car repair shop like Ben's father, if you don't know. I know a girl named Christine Morue and her father owns a collection agency, like who my dad yells at when they call. Christine's father was in *Forbes* friggin magazine. You better believe she knows what the hell job she's going to get. Those kids who went to Flower Hill School, the rich kids, they're going to be doctors or something, or hedge fund managers like their parents. I can say I want to be a doctor or some good type of professional, a manager or something, but I don't know anything about it. Only what's on TV. My parents never talked about the E.R. or the stock market over dinner or at a barbecue. If you're always hearing your parents talk about the E.R. or the stock market it becomes, I don't know, like a real thing. My father didn't even eat dinner at the table with us. He took his plate to the couch and watched the news. Anyway, they could have at least thought of putting me in the movies. You don't have to know anything to be an actor.

"You got little gurly arms…"

"God damn sonuva bitch! Bed, now!" He'd blow up like that. I expected it was coming but even so, it scared me. He didn't hit me too often. Once in a while I'd get slapped across the back of my head. What he liked to do was fold his belt in half and yank the straps together. Smack, smack, like brown lips eating fear. I'd run to my room and slip under the quilt. He'd come after me. His jeans open. Potbelly leading the way. His hair sticking up like blonde fire. My mother gone to work. It didn't matter how dark it was in my room, his wet eyes glinted while he unloaded on the covers. It scared me more than it hurt, smacking the quilt, screaming, "What I tell ya, hah? What I tell ya! Mother fuckin mother fucka! Mother fuckin mother fucka!" Ten swings of the belt, me screaming from one bed corner to the other. The leather thwacked between two beats of my sprinting heart. I didn't feel it. Except once. No covers.

"Okay," I said. "Jesus."

"Larry," went my mother.

"Smack him, Francine," said my father.

"Fine, I'm going to bed," I told them.

"Smack him," my father said again.

"For what? I'm just trying to make you idiots laugh."

Then it was like I'd thrown a stone. I wanted to reach out and grab it. My aim was off and it's going to be bad, but there's nothing I could do.

It was quiet. My dad sits up. He points to the floor by his feet. His socks are baggy and stained. "Come here," he says. I look at mother. She doesn't say a thing. I don't move. I'm sort of frozen. I think about running to my room. "Little bastard don't want to listen, hah!" He points at the ground again. "Here. Now." I go over to him slowly. Stand in front of him.

"Turn around," he says.

"Why?"

"Turn around."

"Why?" I ask again, turning.

"Bend over."

He's not going to use his belt.

I can't look my mother in the eyes. I take a quick squint at her, though, all bent over. She stands there with a comb in her hands, watching.

He pulls me closer by my waistband. Then he pulls my sweatpants down. The pillows stuffed in the legs fall away. He drops the sweats to my ankles. I'm wearing tighty whities. My palms are on my knees. About five friggin minutes pass, it seems. I'm waiting for the spanking. How hard will his hands be? My stomach is boiling and I flex to keep from crapping. I might scream but I won't cry. I realize I'm smiling. If I crap myself he will see it through the white cotton. I'm weightless. The room feels small and the things in it are stupid.

Then all he does, he pats me on the ass. Tap tap. "Go to bed," he says. Real calm and nice. Isn't my mother pleased! I sprint from the room.

I wish he'd belted me. I really do. No sheets, no quilt, and get those purple welts that split and bleed. Instead of making me turn around and bend over. I'd take a punch in the eye rather than that.

I never did a show for them again. Assholes. I stopped performing anything.

# Regular Americans

If you ex*celled* at J. Taylor Finley Jr. High School they invited you and sixty students on a trip to these campgrounds in a corner of New York. The retreat is called Springkill and it's all anybody talks about for the last month in school, if you got invited or not. It's a big deal.

The teachers choose their favorite students. They never tell you which teacher picked you. But most kids knew. I was invited and I couldn't imagine who the hell would've voted for me. I was close to failing every class, even gym. I got suspended for telling my Spanish teacher to eat shit (in Italian). The only teacher who I think liked me was Ms. Berry, from art class. I never made anything, like silk screens or those wheels you mix paints on and create new colors. I didn't draw the objects we were supposed to *study*, like coffee mugs and wood cubes. I drew faces with black eyes and busted lips. Sometimes I drew a bullet through its head. Ms. Berry said I had a good hand. She really praised me. But she was only a substitute teacher and couldn't invite anybody. Anyway, *somebody* picked me.

Meanwhile my father got sicker. He lost 10 pounds a week. You thought he had no more weight to lose, then his arms shriveled up. Three days later his cheeks caved in. Anyone could see he was sick as hell. Every day was something new. Rashes to constipation to the hiccups. He shivered under a pile of blankets as sweat ran down his neck. Then he'd throw off the blankets and yell, "It's hot as ten motherfuckers under here." He stood up to get a drink of water. Halfway to the kitchen he doubled over, his mouth opened, his eyes poked out of his face all red and purple, and a trickle of yellow froth oozed off his blue tongue. He hiccupped three or four times. "I'm so hungry I could eat the asshole out of a skunk." But he couldn't keep any food down.

We call them his colorful days now, me and my mother, because after the puking and losing weight he turned pale as a grub and nothing that oozed out of him had any color at all. He faded gray and empty the way the sky does after sunset. So I wouldn't be allowed to go to Springkill.

The good part was I didn't have to go to school if I didn't want to. I'd tell my mother I was worried or sad and I wanted to stay home with dad and do chores or something. My mother got a second job at the Library in the periodicals section, where they keep the magazines and newspapers. I stayed home and listened to my father sleep. I mowed the lawn or washed towels and made sure dad took his pills. As long as I did *some*thing my mother was grateful. Mostly I watched TV.

This is what I mean about Joey's imagination. How clever he was. He'd find out what his mother was making for dinner. Like if it was Pasta Bolognese. He'd open a jar of tomato sauce and dump it into a plastic cup. You should have seen the kitchen closet at his house. Not the closet, the pantry. There were about four hundred jars of different sauces his mother made from scratch. Joey'd mix old hamburger into the sauce, or whatever leftovers sat tin-foiled in the fridge, and put that in the cup and hid it under his bed. An hour before he was supposed to go to sleep he'd start complaining he was sick. He'd tell his parents he was going to bed early.

Joey kept a rag under his bed to catch his batch. He'd soak it under the bathroom tap with a trickle of water then make gagging noises to get his parents' attention. He squeezed the rag over the toilet bowl. Splash!

He rubbed toothpaste in his eyes to make them red and teary.

"Again, you're sick? This boy. I'm telling you, Paolo, it's how they feed him at school. It's not food. It's petroleum. It's plastic." His mother wasn't born in Italy but her parents were. His father was born in Sicily, I think, but he only lived there until he was six. Their house looked like the middle of Europe. Three hundred years ago. You couldn't touch *anything*. Every bowl in the cupboard was special and you couldn't use it. There were packages of weird meat in the fridge I wasn't supposed to eat. "You wouldn't like it," Paolo told me but that's bullshit because when he wasn't around Joey and me ate tons of it with cheeses and mustards, and oils in bottles with like twigs inside them. They kept their eggs in a basket on the counter, not in the fridge like at a regular house. They never went bad though. I ate breakfast at his house some weekends.

"I'm feeling shitty," Joey'd say. He was allowed to curse once in a while. I would've gotten smacked in the mouth if I said that around my dad. "I'm goin'a bed."

Joey'd wait in his room for ten minutes before gagging again. He'd take out his cup of sauce and pour it right on the floor. And down his arm! "Ah, marone!" he'd go. "Ma. Ma!"

After a couple weeks his mother took him to the doctor. He wasn't allowed to eat school food anymore. She sent him with a cooler bag. He brought Italian meat sandwiches. The bread was the best part. The crust was hard, it hurt the roof of your mouth. The white part was soft and chewy. It didn't dissolve into paste like grocery store bread. I traded my cafeteria peanut butter and jelly for his Sweet Sausage sandwiches. Joey loved PB&J more than anyone I ever met. Italians make good sandwiches. Even if they're really only Americans.

# A Diet Of Worms

When I think about my dad, like what he looked like, he's always got a cigarette in his hand. The memory I have most, how he looked before he got sick, is he's sitting shirtless on the couch watching television, smoking.

The first thing he did when he came into the house was he took off his shirt. It could be two degrees outside but he'd pull it off in the front hallway. His hair stuck out all over the place. Then he'd light a cigarette off the stove. He took long drags and blew the smoke from his nose over his hairy chest and potbelly. Blue, braided smoke rolled off the cigarette's tip and crawled along the tattoos on his forearm. My favorite tattoo was his baby devil. It wore diapers and held a pitchfork and had "Born To Raise Hell" written around it. There were burn holes in the couch's arms. Nobody cared. That was his seat. That's how I see him.

When he ran out of cigarettes he sent me to Cookie's to borrow one off her. "Run next door and grab me a cigarette," he'd send me like she was a convenience store.

Cookie ran a beauty parlor in her basement. She cut my hair when I was little until dad made me go to the barbershop *he* went to. She loved my dad. Everybody loved him. The called him Crazy Otis down at the firehouse. He was the first fireman to win trophies in both the Bucket Brigade and the Fireman's Carry in one tournament. There's a plaque on the game room wall for him, next to the trophy case. So people liked him. Cookie didn't have a lawn mower. My dad cut her grass or he'd make me do it. He shoveled snow off her porch in the winter or he'd make me do that, too. Cookie was divorced. We borrowed eggs off her, or a cup of milk or something. Any time I went over to Cookie's house she fixed the part in my hair with her fingers.

I like the way cigarettes smell before they're lit. They have a sour smell, and they're musky like inside a closet. One time I went to borrow a cigarette off Cookie, my dad must have done something for her because she gave me half an apple pie to bring home along with *four* cigarettes. I smelled them while I walked home, the cigarettes, not the pie.

I went and put everything on the counter but one of the cigarettes was missing. I didn't care because usually Cookie only gave my dad one or two at most, so three was still pretty good. It was hot outside and I didn't want to go looking for a cigarette I'd probably dropped near a pile of dog shit.

I forgot to tell you about the dog pack that roamed our neighborhood. They crapped in the street and ate garbage. My dad swore he'd shoot the next dog that pissed on our cans. He bought a handgun, a .45 caliber. There were always cops in the firehouse kitchen drinking coffee and they told my dad he could shoot a dog if he felt threatened. Cops couldn't do anything about the dogs. They weren't allowed to shoot them unless a dog attacked somebody. It wasn't their job to catch dogs or shoot them. It was up to you to protect yourself.

Dad bought the pistol from Campsite, a sporting goods store a fireman owns. They sell tents, fishing gear, butane grills and ponchos, things like that. And they sell guns. The guys there let me aim rifles at the stuffed turkeys and moose and deer heads on the walls. You weren't supposed to dry fire a rifle but they let me dry fire at animal heads because my dad was a fireman. We never did anything together, dad and me, but go to Campsite or to the firehouse.

He carried the gun in his waistband. Guns don't come with holsters, you have to buy them separate. A gun comes in a box the way an alarm clock does.

He made big threats, too. Like he'd call up the gas company and scream at someone on the phone. "Why's the bill different every month from you scumbags. The fuck is a service charge? I'm paying for your service already! Hah? You're charging to bill me? Let me tell you what I'll do. I'm gonna deduct the price of the stamp every month. I'll charge for my service'a paying you pricks. Cock *suck*ers!" He slammed the phone so hard it broke off the wall. Then he'd have a Jeremiad, that's what my mom called it. It's something from the bible that basically means to rant. His Jeremiads lasted a long time. "Collection agency called and said I owe'm money. For what? A phone bill I stopped paying. The cellphone I had and never used and threw in the harbor when I was fishing with Bill Hullinski three months ago. Remember? And I told the phone company I didn't have it any more and wasn't gonna pay them anymore and now they got a *service* on me! Cocksuckers!" He paced and smoked and kicked the chairs' legs. "Listen, if I had a problem with *another* man, hah, and a stranger come up and get in *our* business, I'd smack'm in the fucking mouth for butting in. But these pricks call themselves a collection agent and think they get the right to shove into another man's business. And charge'm for it, too! Well I ain't paying and I told'm so and if they want blood from a stone they can come and get it and take a round in the fucking chest with'm."

Sometimes it was funny, but not always. Say he was watching the news and a story came on about a drunk driver. He'd yell at the television. "Shoot the motherfucker! Let me do it, shoot em' and bill his family for the bullet. Cock *suck*er. The courts ain't gonna do anything about it. Laws don't stop anybody. The judges run'm through jail then turn'm out. What kind'a country is that, letting anybody in that wants to commit crimes and get turned loose or sneak back where they come from taking American money with'm? They don't care if the country goes broke. Illegals don't pay their share but they still get money from the government for rent and school and doctors. And send their pay to gramma back in her shitty country. We're overrun right here in this neighborhood. Half the block is illegals and more coming. And I hafta pay tax to school'm and house'm. You watch, the government'll force me to feed'm right off my fuckin table. I'd shoot them by the family if this country meant anything, which it goddamn well don't anymore, so help me fucking Christ!"

"Otis!"

"Motherfuckin motherfuckers. Motherfuckin motherfuckers!"

You knew he was finished when he said that.

My mother was nervous about the gun. What scared her was his threats were always different, like he was experimenting. She thought eventually an experiment would work and it would change things, violently, forever.

One day we were sitting around waiting for the chicken to finish cooking. It was about a week after he got the .45. Mom kept checking the plastic popper that comes out of the chicken when it's cooked. Every time she got up to check my dad would go, "It ain't ready, Fran. I'll smell it when it's done. No wonder you're a lousy cook, you can't smell. How the hell you gonna know, hah? You can't even taste. I could feed you hamster food and you wouldn't know. It'd be cheaper." He was only teasing her. She really couldn't smell at all though.

We ate dinner at 5 pm. Most of my friends, like Joey or Ben Croton, they had dinner at 8. That's why Mr. Nailati was always saying, "You won't like it," because I was usually at Joey's when they ate dinner. I'd had my dinner by then and would be feeling hungry again. I can eat constantly. My dad always said, "You don't eat, you graze. Jesus, I can't afford this sonuva bitch." At Joey's house the air was practically made of soup.

"Ma. Why do we eat so early," I asked. She was checking on the chicken. "I get so hungry at night I can't sleep." It was true. I couldn't sleep with an empty stomach. I'd pour a bowl of cereal when I couldn't sleep. My dad would sit on the couch and grumble, "Don't put so much milk in it. You pour half the milk down the drain cos you don't finish it. Or you spill it on the counter like a fucking slob. Eat and eat and eat, that's all you do." That made me angry, getting yelled at, and it was even harder to sleep. Cereal really is my favorite food, though. I could eat it all the time. At night, it didn't matter what I had. I was always nauseous. My stomach squirmed. Like all I ever ate was a diet of worms.

"Your father gets home from work at five o'clock. Then I have to be ready for work by nine. Okay?" My mother didn't say it mean, but you could tell she was annoyed, peeking in through the oven door's burnt window trying to see if the popper popped.

I can't describe the sound. I can't replay it in my mind, either, but I'd recognize it if I heard it again. Gunshots are like a song in a way, if you only heard it once. I remember my mother flinching like she got punched in the ribs, and the way she covered her head, kneeling on the floor by the oven. The shots were so loud they squeezed us with noise, then dissolved into fear ringing in our ears.

My dad was inside the house, in the hallway at the front door, when he fired two shots so quickly it's like one explosion was inside the other, separated by a layer of numbness. "I got the motherfucker," he yelled, and ran out to the driveway, his socks flopping all over the place. There was a blue cloud of smoke. The house smelled like firecrackers for a week. I love that smell.

I found it later. The cigarette I mean. I was going to Joey's, probably to whack off in the fort. It had rolled down the driveway and stuck to a weed in the asphalt. I didn't go back and give it to my dad. You never knew with him. He might change his mind and make me stay home to fold his painty drop cloths. I walked and kind of smelled the cigarette on the way. I put it in my mouth and took unlit drags.

I didn't hide it when I got to Joeys. His father never even looked at you, first of all, if you weren't Italian. He didn't like his son being friends with a boy who wasn't Italian, I guess. He hardly said a word to me if he wasn't telling me to not touch something or that I wouldn't like what they were eating. Joey's mother was in the kitchen making dinner. She spent three hours a day in the kitchen cooking and drinking wine. You always had to knock if you went to the front door. Some families you don't have to knock. You can walk right in like it was your own house. Not at Joey's. I did it once after we'd been hanging out every day for a month. Paolo, Joey's father, went crazy.

"What'a you outta ya mind? Someone walks in my house I take a golf club to his skull, eh. In this neighborhood?" He was a short guy. He had stubby, thick fingers. He could crush walnuts with his bare hand. He made a big deal about how strong his friggin hands were. He could change a car's tire without a wrench, he said. He pressed one of his fingertips against his temple. "Joey, your friend isn't too bright."

Nobody cares if you walked in through a back door, though. That's what I did. Mrs. Nailati was sitting on a kitchen chair, drinking wine from a coffee mug and reading a magazine. You never saw where she got her wine from but the next day there'd be an empty bottle in the recycling bin. She had to hide it from Paolo. He knew she drank wine. It wasn't a secret. But Paolo, he wasn't even supposed to see it ever since they moved into this neighborhood from the old one.

Mrs. Nailati had very nice legs. She wasn't hot like my friend Ben Croton's mother, but she had nice calves and ankles. One of her feet was bouncing over her other leg. A sandal dangled on her toe. She had nice feet, too, all tan. Her toenails were painted pink. There were no wrinkles in the arch of her foot or anything. It was just nice.

"Hello La. You looking for Joe? He's in his room," she said fast without looking up. I stuck the cigarette behind my ear.

"What are you cooking," I asked her. "It smells pretty good."

"You wouldn't like it," Paolo said from the other room. He yelled for Joey. "Come get your friend." He never said my name. Larry wasn't Italian enough.

Even Paolo liked my father. The only time he talked to me was when he asked about my dad. "How's your poppa" he'd say. I'd say he was feeling better or that he wasn't doing too good, depending if he'd yelled at me that day. When they first met my dad wasn't very sick. He'd only had the surgery. And plus, Paolo was in a rage over a man who tried to kill Joey.

# Curses And Dirty Phrases

Joey had a black BMX, a freestyle bicycle, with thirty-six-spoke wheels and pegs I stood on while we rode around the neighborhood looking for dumpsters, or just to hang out on the train tracks behind the foundry. I didn't have a bike. I mean I did, but I never told Joey about it. First of all, I liked riding on his pegs. And second, my bike was a piece of crap. I got it for Christmas one year. It wasn't even new. A real cheapo, ugly and embarrassing. The kickstand stuck out like a broken insect leg, and chrome flaked off the chain guard. My dad probably took it from someone's yard while their house was on fire. There were reflectors all over it and stickers saying Racer and Lightning. That bike had no lightning in it, I promise. Joey's bike frame had El Centro painted on it properly. It was quiet when you rode. Mine clicked through every pedal, and the sprockets grinded. I let it rust behind the shed in our back yard, covered with a torn blue tarp.

The day Joey's and my dad met we'd been riding around the neighborhood looking for bundled up magazines or gym equipment or dumpsters. We only looked for good garbage, like when someone's cleaning out their basement or they're moving out, not regular trash in white bags with potato peels and coffee grinds.

First we found a rolled up carpet on 11th street, which usually means there's a lamp, too, or a dartboard or something. But when we broke the strings and unrolled it in the street all there was inside were expired bags of fertilizer. We rode a little further and saw the dogs at a corner.

Some stared, and some sniffed a bit, squinting and pointing their ears. All you did when you saw the dogs was whoop and they usually ran off. If you didn't scream they stayed, but they backed off to let you pass and checked if you were one of the people in the neighborhood who was kind to them. There wasn't enough garbage in the town for the pack to eat. Some people had to be feeding them, which gave my father the Jeremiads. "I hope I catch the cocksucker leavin food. I'll stuff the shit off our lawn right through his goddamn mouth."

We found a pile of black bags on 4th Avenue and 9th Street, three blocks from my house. There were hard straight lines pressing through, and corners. Man-made stuff. That was how Joey found the *Hustlers* for the fort and where we got a radio to put in it and a little fan, he'd seen the magazines' edges in bags.

Joey took a glass bottle from the gutter and broke it over the curb and we used the pieces to cut open the bags. There *were* boxes, too, but they were empty, mostly Christmas ornaments and dry-soap containers. Plus there were diapers and then regular trash, coffee grinds and all. Joey got mad and kicked the crap all over the street.

We rode around the neighborhood a bit longer, me on the pegs, talking mostly about what we needed to put in the fort, and we talked about girls. We found a dumpster behind an empty house on 10th Street and dropped the bike in the driveway and climbed on.

A man sat on the curb across the street. He wasn't doing anything, just kind of picking at his broken boots. Once in a while he stood up like he was going somewhere, made a forgetful face, then sat again. The dumpster had electronics buried under asphalt shingles and dusty two-by-fours. The man on the curb didn't live in the neighborhood. He didn't look homeless. He was dirty but not homeless dirty. We were a couple blocks from the gas station on New York Avenue, where day laborers wait for landscapers and roofers to pick them up. That's the kind of dirty he was, day labor dirty. They lived on the *other* side of New York Avenue.

Joey found a busted speaker. "The sound part's torn, the fabric bit," I said.

"Yeah but speakers have magnets in them."

"So what do we want a magnet for," I asked.

"To sweep the ground in the fort and pick up the nails and staples we're always kneeling on and can't see in the dust."

"Magnets are good for your blood, too. You stick them on your wrist or your back or somewhere and it heals your blood."

"I don't give a shit about my blood."

That's when the man started walking up the driveway. We didn't pay attention, just saw him moving along the hedges past the mailbox and recycling bin. Day laborers, I'd see them in the morning holding styrofoam coffees at the gas station and staring into passing trucks. My Uncle Lloyd takes care of trees, fertilizes them and prunes them, or cuts them down. He picks a day laborer from the gas station a couple times a week. He says they're like the Invisible Man, you don't see him until he's covered with paint or dirt. I don't mean this man was *invisible*, we saw him, we just weren't paying attention.

We dug deeper and threw a thousand shingles and pipes from the dumpster and hit the jackpot. There was a heavy punching bag, taped where it was torn, a bar-bell but no weights, a dozen paint cans, kinky extension cords, a hair drier, knives and forks mixed into everything, a boxy television with a screen perfect for smashing with a rock or maybe the bar-bell, three coffee makers, a tennis racket, a dresser drawer full of a woman's shirts, a tire, enough books for a bond fire, a bike frame, and that's only half. We wanted to take it all but it wouldn't fit in the fort. We'd've dragged the whole dumpster back to Joey's if we could.

"Let's take the knives. And a box of candles."

"I want to smash the TV."

"You can use the glass for the fort door's trap," I said.

"We can rip out its electronics. And take these chords, too. I want to electrocute mother fuckers tryn'a sneak in."

I bet Joey would've figured it out, too. He'd electrocute the whole garage if we'd got the things we wanted. But the laborer was literally standing on Joey's bike.

He might've been forty. Drunk. You couldn't smell him but it *felt* like you could, you know? He tried to say something. It wasn't English, though. He was speaking and breathing through his nose at the same time. I've heard firemen talk that way at barbecues and after tournaments. He was some kind of South American, from one of those countries where the government is corrupt and America has to save everyone. He was very pissed off. Which is the opposite of my dad when he got drunk. The only time my dad wasn't angry was when he was drinking at the firehouse.

He yelled and stomped. His body wiggled from his heels to his speckled forehead. He reminded me of a baby that just learned to stand.

"Hey, barbone!" Joey knows Italian. "Che cazzo vuoi, eh?" He busted the drunk's balls.

I didn't care as much as I would if Joey was talking English, because then it would *mean* something. Joey taught me how to say things in Italian, like "kiss me" and "nice tits." And I could go and say it to girls because it may as well have been Martian. It was only sounds, and didn't mean anything. If I said the same in English I'd've gotten slapped. The man though, he understood Joey. He stomped his foot and got Jell-O-y, sagging and bending like a band of phlegm. And he yelled back in Spanish.

"Italian and Spanish are practically the same language, Joey. You're pissing him off." It's like growling at a dog. It doesn't mean anything to you, but you'll end up getting bit.

"Italian ain't nothing like Spanish, retard." Then, to the man, he goes, "Tua madre si da per niente. Vaffanculo!" Joey didn't really know Italian either. Just curses and dirty phrases.

The man grabbed the handlebars and lifted the BMX but stumbled. He was too Jell-O-y. He couldn't keep his balance. There was garbage all over the place and demolition debris. There were two by fours and broken glass, like a bomb had gone off. The man half looked blown up he was so dirty, and still dizzy from the explosion.

Joey climbed off the dumpster. He kept yelling Italian. He's a clever one, I'm telling you. Insulting the man without really doing it, you know, without getting in the man's face or even using the English language.

Then the man picked up a plank. It was rotted. He could barely hold it. He swung it once and fell. The bike was way behind. Joey kept stepping backward. He wasn't scared but he wasn't having the time of his life, calling the guy a whore in Italian and telling him to suck his sausage. But so the man followed him step for step, swinging the plank and breathing heavy, going deeper into the yard.

I snuck around the house, grabbed the bike and swung myself onto the seat. Then I beat it. I took a squint at Joey backing away from the man's raised arms and the plank of wood overhead.

My heart was all over my body, pounding in my temples, my neck, kicking around my belly like I'd swallowed a rabbit. I pedaled hard. All I could hear was rushing wind. I was full speed in half a block, sand and broken glass whirling in the spokes.

I shot around the fence at the corner. My heart stopped on the other side.

The dog pack had ripped open a garbage bag and were pawing through it. I nearly broke my ankle trying to avoid smashing into them but I drove one down with a yelp. Everything got still for a second. I hollered, "Sit!" for some reason but they burst out barking. They almost sounded jolly about it. "Hey. Look who it is," they said. "The son of an asshole with a gun!" Their ears pointed up like rockets and then all of them—minus one, thanks to dad—stalked toward me, snarling.

I jumped on the pedals. A dog got hold of my jeans. Tearing loose, the others came from behind, lunging at the wheels. Claws clattered. Big barks and little squeaky ones. "Sit," I kept screaming like a moron. Growling and biting each other's ears. Spit flinging. A smaller dog's paw went under the wheel with a crunch and he scattered off howling.

Didn't they know? I was the top of the food chain! On a bike, which is a tool Man invented, a tool like the gun that shot them down. Even dogs were an invention, and they were biting their creator, in a way. The thought turned my panic into outrage.

I'd always liked them, because each dog started as somebody's pet probably, and got beaten too much. So it ran away. Maybe it was thrown from a car on the way out of town. I felt sorry for them. I left bologna slices and raw hotdog pieces by the corner hydrant. If Joey had leftover puke I'd leave that, too, down the street from his house. The dogs didn't know. There was a limit to what they understood, and when they reached it they attacked. Sure, I thought it was unfair that my dad shot a hungry animal for destroying our garbage. But I already hated him, so there was only one way to feel about it. Just plain old sadness.

They gassed out pretty quick, except for one. She was skinny, with a head so wide and flat she looked more like a monkfish than a mutt. Long black nipples swung from her belly. She had a hoarse voice, and her barks went *haba haba*. She had no trouble keeping up with me, running sorta sideways and snapping at my ankle. A flap of denim stuck between her teeth. My burning thighs couldn't pedal harder. I wished Joey was there because *he'd* have an idea.

When I got to Fat City the monkfish had lost a step. An arm's length from the fence I jumped off the bike and climbed ten feet up the chain link. The guard dogs saw me and trotted over, curious. The monkfish leapt, her wide jaws snapping beneath my sneakers.

You never saw anger turn on so quick, like electricity. The guard dogs charged, buckling the fence. Monkfish forgot me and haba haba'd in Fat City's dog's faces. Spit and blood boiled.

Monkfish's paw must've slipped through the links into a guard dog's jaw because next came a scream I can't describe, like tires screeching. I heard the crackling sound of something hard being torn and then the Monkfish howling down the street for all she was worth.

I was afraid to come off the fence. My scent was well known at Fat City and the guards were on familiar terms with me, normally, but now they were frenzied, fighting each other. I jumped. From that height it was more like falling, but I wasn't going to climb down cool and slow and get my toe ripped off. I plunked down beside the BMX and the dogs charged again, bowing out the fence like a fishnet in a current. I hopped on the bike and they chased me along the chain link, barking until I was out of sight.

"That's fighting fire with fire," I told myself.

I was worried about Joey. But I knew he'd be fine. Like I just knew it. He was smart and strong, more than me at least. I dropped the bike at his front porch and ran in through the front door. "Mr. Nailati! Mr. Nailati!"

I didn't see Paolo right away. I stopped in the den to catch my breath. "There's a guy after Joey," I yelled. "Tryn'a hit him with a stick."

Paolo's big feet pounded down the stairs. He wore a windbreaker jacket zipped to the neck and a pair of loose blue shorts over black spandex stretched around his thick dark thighs.

He aimed his nostrils aimed at me. "Listen to me. Slow down. What'a you saying?"

"A drunk guy's hitting Joey."

Remember the cartoon, when a guy unzips his entire body and a different character steps out? Mr. Nailati grew eight inches. His face turned maroon! He leapt from room to room, gained ten pounds with every door he slammed. I followed him around, explaining it. I was working him up big time. I knew he appreciated it, that he didn't have to ask a lot of questions. He could get fired up and angry and collect reasons to kill without thinking hard.

He found what he was looking for, a golf club as long as him, and sprinted out the door. He had this car from the middle of last century. Paolo wasn't supposed to drive. The motor turned over, trying to start. "Son of a bitch," he yelled.

I stood on the front steps and caught my breath and coughed and spat on the bricks. My ankle itched so I scratched it. My jeans were torn there and some blood had trickled. It hadn't occurred to me to run to my house, to yell out for *my* dad. We lived even closer to Fat City than Joey.

"Start, putana!"

I'd only seen dad's .45 once, but I thought about it every day. Not in a serious way. I thought about the gun the way you think about a frying pan when you see eggs, or a match when you see a candle, because there was one time he'd gotten pretty depressed, my father. When he found out he was sick again. The surgery didn't work. I don't like to talk about it but since I brought it up I'll tell you.

One day I was making oatmeal with my mom and sister when my dad came into the kitchen. "See this," he said. He was holding a bullet, fat and brassy. He tapped it against his forehead. "This is the bullet I'm going to kill myself with." He put it on top of the refrigerator and left the room. It stayed there for months. After a while it became like anything else, sort of decorative, meaningless. Anytime you went to the fridge for orange juice or to make a sandwich, the bullet was there. It only reminded me of the gun though, and not what he said. Sometimes you were angry and you slammed the fridge door and the bullet tipped over. You'd stand it up again. You didn't even think about it. The only time you think about a bullet is after it's gone off. They aren't scary when they're just sitting on top of a refrigerator. If I saw a spider though, forget it. I hate spiders. They creep me out. I can't even think about a spider without spitting. I feel like they're in my mouth. My whole family is like that. My sister's afraid of heights. My mom hates small spaces. We can't keep the vacuum cleaner in the closet because she'd have to stick her head in there to get it. We keep the vacuum on the landing to the basement stairs where you trip on it anytime you get the laundry. It's natural to be afraid of spiders and heights and small places because of evolution. Those are things that would kill you a million years ago. The only thing natural about a bullet is the noise it makes. It's scary as hell.

I got back on the bike and pedaled home.

He was lying on the couch when I ran in screaming, "Dad! Dad!"

"What! Christ with the screaming, hah! What?"

I told him what happened. About the laborer, I mean, not the dogs. He seemed concerned, I have to give him that. He got his shirt from the kitchen table and put that on, then he walked down the hall to his bedroom. I heard the closet door open. He could've been getting his axe handle. I wasn't sure. He'd lost weight. His potbelly wasn't so big anymore. When he came back empty handed, I knew he had it tucked in his waistband. "Stay here," he said, but I rode the bike behind him.

Paolo was pulling up in the old Buick when dad and me got in eyesight. The laborer was at the end of the driveway. I didn't see Joey right away, which made me worry.

"Is that him," Paolo screamed through his car's window. "Was it you? You fuck with my son!" He went to turn off the ignition but the car was in gear. The Buick rolled forward. When he tried to get out the door was locked. Finally he got out and grabbed the golf club from the back seat.

It tangled in the seat belt. So then he walks over with nothing in his fists. His eyes were about level with the drunk's Adam's Apple. Paolo poked him on the chin with his stubby finger.

Now my dad was on a sprint, holding his elbows out from his body as if he had sore armpits or something. I'd never wondered what kind of an athlete he was at my age. It never occurred to me he ever *was* my age. I pictured him running like that during gym class and everybody thinking he was spastic. He was pretty fast though. I had to peddle hard to keep up with him.

"You fuck with my son! I'll kill ya! I'll kill ya!" Paolo stomped in circles, yelling, "I'll kill ya!" His calves were big as softballs. "Joey," he said, "get over the car."

Joey came around the side of the house, smiling. I swear he loves that kind of stuff. He untangled the golf club from the seat belt and handed it to Paolo. They gave each other this teammate look. It was quick but I saw it. Paolo loved his son. But also, him and Joey were partners. I knew my dad loved me or whatever. He had to. But Joey and his dad *liked* each other.

You know about the visible light spectrum? If a band stretched out a mile long represented all light energy, visible light would only be two feet. I learned that from Mr. Brush in Physical Science class. That's what *love* is, all the miles you don't see. *Like* is the two feet you do see. The thing is, all the light you don't see doesn't matter. It's what you see that's useful. I'd rather be liked than loved.

I pictured Paolo slamming the club over the guy's head, and meat spraying from his ears. I was sorry I'd worked him up.

"Whassit for," the drunk asked. "Whassit for?"

"What's this for? What's *this* for? I'm gonna break your fuckin hole!" Paolo held the club with both hands. "Did he touch you! You got'ny marks," he asked Joey.

Joey didn't say anything, just shook his head no.

"If I find a mark on my kid, I swear to fucking Christ, I'll kill ya. Anyone knows me'll tell ya. You don't fuck with my family." Paolo didn't hit him, he just repeated himself, "You fuck with my son! I'll kill ya." He walked to the Buick squeezing the club in his stubby hands. Bang! He slammed his own car. Bang, bang! He put two holes in the hood. The club stuck in the sheet metal. He couldn't pull it out. He tried like a madman, pulling it everywhichway.

I saw my dad beat a man once, on our way to the Fireman's Fair. My mother was pregnant. You couldn't tell, though. I remember her dress's color, lilac, because we had a lilac tree next to our driveway and that day my mother had gone and stood next to it and said, "Somebody take a picture." Nobody did, though. Anyway, we were a block from the firehouse, driving, and my dad was singing along to the radio, messing up the words on purpose, saying dirty things to make us laugh. Then he blew the horn.

People blow their horns when they're crashing. It doesn't help. My mother didn't scream when the car smashed into her door and knocked her into the back seat on top of me and my sister. We did, though. Me and my sister screamed.

Firemen pulled her out first, then me and my sister. A few of the guys stayed with her, kneeling and holding her hand. The rest evaporated. That's how it felt, a wall of men and jeans broke apart and there was light and space and yelling. "Otis, stop it, Otis! That's enough." My dad kneeled over a man, holding his collar, dropping short, hard punches. At first there was a little blood. You couldn't see where it came from. Then there was a lot of it, like just *suddenly*, and the punches' sounds changed from thuds to pops. It took ten firemen to pull dad off. Seriously. Ten. He was strong back then.

That man my father beat, he was a drunk.

So now, dad went and took hold of the laborer's collar. My guts flushed because I half expected him to pull the .45 and blast his brains on the street. The laborer kept quiet. He was only tough with kids.

"Check it out," I showed Joey my ankle.

"What's that from?"

"Dogs, bro. One of'm bit me."

"Your dad gonna shoot him?"

"Joey, get in the car," Paolo said.

They were in the street, my dad and the laborer, and cars were lining up. They didn't blow their horns. People always blow their horns. It's the same as screaming at somebody, screaming, "You're an asshole." They never do that in line at the grocery store, do they? You never hear someone scream, *Move it, dickhead!* waiting in line at the bank. I kept waiting to hear those cars blow their stupid horns to get past Paolo's car on one side and my dad and the drunk on the other and it was pretty much entirely my fault that it was happening, which gave me the butterflies.

So then, they were like having a tug-o-war, dad and the laborer, with the laborer's collar. One drunk leg gave out and his body sagged in places you'd think a body couldn't sag. If it's possible to stand with a limp, that's what he did. My dad didn't look too sturdy either. I mean, the laborer could hardly stay upright, but he did, goopy as it looked. At least his body *could* goop, *could* sag. He had the flexibility. The health. Where the laborer sagged my dad was rigid. He had ceramic bones. I wanted to laugh because it was funny, but also from nerves.

"Whassit for," the laborer said. Dad pointed to the curb and told him, "Just sit the fuck down, hah," then turned pale and coughed with his palms on his thighs.

What'd he get? For coming after Joey and me for no reason, chasing us with planks and calling us whoknows-what in Spanish? Big deal, he got yelled at, and poked in the chest. It didn't bother him any. Our fathers weren't his father, and he wouldn't get belted across his ass. He'd be waiting at the gas station in the morning, holding a styrofoam cup. It was plain unfair. He should'a got a beating.

"Look at my leg," I told my dad. "He hit me with a nail. It was stuck in a plank and he cracked me on the ankle." I lifted my heel to show where the skin was torn above my ankle knob. "You see that?"

"Calm down a minute," dad said.

"He hit me."

"Just calm down."

"But he hit me!" That was nothing to dad. He hit me, too. He'd probably high-five him if he could talk Spanish.

"Well hit him back, the cocksucker. Hah? Why don't you punch him in the fuckin nose? He can't even stand." My dad didn't look real mean then.

His eyes were red but they'd been that way for weeks. He breathed heavy from the tug-o-war. "Wud'ja do, run from him? You don't run away! You stand your ground and fight! Why couldn't'cha hit him back?"

Man, I wanted to cry. Badly. My face was on fire. I wouldn't do it with Joey watching.

"Here he is," dad kept saying. "What'a you gonna do?" He coughed like he was holding change in his lungs. Then he took a knee.

I'd made up my mind to take a running kick at the laborer's teeth. But then something stopped me. I thought about my mom, and what the Lord says about forgiving your enemies and not repaying evil with evil. That made me feel better. I couldn't hit him even if dad and me both wanted it. Forgiving him was the only thing I *could* do. It made me sick to forgive him because it wasn't real forgiveness.

The truth is, I was too scared.

"You gotta kick him now," I told myself, "or you'll be awake all night, regretting. You won't sleep for a week!" It felt like a long time passed while I tried to force myself to hit him, before forgiveness made a coward of me. It was too late.

One of the passing cars pulled over. Four men in boots and cotton shirts got out. Hard looking men, not tattooed and shaved heads and prison looking, but in the way they walked straight at us. They were brick colored, with dirty hands. They surrounded my dad. I wished Paolo would get out of the Buick and pull the golf club out of his car's hood. We were in real trouble now and I expected he'd have reason to swing *this* time.

One of the four, the brick coloredest, black hairiest one of them stooped over my dad. I felt the butterflies whirl up my throat, spicy and sour. Here came the other three, circling.

Dad played it very cool, like all doubled over with a hand on his gut, clutching the .45.

"You okay, mister? You needing help?" That's all he said.

The other three went over to the laborer. I couldn't understand what they said but they weren't blessing his soul. They lifted him, hard. One of them kicked him in the ass. They cursed him beautifully. They kept repeating one word, Vito, which I guessed was his name. Vito kept saying, in English, "Take it ease. Whassit for?" They knew Vito and what a crappy drunk he was.

The brick colored man got a bottle of water from his car's trunk and gave it to my dad and said he'd take care of Vito, that he wasn't a very bad guy. "Just too much drinking." He made so many apologies you'd think it was *him* that caused the trouble. They put Vito in the car and drove off.

The police came. It was all over. My dad knew the cops. Knew their names.

"How's it going, Nolten? Hey, John. Yeah, some prick come after my son and his friend. We took care'v'm, the motherfucker."

That's how Joey's and my dad met. They didn't become friends or anything. They just asked about each other sometimes.

Me and Joey climbed into the fort. Twice the cigarette fell off my ear and I had to go down the crappy ladder and almost break my legs jumping over the workbench to pick it up. Then I put it back behind my ear. I just liked it there. I didn't want to smoke it or anything. Every now and then I took a few dry drags.

"Can you get a buzz that way," Joey wanted to know.

"I don't think so." I handed him the cigarette. He took a drag and held his breath.

"Shit's nasty," he said.

"I like the smell."

"It smells like a pile of raked up leaves. Why don't you light it? You look retarded with it hanging off your lip."

"I don't have matches."

The thing was, I didn't like cigarettes. I'd taken a thousand drags. Mostly from my dad, when we were at the firehouse or driving somewhere. I didn't call it a *drag* because I didn't know what a drag was. I'd ask him for a sip. I only asked him when we were alone, and he always gave me one.

My dad threw butts into the lawn after he smoked at the front door, looking into the street. He kept the door wide open, even in the middle of winter, when he smoked, with one hand on the doorframe. He wouldn't put his shirt on. He stood there letting in the frozen air. He had a hairy chest, so he didn't get cold. If I left the door open he'd have a *Jeremiad*! I picked butts out of the grass in the front yard. I lit them and watched myself smoke in the car window's reflection.

Once my sister and Sexy Lexy were standing out front of the house. I was inside watching TV with my dad. He was smoking on the couch when I asked him for a sip. He gave it to me without looking away from the screen. I didn't inhale it. It sat in my mouth getting spicy while I ran outside to blow the smoke in front of Sexy Lexy. The smoke had disappeared, dissolved into my saliva or something. I ran back and forth getting sips from my father's cigarette and running out.

"What are you doing, Le Perv?"

"Smoking," I told her.

"Go away," my sister said, "you're annoying. Sheesh!"

Sheesh. I hated that word. She used to say Jeez all the time but my mother thought it sounded too close to Jesus and made her stop.

I took one more sip from my dad. "Jesus Christ, watta you want your own fucking cigarette?" He looked around, probably for my mother. "What the hell are you doing running in and out of the house? Stay in or stay out."

"Alright, can I have one more sip?"

"Alright! Here," he said, and handed me the butt. I ran out of the house. "Don't throw it in the lawn," he yelled.

I blew a cloud in Lexy's face.

"Asshole," she said, fanning her eyes. "You know what that means, you nasty perv."

Blowing smoke in somebody's face means you want to beat that. She thought I was being a pervert. It makes sense though. There's something sexy about smoking cigarettes. You light a cigarette and the next thing in your mind is a girl. Or maybe she was there all along. I don't know why. Maybe it's advertising.

Mrs. Nailati started asking where her tissues went. They were scented tissues, the kind that won't make your nose sore, expensive. We had to steal newspapers off the neighbor's porch and shoot our batches on them instead. We didn't put them in the garbage where Joey's parents would find them. We stuffed them into corners, especially where there were cracks in the roof. It was getting cold outside. The fort looked like a squirrel's nest.

We joked around after we played with ourselves, and talked about school or baseball. We liked the Mets. The boys in our school were mostly Yankees fans. They're the other New York team. If you were a Yankees fan you always felt like a winner on account of the Yankees played in so many Pennants and won a hundred World Series. The Yankees could be in last place but it didn't matter, they still won more World Series than anybody else's team. It didn't make sense being a Yankees fan because we lived on Long Island and that's where the Mets played, at Citi Field, Queens. So we'd talk about things like that. Not the day I'm telling you about because after we finished whacking off Joey got a match and I lit the cigarette. I didn't inhale much, just like Amanda Voyage. I inhaled every other sip. There must be a link between cuming and smoking. As long as smoking makes you want a girl and vice versa people will always smoke. Especially kids my age, like sixteen. It doesn't matter if you don't use cartoons in the advertisement, or if you tell us it'll kill us. No teenager thinks he can die. Put the skull and crossbones on a pack of cigarettes, it'll only make me smoke more.

# Booze and Cola

He got sicker by the hour. My parents didn't talk about it. Not to me at least. My mother talked to the Lord and to Pastor Lynn and to her church friends. Big help! You could almost watch life slip out of him, blood speckled, and it didn't smell nice either.

For a while there were raffles and bake sales or car washes at the firehouse, trying to raise money to help pay his bills. Too late. We stopped going to the firehouse. They started coming to our house instead, bringing coffee, sitting with my dad on the couch and telling him about fires and car accidents, never holding back a curse word, and saying *look at the hangers on her* when a girl with big tits was on TV.

He didn't yell anymore. He was mostly friendly. Nobody'd give him what he wanted if he copped an attitude. He drank all the time. No one knew but me. All he wanted was cigarettes, Coca Cola, and booze. He wasn't allowed to smoke or drink, which was stupid. If he was going to die who cared if he had a cigarette? When nobody was home I slipped over to Cookie's house and got a couple smokes off her.

"He's not supposed to." Cookie had boney hands. She dug into her purse for a pack of Turkish Gold. "Larry, you haf'ta show you love him. That's the most important thing. He's a guy who knows you love him when you break the rules for him." Her voice was deep in her chest, grainy. "I've known Otis since way before you were born. You're a lot like him," she said. She probably thought I liked to hear that.

Cookie never brushed her own hair. She ran her fingers through mine and played with the part. She probably dyed ten heads a week but her hair was always messy and oily. It was a weird color, too, blonde and grey. She used to sing at a crappy bar a few blocks from my house. The guy who ran it was an old cop.

"You were towheaded. Your mother liked your hair feathered. You'd ask me for wings over your ears." She played with a curl near my eye as she said it. I pretended to sneeze so she'd stop. "Tell your father I hope he feels better. I'll come over tomorrow with some eggplant parm."

I ran out the door.

"Show him love," she called after me.

She never came over though, and saw how bad he looked. Every time I borrowed cigarettes off her she promised to visit. One time she walked into the pachysandras between our driveways. I saw her. She didn't have an eggplant or anything. She looked at our front door a minute then turned around and left.

He was sleeping anyway, on the couch. He slept so deeply, and he was so thin, he was practically another sheet, pale and wrinkled. You thought he was practicing for death. He wouldn't've known Cookie came.

When he woke up it took him a while to recognize where he was. He looked around the room. Then right in my face. "Hello," I said. He twitched and blinked.

"Jesus Christ," he said after a while. "Get me a cigarette." He said it like a question though, real sweet. I gave him one, lit it, then lit one for myself. I sat next to him on the chair with the burn holes in the arm.

"I want to go to Springkill. It's in a week, this trip. I got invited. Like one of my teachers recommended me. Joey's going, and so's Ashley, too, Rusty's daughter. You know her," I said to him one day home from school.

"Go to Springkill. What."

"Mom says I can't because. She doesn't want me to go. Plus it costs a hundred bucks."

"A hundred bucks? Why the hell we paying property taxes for? It's school, ain't it?"

"I don't know. It's for gas or something. I have some money for it," I told him. I had fifty-seven dollars saved from working with Uncle Lloyd. "But mom won't let me go."

"Fuck her."

"That's what I say. I mean, that's what I say. But she thinks…"

"Get me a drink, hah?"

"What kind?"

"Vodka Coke."

I went and got the drink. When I came back he'd fallen asleep again. He dropped ashes all over his sheet. The cigarette was on the floor burning. Smoke faded from his nostrils. I had to get the sheet off him. I'd be in trouble if my mother knew I let him smoke. One of his arms was twisted in the material.

"Goddamn son of a bitch." He woke up that way sometimes. Sometimes he took a long time with the death practice and sometimes he'd wake up angry. "What the hell'a you doing?"

"You burnt the stupid sheet," I said. "I have to put a new one down before mom comes home."

"Get me a drink."

"It's on the table, look," I said with a real attitude.

"Hand it to me."

"Take the sheet off first." He let me take the sheet. I put it in the laundry basket we keep next to the toilet. We don't keep it in the closet because my mom does the laundry and she hates closets. Our bathroom always smells like dirty socks.

When I came back he was sitting up. He'd almost finished the vodka Coke. It wasn't a weak drink either, the way he took it. The Coke was only like a tint or something, in it for the look.

"It's all I can keep down," he said, shaking the ice.

"Want another cigarette?" I wanted one. He only wanted another drink. I got that and put the new sheet at the end of the couch. "The Springkill trip is in a few days," I told him. "Mom won't let me go. She thinks she needs me here. Or like you need me here."

"I don't need you."

"That's what I keep saying."

"What do I need?" He looked at his bare feet, white and cracked like a dried out soap bar. He didn't cry but his eyes were red and wet. The tears leaked into the wrinkles weaving towards his ears. Piles of wrinkles gathered on his cheeks over the months. His face was climbing through his eyes. I didn't feel sorry for him, I only felt uncomfortable. He kept looking at me, mouthing words.

If he just rolled to his side and cried I would have felt bad for him. But he stared at me. I hate it when someone stares at me and mumbles. I wanted to get his permission to go to Springkill. He could have talked to my mother. She did anything he asked her to do, except give him cigarettes and booze. All he had to do was say, "Listen, Fran. Larry wants to go to Springkill with his friends. It's important for a boy to do those things." That's all he had to say. And she'd have let me go.

"Will you talk to mom, then? About Springkill? Just tell her you think I should go. She'll let me go if you tell her."

The thing about my dad is, you had to ask him twenty times before he answered. Like if I wanted to play kickball in the street with my friends. I'd stand at the front door ready to go and ask, "Can I go outside and play kickball, dad?" He'd stare at the TV. Even if there was a commercial on. I knew he wouldn't answer me right away. That's what was so irritating. "Dad? Dad, can I go play kickball?" It drove me nuts because I knew what was coming. Standing there like an asshole, right next to the door, I'd keep asking, "Dad?"

"What! Yes, Jesus Christ, go and leave me the fuck alone!" I'd bolt out the door. It put me in a crappy mood though. I wouldn't even want to play for a little while. I'd watch from the curb and feel angry.

That's what I expected.

"Will you tell mom? To let me go to Springkill?" He quit trying to say anything. He looked at the coffee table where the last cigarette was. "Dad?" I kept asking him, "Dad, dad, dad?" I said it over and over. "Dad, dad, dad, dad." Like that.

"Hand me that cigarette."

"Mom said you can't smoke," I said and snatched the cigarette away.

"I don't give a shit what she says. This is my fucking house."

"Not for long," I said.

"Who you talking to you little bastard! Hah?" He looked around the room. I'll admit, I got scared out of habit.

"What're you looking for? Your belt? You wanna hit me," I said.

"I'll rip your fuckin heart out."

I stood up slowly, went and picked up his lighter from the end table and put it in my pocket. I slid the cigarette behind my ear. Then I bent down so my dad could see my face. I was allowed to hate him now. We were eye to eye. "Fuck you," I said. He didn't move. He didn't say a word as I walked out the door.

I went over to Joey's house, checking the streets for the dogs as I walked. Joey played sick the night before so he could stay home from school. I wasn't sure he'd be home because he had to go to the doctor every time he pulled the fake puke gimmick.

I stood on the deck railing and looked into his bedroom. He wasn't there so I climbed into the fort. I didn't switch on the bulb or anything. It was pretty dark. There's one little window with a fan in it blocking most of the light. I sat on a spackle bucket we'd found in a dumpster and rolled the cigarette between my palm and my knee. What I felt like doing was going back home and giving the cigarette to my father. I kept thinking about what I said to him, "Fuck you," right in his face. I wondered if he was crying. If his eyes were getting watery. Was he sleeping? I felt rotten.

Joey's mom's black Jeep pulled into the driveway. You could see pretty clear through the window, even with the fan in it. Joey got out of the car with a fistful of keys. His mother stared through the windshield looking bored. It's hard to imagine what a person is thinking. You can only put your own thoughts in their head. I didn't know much more about Mrs. Nailati than she spent half her day cooking and the other half getting her toenails polished or babysitting some brats in Flower Hill where the Nailati's used to live. I tried to think of something to put in her head besides cooking or worrying about Joey but I couldn't. A person's mind is blocked by more than skull bone.

The more I thought about it, sitting in the fort watching Mrs. Nailati, I started getting this feeling. First it was only a nauseas feeling, which happened twelve times a day, but then a vibration started in my guts. Just in one spot. The buzzing grew bigger. It filled my stomach. Then it broke open, like when a sausage pops on the grill and meat squeezes out sizzling.

Joey went back to the car and handed the keys to his mother. She said something to him I couldn't hear. She probably asked what he wanted for dinner, then she backed out of the driveway and drove off.

I worried that Joey would call my house. He'd always call when he was home alone and then I'd come over. We kept the phone next to the couch where my father laid his head. That way my mom check on him every few hours, or if he needed to call someone he didn't have to get up. He'd been falling. Now, if Joey called, my dad would wake up and answer. Joey'd hang up even though my dad wouldn't care if Joey dropped out of school. It made me sick to think about him answering the phone. The sausage broke in a dozen places, with worms stretching out of the holes. I lit the cigarette and took deep drags.

Joey came out to the deck and looked up at the fort. I pulled away from the window so he wouldn't see me.

I hid behind a cardboard box we had up there and soon as Joey's knees were through the fort's door I jumped on his back. "Gotcha, motherfucker." He threw me off though. He's stronger than me.

"I knew you were up here," he said. I was pinned.

"No you didn't."

"Yeah, I saw smoke coming out the window. Where's the cigarette?"

"It's on the soda can by the bucket. Get the hell off me. I'm on a nail."

"You whack off already?"

"I just came in. Get off." He got off me. It was true about the nail. I had one of those bubblegum looking marks on my skin."

"The doctor took my blood today." He showed me a red dot on his arm. "They gotta do all these tests. Only cos my mom's worried. The doctor knows I'm not sick, I think. He's always asking why the hell I'm in his office again. He's alright though. He won't say shit."

"He's alright," I said.

"What the hell's a matter with you?"

"Nothing. What? I got a scratch from the nail you threw me on."

Joey wiggled his finger over a picture on the wall. "I can't wait until Springkill, bro. I'm definitely fucking Alicia."

That got on my nerves. "I doubt it," I said. You shouldn't talk about fucking girls in Springkill when your best friend can't go.

"Yeah right."

"Seriously," I said. "I doubt it."

"You're jinxing me. Don't be a dick."

"You had the chance last week. Right in that corner. All Alicia did was flap her gums at Ashley, and cock block. If she cock blocked me here she definitely won't let you beat it up in the woods." Joey and me snuck the girls into the fort the week before. I don't know, maybe he had a chance. I was pissed off, that's all.

Joey was in love with Alicia Miller. I could tell she didn't like him the same. She always hung out with her friends, seven of them, all at once. You could never get one of them alone. Except at the movies. I kissed half of them at the movies. If you tried to feel them up, even over their shirts, they'd bite your face off. At first she'd slap your hand away. Not slap, push. She'd move closer to you and press her chest against yours, airtight. You couldn't hammer a nail between you and her tits. Sometimes you ran your hand along her side and felt where boob squeezed out. You were allowed to rub her squeezed tit but you couldn't palm them. Nipples were strictly off limits.

They aren't that way these days, the girls in eleventh grade. I'll tell you about it later if I get a chance. A pack of skanks.

"Are you coming to Springkill or not? Did you talk to your father," Joey asked.

"Yeah, I talked to him."

"And?"

"You really think you're gonna fuck Alicia?"

"I'm telling you, she promised me. You gotta get'm to sneak out. That's the hard part. My brother's been telling me. The girls are scared to sneak out, but they're not scared to fuck."

"Maybe that's why she promised you. She can pretend she's scared to sneak out when you get to Springkill, so she won't have to do it. And for now you'll stop bothering her in school. Girls are just as tricky as you, Joey."

"Why won't she want to? Lookit what happened last week. Just cos Ashley don't want to talk to you anymore doesn't mean…"

"You don't know that. If she doesn't want to talk to me."

"Yeah, okay. She hasn't talked to you since last week. You freaked her out."

"You and Alicia still talk and you did the same thing as me."

The funny thing about a fire is you don't take it seriously at first. You can be afraid of closets or spiders but a little flame barely catches your attention.

"Oh shit, bro." Joey saw it first. He crawled to the flames. You had to stay low in the fort. We were always banging our heads. The flames were around the soda can and in the middle of them was my cigarette. The filter was burnt black.

Joey made a big mistake. Anybody who didn't know about fires, if their dad wasn't a fireman, would've done the same. He tried to *blow* the fire out, like it was a candle. Wood dust flew in the air. The fire jumped into it, then hopped like crickets from the floor to the walls, eating the magazine pages. Magazine pages burn blue, if you never saw.

"Stop blowing it," I said. I took off my shirt. That's how you put out small fires, you smother them with a blanket or shirt. My hands banged against the rafters as I undressed in a hurry. The shirt snagged a roofing nail. Joey kept blowing at the fire, spreading it, and when I finally threw my shirt on one part of the fire two more had started. The fort was filled with smoke.

"Bro, let's get out. We need a fire extinguisher. Joey!" I mean, we needed an extinguisher, or a blanket even, and then I could've put out the fire.

The magazine pages came apart. Black feathers with glowing edges spread all over. Then the crumpled newspaper pages and crusty old tissues wedged in the rafters caught fire fast and bright.

"Joey! Let's go." I kept saying that, "Let's go!" I dangled from the fort's door. Finally Joey started backing out.

Before the fire trucks pulled up along the curb in front of the house the garage had col*lapsed.* I knew the firemen. Every one of them. A garage fire is usually fun, because of the gas tanks in cars. Sometimes there are kerosene heaters or butane tanks in a garage, and they explode. Joey's garage only had tools and garbage. The fire was out in two minutes. It took one engine, the American LaFrance with its hale pump, to extinguish it. Another pumper showed up anyway and a few police cars and the Chief's Suburban, all with lights spinning. "Hello Larry. Hey, how's the old man?" The firemen asked about my father.

It burned to the ground. All that was left was the cement foundation and a few broken studs poking out from the rubble with the raw, white look of bones. The hoses rinsed the ash and the old dirt off the handles on the lawn mower and weed whacker and they shined in the sunlight and soggy ashes.

"Were you in the garage," Eddy Bird asked me. He's one of the firemen. He was Chief about five years before Steven Lundgren got it. He had a round, dull face, nothing like a bird's. His last name should've been Coon or something.

"Nah. We weren't in there," I told him.

"It started up top," he said. "That plywood is burnt on one side. There was a floor laid down over the joists. A loft space caved and knocked out the wall on that side." He was pointing at the wall and looking at my face.

"Yeah, we had a fort up there."

"And you weren't in it today?"

"Nope. We had a couple extension cords for lights and…"

"It's a school day, isn't it? Garrett's in school. Why weren't you in school?"

"Stayed home for my dad."

"What about your friend?"

"He had a doctor's appointment."

Eddy was making me nervous.

The whole neighborhood watched, in the street or through their windows. People always watch a fire.

"Why're you here if he was at the doctor's and you're supposed to be home with Otis?"

"I already did a lot today, changing dad's sheets and choreing around the house and he said he was feeling pretty good and I should go for a ride on my bike or something because I've been staying home from school a lot and it's boring. I knew Joey would be home after a while so I came over here and played video games instead of riding my bike and getting chased by the dogs."

"Where's the video game?"

"In his house. Where else?"

"What game did you play?"

Normally I could have rattled off the names of a dozen games but on the spot I couldn't think so I said, "Jinx On The Captain," which doesn't even sound like a video game but more like a board game people sat around playing after dinner fifty years ago.

"What kind of game is it?" Of course he'd ask me that! And I could've described as many first person shooter games as I've got knuckles but instead I told him it was a space invasion game.

"Garrett plays those damn games all day. Loud. I can't stand it sometimes." Garrett is his son, about two years younger than me. "I got to find him a quieter game. Jinx On The Captain? Sounds like a strategy game."

"Oh yeah. Exactly."

"Must be quiet. I should look at it."

Now I saw my toes were on the line.

"No, it's not quiet. That's why me and Joey were playing it today, because his parents weren't home. When they're home they make us turn the volume down but it's the kind of game where things either creep up on you or the music'll change to clue you something's gonna happen so you gotta have the volume way up, and then it gets explosively loud."

"Which room were you playing the game in?"

"The den right there." I pointed at the windows in the front of the house.

"You can't see the garage from that room."

"Nope."

"Tell me. At what point did you notice the fire? Couldn't hear it. Couldn't see it."

He had me stumped again so I pretended I'd just spotted Aaron Wilcox sitting on the pumper's bench pulling off his boots and I waved hello and thought for a second, then said, "Joey and me were playing for an hour straight and he started getting hungry. His dad just got meat and oil and olives from Italy a couple days ago and I'm never allowed to eat it while his parents are home, so we went in the kitchen and saw the smoke through the windows and that's when we dialed nine-one-one."

"Alright, Larry. Alright," he said, "run home. Your father's sure to hear this over dispatch. He's probably worried about you now. Get right home and tell'm we miss him and I'll come by with coffee."

I left kind of glad and worried at the same time. I heard enough stories to know insurance and investigators get involved and their job is to blame somebody, and make them pay. I only had fifty-seven dollars and couldn't even buy a stack of roofing shingles.

My mother came home and started crying soon as she got her arms around me. She sat on the couch and held both my hands and prayed. She didn't pray out loud or anything, she just closed her eyes. I closed mine, too, but all I could think about, I was worried Joey's parents would be angry and not let us hang out for a while.

My father came from the kitchen. He had the sheet I got for him wrapped around his shoulders.

"I heard," he said.

He's got this alert. It makes a bunch of noises that sound like car alarms. They're signals for different fire districts. Our district is called Huntington Manor. The alert makes a noise and then a voice comes on and announces what kind of fire is happening and what size it is. The voice is the dispatcher and he's sitting in a little room at the firehouse. It's all done through code. My father always kept it on. I can still hear the sound it made for Huntington Manor. It's like an old song you can't forget. And I remember the way my dad turned down the television when the alert went off and squinted as he listened. He'd get off the couch, put on his shirt. He'd light a cigarette as he walked out the door then jump into his black van, pop the blue light on the roof and gun it down the driveway. The firehouse opened its foghorn over Huntington Manor about two seconds later. And as dad rolled through the corner stop sign the last thing you saw was his American flag bumper sticker disappear around the corner.

Dad walked down the hallway. He closed his bedroom door.

I didn't have to ask again. My mom let me go to Springkill. Fires, good or bad, they change things completely.

# There's Money in the Woods

For a long time, Ashley was this annoying kid following us around, me and another boy named Steven, when we went camping. She looked younger than other girls her age. She was thin and straight. My mom called her rangy. She looked like a ten-year-old boy. Her blonde hair was so oily it could slip out of her scalp. We had a broom at the house and when the handle broke my dad fixed it with duct tape and made a bulge in the middle. That's what Ashley's legs looked like, broken broomsticks.

We always went to the same campgrounds, upstate New York, maybe next to Springkill. All those places look alike; the same people, same sky, and way in the distance the same wooly mountains. Mostly it's the smell of the campgrounds that's the same. I don't know what it is. The damp earth maybe, or moss. And the smell of horseshit, of course.

There was a stable and corral at the camp's entrance. The cars pulled into the dirt lot together. The men got out at the same time. As if they'd just arrived to a fire. They registered their cars while kids and wives watched the horses stand around and chew. You could rent a horse if you wanted. None of the firemen did.

The thing for kids to do was explore. Sometimes you found a paint pot or an arrowhead near the lake from some Indian hunter in prehistoric times. You'd bring that back to the campsite and everybody got excited. They'd tell you it was worth a million bucks. I don't know who you sell an arrowhead to. You always had some firecrackers in your pocket. They weren't for fun but for safety, to make noise if you got lost and had to wait for someone to find you. We used them to blow up beetles sometimes.

I liked searching for dead animals. A dead animal doesn't last in the woods. Other animals eat it. When you find a good one, a fresh kill or a kind of animal you'd never seen before, you look at its fur and in its mouth. You turn it over and play with its ears. Sometimes you found a skull with patches of leather and fur on it and the spine tailing off. You weren't supposed to touch dead animals in case they were diseased. You used the end of a stick to move it around. You always had a walking stick with you. It was the first thing you did when you got to campsite after helping your dad unpack the suitcases and tent from the car. You found a good strong walking stick. A walking stick was also good for poking around the fire at night, moving logs and trash closer to the center.

There was a lake to swim in and you could fish it, too. None of the adults fished. Only the kids fished. I don't think there was anything to catch though. Fishing kept us out of everyone's hair while they cooked, drank Coors Light and told stories. When the sun set a chill crept from the ground. Everybody got chairs and sat around the fire and told stories about car wrecks, and structure fires, and how badly someone was hurt or killed. The women held a hand over their mouth and crossed their legs a thousand ways. One of them would say, "Oh, I can't listen to this part," and she'd turn away in her seat. She wouldn't leave the conversation or close her ears, she'd just turn away. That's how you knew who to call Missus so and so, if she couldn't listen to the bad parts of stories. If they listened to the bad parts you could call a fireman's wife by her first name.

That's how I knew Ashley, from camping trips. I didn't know we were the same age. She followed me and Steve Lundgren Jr. around. Steven's father was Fire Chief for a while. Steven was a few years older but he hung around with me anyway probably because one, he was dorky. He was an Eagle Scout and everything. He could survive in the woods but he couldn't make it a day without getting his ass kicked in school. My sister told me about it. They went to high school together. And two, besides Steven, I was the oldest boy there. Anyone near Steven's age stayed home and called girls over to the house while their parents went into the woods to drink on Labor Day weekend.

He stuttered when he got excited, like when he talked about survival, and making fires and shelter. Or fighter jets. If he wasn't talking about survival he was talking about fighter jets. He knew everything about them.

One camping trip Steven came over to me stuttering like crazy. We finished building the tents and put our sleeping bags down and had unloaded the crap from the trucks about two minutes before. "Dude, I found two p-p-puh-perfect walking sticks. They were gonna use'm in the fuh-fuh-fire," and he stuck one in my hand. He was super excited about something.

We walked into the woods. Ashley was behind us even though no one invited her. Steven and me were walking fast. She was looking for paint pots or arrowheads or something. The whole time, Steven told me about the A-10 Thunderbolt, an airplane that was shooting up tanks in Iraq, and how it was nicknamed Warthog because it was ugly.

"It's a single seater," he told me. "The pilot basically sits on top of a thirty muh-millim-muh-meter Gatling cannon. It shoots thirty-nine hundred rounds a minute. The gun's suh-so strong it slows the plane down, like air brakes." He had to stop to explain it. He snorted like he was scratching his throat. "That's how it sounds. Like a hog." While he talked I smashed old branches off trees with my walking stick. "By the time I'm a pilot we'll be fighting Chinky China. I can't wait till I'm fuh-flying an A10 and spraying holes in Nip tanks."

We didn't notice Ashley was gone, we just heard firecrackers popping. So we went back. Steven was mean when we found her.

"The biggest risk to a soldier is someone doing something stupid like getting l-luh-lost or hurt," Steven said.

"I wasn't lost, you dork. Look." Ashley was a brat back then. "I found a horse."

You couldn't see it at first, where she was pointing. A white and brown mound, half buried in by fern and other stuff. You could smell it though. Horse shit! There was a dark haze around it, like its shadow had fallen out and sunk oily into the brush. She had no eyes, just stringy black holes. The lips rolled up her teeth and her tongue hung out all dry and hard. Her skin was drum-tight over her bones, split down the side and showing white ribs and spongy darkness. Her front legs were bent as if she'd jumped into death.

Under her tail were dried out clumps of crap. It made me sad to see it. That was the only thing that was real about her. Old hey someone who loved her had fed her.

"She must have jumped the corral," Steven said.

"Don't poke her," Ashley said. Steven was poking it with his walking stick.

Then a howl rolled through the forest.

Most firehouses have a dog. On television a firehouse always has a Dalmatian, but that's bullshit. The firehouses I know, the ones on Long Island I'd see at tournaments, they have all sorts of dogs. Sometimes there'd be a Dalmatian, but not mostly. Most firehouses, if you really kept track, have bulldogs.

Our firehouse, Huntington Manor, had a black and tan Coonhound named Bonkers. His nose was keen as a shark's. He couldn't hear very well I think. His foot-long ears hung down like he'd been in the laundry and got a pair of pants stuck on his head. He was always scratching his ears. Anytime I was at Station One—Huntington Manor has three stations—we played together for a bit, Bonkers and me. Then he'd go and lay down next to the Heavy Rescue truck on his blanket. I'd climb all over the Engines and Tower Ladder. My fingers stunk like ear infection after I played with Bonkers. I had to wash my hands, twice. It must be terrible to have such a strong nose and always smell your own ear infections. I guess he got used to it.

They heard Ashley's firecrackers at camp and sent Bonkers out with Terry Ward and Ken Hertig, two of the firemen, to find us. The howls got closer.

"Should I light off more," Ashley asked.

"We're not even lost! Nice job!" Steven was pissed.

"We can't leave until they find us or else they'll keep looking and everyone will get scared, Steven. We have to wait."

"They're going to think we got lost!"

Ashley went to light off more firecrackers but Steven said, “Gimme those,” and tore them from her hands. He lit the fuses and threw them in the air. They went off over our heads. A few minutes later we saw Bonkers at the end of his leash, sniffing low and high. “Bonky boy,” I called but he couldn’t hear me. He got closer, stretched his neck and pointed his nose.

“Good boy, Bonkers,” Ashley said.

“Who’s a stinky boy,” I said.

“You guys found us so fast,” Ashley said to Terry and Ken.

“Old Bonkers got the scent and took off like an arrow,” Ken said.

“He knows his family,” Terry said.

“Do you guys often rescue lost kids,” Ashley asked.

“All the time,” Ken said but you could tell he was lying. “Most times kids run away and their mothers call the police and the police call us. We take old Bonkers and he usually sniffs ‘em out behind their garage. They don’t go far.”

“We found a horse,” Ashley said. Her ankles pressed together. “Over there. See her?”

“Shit, look at that,” Terry said. He walked closer. “It’s smiling. Goofy looking sumbitch. They call that a Roan horse. I know them kind a horses. We should call down let ‘em know. They’re expensive them things.”

“Shit yeah,” Ken said. “Like ten thou apiece.”

Arrowheads and horses, there’s all kinds of money in the woods.

“Can we finally go where I wuuuh-wanted to,” Steven got all stuttery. He stutters when he’s mad.

“We gotta bring you back,” Terry said.

“I’m not going. I’m taking Larry, too. We’re not lost. I didn’t get lost.”

“Chief will murder me I don’t bring you back.”

“We’re not even lost,” Steven said again. “It was Ashley. She’s retarded.”

“I’m not retarded. I found a horse.”

“Go tell them that. Go back to the camp and tell them about the horse!”

“I don’t want’a go back. I’m going with you guys.”

“Hey, look at’r hoof,” Kenny said. He was standing way the hell over by where the horse’s leg was. He picked it up. It was stiff as a branch. He turned it over, sniffing and smiling. “Doesn’t stink,” he said. “Terry, let’s take the leg bones back to camp. We tell Big Steve about the horse and call down to the barn. They done the right thing."

Terry took a squint at the bones. He pulled a strip of clear leather, like cigarette paper, off the ankle. "The hoof is hollow. I didn't know they had hollow hooves. I thought they were like rubber. How do they make glue out of hard-old hollow hooves?"

Bonkers wouldn't look at it. He walked all over sniffing the air, then dropped his head and dragged his ears in the dirt.

"Alright," Terry said. "Let's take the bones. They'll prolly comp us a night for finding her. Steven, don't let'nybody light off no more poppers unless you're lost. Unnerstand?"

Where we went, Steven took us to an old slate quarry we'd found the year before. A river runs through it, shimmering flat, then branches out around bright pebble dunes a hundred yards before funneling into a channel.

"Who gives a crap," I told Steven. "We already knew about this." We'd been there the year before. There was a waterfall and weird tunnels going in and out of steep bank walls. There were deep sockets in the riverbed you could see along the water like sunken shadows. The streams were mostly knee deep but the sockets were deep as your chest. The water in them was black. There was an old sign nailed to a tree that said *No Trespassing!* overgrown with vines. That was pretty cool. Not cool, ironic. But it was nothing to stutter about and yell at people for getting lost.

"We didn't come to see the stupid quarry." Steven walked along the deep part of the river near the falls, stopping every ten feet to look under these long slices the river cut into the rock bed.

"Why're we here," I yelled across the quarry.

Steven belly crawled, reaching under the blue slate shelves, feeling for something. Then he dunked his body in the water. "Fuck my ass, that's cold," he howled. The water under the shelf was dark as coffee. The river swept over Steven's shoulders and neck. His two feet kicked pebbles all over the place. I didn't worry because he's an Eagle Scout Big Shot with fifty honor badges and dunking yourself in black river water was probably some test he passed.

A glassy water tube tangled in his shirt. He was wearing this triple extra-large *Huntington Manor Hook & Ladder Company* T-shirt and it filled like a parachute. It dragged him off the shelf into the stream. He clutched the ledge with his fingernails.

"Help him," Ashley screamed.

The water bit my ankles. My shoes filled up and weighed a hundred pounds. It was slow going, even across the shallow parts of the stream. Steven got a leg on the shelf and the one arm in the river breast stroked like crazy to keep his nose above water. It wasn't funny I guess but I laughed as I ran. I don't know, the river could've sucked him into the hole and he'd drown but I'd never seen someone die and I couldn't imagine it happening. That's why I don't care when someone gets killed in a movie or on the news, because I've never seen it for real, never seen someone die the way I've seen a dead horse, or a squirrel hit by a car, or a dog shot. It's easy to imagine animals being killed. You see it all the time. They're roasting in the oven. You wear them on your feet. Every time an animal gets killed, like on the news or in a movie, I wish it were a person instead.

Finally I reached Steven. I pulled him by the shirt. It tore a little. He came up with something dangling from his hand, a fish or something shining. He rolled onto his back and coughed.

"That's the most dangerous thing a solider can do, Steven," Ashley yelled from across the river. She was upset.

What it was though, what Steven had caught, it was a six-pack of Coors Light. "I hid it here luh-last year. Before we broke camp."

Broke camp. What a cornball.

We sat on the riverbank and drank beer. Coors Light, it's my favorite. Steven had three and I had two. We gave one to Ashley so she wouldn't rat.

That was the last year the three of us camped together. Steven went to military school. It was his dream to fly fighter jets. He never got to be a pilot though, because he stuttered. You can have a million badges of honor but you can't fly fighters with marbles in your mouth. Ashley got bored of camping. Girls don't like it after a while. My sister for example, she never camped. So I didn't see Ashley for two years, until we met again in Finley Jr. High.

# Hung Christ

We made it through Junior High. It was the last week. We were all friends after two years together, familyish. We knew what we could get away with on the bus ride to Springkill, like grabbing tits in the back seat and cursing under our breath. I mostly sat with Ashley, my girlfriend for five months. Joey sat with Alicia Miller.

Our chaperones were two teachers. Mrs. Ackerly and Mr. Brush. They sat up front talking to each other and with a Japanese kid we called Moto and another nerdy fat kid, "Chops" Lambert. For a while Mrs. Ackerly sewed. She had some red fabric and a three-feet-long bamboo stick thick as your thumb.

Ackerly and me were enemies. She taught Home Economics. She hated me from day one. Before that even. The first time I walked into her classroom she pulled me aside. "Follow me," she said. She hadn't even taken attendance yet. The other kids talked and messed around while I went to the empty classroom next door with Ackerly. She was going take a *peremptory strike* at my *insubordination*, which was a gateway crime in her book that, if she stopped it early, would save the world a lot of trouble from punks like me.

We stood just inside the door, with the lights out. "You make a lot of jaws jabber in the faculty. And bottles of aspirin are in demand. So let me make it clear to you. In my class you will show respect!" That's exactly what she said. "Now, you're going to explain to me how you'll do that. In plain English! So I'll understand."

I didn't say a thing. If she wanted to yell, she could knock herself out. I'd heard it all before, and she had nothing on my dad. But I wasn't going to *participate* in my own punishment. Instead, for no reason, I smiled.

No one had ever seemingly enjoyed her *peremptory strike* before. She snatched at my face. "Look at me!" One blue fingernail scraped my chin. "How dare you! Giggle! While I'm striking at you. When I'm speaking, that's the last thing you will do. You will not interrupt. You will not speak. You will not cough, sneeze, or squeak!"

I felt a cold sting on my chin while Ackerly *upbraided* me. I never learned a thing in her class but synonyms for crime and punishment.

When I got home from school the scrape had scabbed. My mother asked what happened. I didn't tell her. She would have asked why Ackerly was forced to yell at me instead of caring that I'd been scratched. I could have made a big deal about it, like gone to the principal and ratted. But I didn't think about it until long after because even though I was smiling in her face and acting like I was having a good time, really, then and for the three periods after she yelled at me, I felt sad and little scared. I'd never met Mrs. Ackerly, but she knew me. My other teachers had told her I was an asshole, and that she should tear my face off before she even counted the students in her class.

I should have told on her and got her fired. But I wasn't smart and quick enough. You have to be smart and quick if you want to be mean.

We were on a regular school bus, a yellow one. The only place to put your suitcase was under the seat. They warned us to just take the necessities, whatever you needed to walk around the woods and to wash yourself. Plus some snacks. Ashley packed her entire closet. Her suitcase took up all the space beneath our seat. I had to jam it under there for her while she moaned, "Careful, god," because I used my feet to shove it. She didn't say thanks or anything. I only had a duffle bag my mom packed for me. I put it under my feet and sat with my knees against my chest. Ashley didn't even sit. She was on her knees resting her chin on the backrest, talking to Alicia. She just kneeled there ignoring me.

Joey broke in on their conversation once in a while asking are you hungry or something. Or he butted in to kiss Alicia. While her attention was broken for one second I'd ask Ashley if she was comfortable. I was being sarcastic. I brought my knees up to my nose. I pretended I couldn't breathe. She smiled and turned her face to the window.

Joey put his fist against his mouth and stuck his tongue into his cheek, faking a blow job.

"Lame," Ashley said when I laughed.

"You don't even know what I'm laughing about."

"Whatever, it's lame."

"It's funny."

"Lame."

"Funny."

"Lame."

"Are we going to sneak out tonight? I think we should the first night," I said.

"Laaame," Ashley moaned. Her and Alicia cracked up.

"Wanna to listen to The Zeros, Ash?" Alicia and Ashley were into 70's punk. They were really two very cool girls. Jesus.

"Yes! Put it on."

They shared the headphones. Ashley had the left ear and Alicia had the right. After that you couldn't talk to them.

"I told you it ain't gonna be easy get'n'm to sneak out. My brother said it's the hardest part," Joey said.

"What are you wearing?" I noticed Joey was dressed different. He wasn't wearing his big white Nike's. He wore brown pants with extra pockets, and they fit tight.

"What? Clothes," he said.

"You got a vest on. What's it made of." I pinched the edge of his vest. "What is that?"

"It's wool, dumb ass."

"Why you wearing a wool friggin vest? And fancy boots?"

"They're not fancy." Everyone hates being fancy. "We're gonna be on a mountain hiking in the woods, retard."

"Big deal! I hike in the woods all the time. I never needed a wool vest. Look at the Indians. Native Americans I mean. They wore moccasins, which were basically leather bags on their feet."

Nobody else wore a vest. It was only Joey. He was trying to look hot shit for some reason. I let it go after a while. So he wouldn't feel weird.

You only saw highway for five friggin hours, and those rest stops where prostitutes get murdered. We were in a regular school bus, like I said, not a silver liner where people sit higher than a tractor-trailer with their luggage in a bunker underneath them. Those busses are practically yachts. They got televisions and everything. Bathrooms even. I went to Vermont in one of those busses. My dad's cousin Ray lives on a maple farm with his wife. They make syrup. Every year around Labor Day my dad and mother and sister and me went on vacation. We mostly went camping with the firehouse. But one year we went to Vermont instead.

I had to call my dad's cousin *Uncle* Ray because he was even older than my dad. I can't stand things like that, calling someone Uncle because they're old or something. I'd never even met him before and I had to call him Uncle. I don't remember his wife's name but I had to call her Aunt, like to keep things balanced and respectful. She was Ray's third wife. My dad never even met her, but still. I didn't want to call her Aunt, which she wasn't, so I never called her anything. My mother makes my friends call her Misses Morvan. She introduces herself that way. "I'm Misses Morvan," with a big smile. My dad though, he didn't give a crap. You could call him anything you wanted but my friends ended up calling him Mister Morvan because my mom made things awkward. He was pretty cool in a way. He was a joker with everybody, especially with my friends. But mostly he was a dickhead with me. Anyway, the whole ride to Vermont, mom asked dad questions about the maple farm. What kind of animals did they have? Do they still take in stray cats? Are they building a bed and breakfast on the property? How many acres have they?

"I don't know, Francine, shit." That's how my dad answered.

"What's the name of the farm?"

"Something with the word sugar in it. Who the hell cares?" He got a kick out of not answering her. Sometimes he looked at me and winked. We teased my mother quite a bit. That's the only thing we did together, tease my mom.

"Did Ray mention there'd be an antiques show this weekend?"

"I hope not. Antiques. Christ!"

"Please, Otis."

"Jesus H. Christ! Hey, tell me what the 'H' stands for, Fran. They teach you that in bible class?" Then he gave me the wink.

"Holy," my sister said. "Jesus Holy Christ."

"Enough. Cut it out right now!" My mother was sensitive about religious things. Ever since she lost her baby, all she talked about was Jesus and the Lord. She never even said "God," only "the Lord."

My mother was saved and went to church every Sunday. Sometimes more. She made my sister and me go to bible study, which is even more boring than regular school. I learned about Jesus's miracles and how he went ministering around. The pastor's favorite stories were about how the Romans *hung* Jesus on the cross. She sort of sung the word with her eyes half closed. Her eyebrows practically flew off her face. It's a funny word. It barely gets out of your throat. It's probably the only English word you don't need your mouth to say. Anytime someone said *Jesus H. Christ!* the word *hung* popped into my head. Guys said it all the time at the firehouse. They had terrible mouths.

I thought a lot about my dad on the way to Springkill. I wasn't worried or anything. I was just thinking about him. Everything reminded me of him. I almost missed the trip. That reminded me of him, too. Anytime someone asked if we were almost there I'd remember we were going to Springkill. Then I'd remember I almost didn't go. Then I'd think about my dad. He'd been locked in his bedroom for a few days. I hadn't seen him since the fort caught fire.

The bus slowed as it climbed up a mountain. It got dark, then light, then dark again closer to the Springkill campgrounds. You could see a hundred miles across the Allegheny Plateau. You feel your eyeballs stretch when you look across the valley to the clouds clinging to the mountains. After a while we turned onto a road no wider than the bus. We could see over the road's edge to the valley streams snaking around cat skiffs and spotted with puffs of shrubbery. Each time we turned a corner me, Joey and Robby Morales jumped to one side of the bus and tried to flip it. The girls shrieked and laughed until Mrs. Ackerly told the driver to stop. She stood in the aisle, her thighs brushing the seats each side of her, and she stared us in the eyes. She didn't say anything she just stared and shook her head, slowly floating it from side to side like a buoy in Huntington's harbor tide.

"Look at her fat chin," Alicia said when the bus started moving again. "Are you okay Mrs. Akerly? Even her ears are fat. Like, is your face okay?"

"Even her fat is fat," Ashley said giggling. "Is your lard okay?"

"It's like her fat is wearing a turtleneck," Alicia said. "Is your neck okay?"

They kept that up a while, making fat jokes and cracking each other up. And ignoring me and Joey.

Mostway up the mountain we turned onto a dirt road with a parting of grass up the middle. We drove along until we came to a gate, which was a long log tied to a pole on one end and a wheelbarrow tire on the other. Next to the gate there's a little shed with a man inside. He came out with a clipboard and talked to the bus driver. Then he rolled the log gate away and waved us through. He kept waving to us as the bus passed, like we'd just arrived at Disneyland. Tree branches brushed against the bus. Dust whiffed through cracked windows. Joey jumped when the bus hit bumps and catapulted against the ceiling. His shoulders banged against the roof like a drum. He had us laughing in the back rows. Ackerly kept turning to glare at us. Joey sat still, innocence oozing out of his face, looking guilty as hell.

Gravel crattled under the bus's tires. We were all quiet and fidgeting on our knees with our faces pressed against the window as we pulled into the parking lot.

You'd see one kid and you'd recognize him from a little league team you played third base for but you're too shy to walk up and say hullo, remember me? It's easier for dogs, they know right away if they like you or not. That's why I like them I guess, like Bonkers. Kids, too, the little ones, because they're just like dogs. If they like you, you know it. They practically slobber on you. They even get annoying. When they go back to their moms you know they aren't going to bad mouth you. You don't know that with older people.

There were other busses in the parking lot, from Woodhall and Washington. And from Flower Hill, where the rich kids go. The schools stayed together at first. Then some girl would look over and recognize somebody. Girls are always recognizing each other from a dance class or a theatre camp or something. Then the girls, both of them, squeal and sprint to each other and hug and swing around in circles. Two guys couldn't do that. When a guy recognizes somebody he nods and says, "W'dup, son?" And the other goes, "Oh shit, what up?" They slap hands, one-arm hug, and generally act like they don't give a shit.

Finley kids didn't have a chance to slap hands or one-arm hug anyone because right away Mrs. Ackerly yelled, "Finley Junior High." She has a sack under her chin. It jiggles when she talks. She stepped up on her suitcase. She wasn't too graceful, either. She's round in the middle, with short legs and arms, like a turkey. The suitcase hissed air while Mrs. Ackerly wobbled around for balance. It deflated. It sagged so low she was practically on the floor. "You are going to gather your belongings and follow me to our cabin. Before you do so," she looked around. "Before you do so," she repeated, with a pause. A serious look drooled over her face. "Notice the white van." She pointed across the parking lot. The van had a sliding door on the side like my dad's black van only this one had windows in the door and seats in the back. My dad's had buckets and drop clothes in it. "It makes daily trips back to Long Island. You will be*have* yourselves. You don't want to ride in that van. It is a privilege to be here at Springkill and to be sent home is to humiliate yourselves and dishonor your school, an offense that is marked on your permanent record. If you misbehave, children," she paused and stuck a finger into the air, "you will have to deal with Ackerly. Now," she snapped a red flag up over her head. "Follow me."

Who knows how long the other students were milling in the gravel before we got there, waiting for us to show up and see who they'd be spending the next three days with when Ackerly started gobbling without even giving us a chance to tie our shoelaces or wander off and finally let a fart go. She made us look bad if you ask me. When she made commandments, her neck jiggling like some weird chin tit, we were stunned like morons. The other districts practically snapped their necks looking at her. A few of us huffed and rolled our eyes to show the other schools we knew what a bitch she was, and we weren't clueless. Mrs. Ackerly held up her red flag and led the way. All a sudden Ashley was on my arm. She hugged my elbow while we walked through tall grass that grabbed our feet and tripped us. We followed Ackerly's flag through pines, down a dark path with patches of light twitching on the mud. "Look around you," Ackerly said over her shoulder, breathing heavy. "There are thousands of acres of coniferous and deciduous trees. Ferns. Wild grasses. Lichens! Legumes! Flax. There are animals and algae and bugs and…" she took some deep breaths, "…worms and fresh water trickling down the mountainside. Each of the Springkill counselors you meet …can survive in this forest without ever going to 7-Eleven. They don't need one iota, not a cent! Nothing." She huffed and coughed. "Can you imagine that," Ackerly continued. "And all their waste is *good* for the environment. They are completely plugged into the cycle." Me and Ash joked about camp counselors crapping in holes and burying it the way Indians taught the pilgrims to bury fish where they planted corn. Ackerly went on with her speech while everybody walked behind her carrying luggage.

Mr. Brush walked funny. Like he was made of broomsticks and twisty ties. His clothes flapped all over. He looked like someone you knew, but you couldn't remember who. He walked about in the middle of the group. Kids kept getting closer to him. Little magnets. Around Brush you could talk quietly and shove each other a bit. Brush stared at his shoes. They had mud on them, or maybe it was goose crap.

At the end of the path was a field. There were cabins built on stilts with different sized windows colored by the darkness inside. "They're empty," I said, but that was obvious. They weren't facing any particular direction. They weren't in a line or anything. They had the lost look of cows in a new pasture. Mrs. Ackerly adored them. She stopped to lecture about the cabins. They were made from sustainable materials. From the very forest we'd be exploring. That's her words, "The very forest you will be exploring." You can't explore a forest full of paths and signs and colored arrows where a million other schools have marched through.

Ackerly talked a little more about the forest and the Indians who once lived and hunted there. They didn't have any laws but they weren't savages, she told us. She had a crush on the Indians.

"My shoulders are savage," Joey whispered. "This suitcase is pulling my arms off."

Finally we went inside, into a slate and brick common room with a black pot-bellied stove in the middle. I like those stoves. We had one in our house my father lit in the winter. He peeled oranges and set the pieces on top. Our house smelled like citrus and burning wood. I was really thinking a lot about my dad. He'd locked himself in the bedroom. Only my mom went in. She brought him food. I heard them argue. She came out crying and wouldn't look at my sister or me for a long time.

One side of the cabin was for the boys and the other for girls. There were two bunk beds in each room. The boys hall was to your right, the girls to your left.

No matter how much you loved Mr. Brush you filled your room so he couldn't bunk with you. Who wants to sleep in a room with the teacher? Nobody, it's uncomfortable. You can't talk about girl's tits or tell jokes about fags and Chinese people. You always have to watch your mouth. Anyway, he knew how it was. He stayed in the common room. He shot the breeze with a camp counselor and let us choose for ourselves. We stuck him with Chops and Moto.

There was a room with only three boys and one room with two and they felt lucky. But I liked sleeping in a full room. Some people hate that. Like my sister. My mother was pregnant when I was about seven. My sister got all upset. "What if it's a girl," she complained. "You're going to put her in my room. I'll have to share my room!" We only had three bedrooms in our house. Not like the Flower Hill kids. Their houses probably had ten. My sister was so upset about sharing her room she couldn't get excited about having a little sister. I don't get it, because when I was little she always wanted to dress me up, like I told you.

# Hearts Like E.T.

Remember I said some of us knew kids from other schools? I knew one. From Flower Hill, for Christ sake. We went to church together. Jonathan. His parents *had money*. That's how people described them.

I went to Jonathan's house after church one Sunday because his mother had a picnic. Where I live, in Huntington Station, the streets go up and down, left and right. It's a grid and we live on flat blocks. Jonathan's neighborhood was all hills and winding streets with no street lamps. The houses are far apart and sometimes set back from the road so far, with trees and fences, you can't see them. Jonathan lived in a house like that. An invisible house, me and my mother called it. You can smell the Long Island Sound as you get closer. The street names are written on white posts about three feet tall, not on grey posts with green metal signs like in our neighborhood. We kept slowing down the car to read them. My mother turned the radio down. Women turn the radio down when they concentrate on driving.

When we got to the Invisible House I thought we were at a golf course. Seriously. All you saw was grass and trees. It would be pretty cool to live on a golf course and collect golf balls and play manhunt all day but it wasn't a golf course. It was just their yard and the neighbor's yard.

Everybody was out back on a patio, eating shrimp and fruit and cheese. Some picnic! No one was my age. Jonathan wasn't even there. He was practicing to ride a horse or something. I walked around the house while I waited for him. There was a long hallway down one side of the house with doors all over the place. Some doors went into the same room. One room with two doors seems pretty stupid to me. That's how people with money are, I guess. They get excited about doors and mirrors and cloth napkins and riding friggin horses.

I found a room with only one door. There was baby furniture in it. The walls were lilac, and yellow bunting drooled over everything, all Eastery looking. There was one of those lamps that rotates and has different shapes and scenery on it. This one was glass. I picked it up. It was heavy. The lamp we got from the attic when my mother was pregnant, along with all the junk from when I was a baby, was plastic. It didn't rotate. It just glowed and showed pictures of giraffes and animals from Africa. The glass one at Jonathan's was better. The shapes were more scientific than pictures of animals because a baby can't recognize African animals. Scientists figured out how to stimulate baby brains with shapes. That's one reason rich people are smarter than normal people. Science helps them.

I heard someone call out, looking for me. The hallway stretched the sound and the words vibrated back and forth, like when you cough in an empty church. I shouldn't have been in the room. There was no baby anymore. I don't know how it died. It wasn't from a car wreck though, like how my mom's baby died in her. Jonathan's sister was born. "Larry," I heard again.

I put the lamp back on the table but it had little brass feet on the bottom. One of the feet caught an edge. There was a rug on the floor so it didn't explode into a million pieces. It fell on the ground and inside the thump was the same crack sound you hear when you bang your head really hard. I picked up the pieces and balanced them together on the table. A burp could've toppled it. Then I went and hid in what I thought was a closet as the footsteps came closer.

And now, what creeped me out, whoever was looking for me started laughing. It wasn't a normal laugh either. It was a *cachinnation*, which is laughter set on fire.

I wasn't in a closet. It was a kind of getting-ready-room. There's a name for it but I forget. It had a back door that opened into a bedroom.

The footsteps came closer and closer, and the laughter turned into singing. Singing my name. "Larry?" It was playing a game.

The reason I bring this up. While I was in the getting-ready room listening, I got this chill. It was summer and the house was about ninety degrees but I got all cold feeling like when you bite an ice pop and it gets packed into your molars. I even stopped sweating. I knew I was hearing a witch.

Witches aren't even scary. Not like clowns or stranglers. This one scared the crap out of me anyway because *I know* witches aren't real. That was the disorienting part, I was wrong. Here was a witch, the least spooky part in a movie, or a haunted house or something, and it was all a sudden real. Looking for me. Playing with my fear. And my only defense was to *believe* she didn't exist! Then I heard a knock and a heavy thump. Later I realized it was the lamp tumbling over again but when it fell I bolted scared for the door into the big bedroom then sprinted through the hallway, down the stairs and out of the house. I didn't feel safe until I was on the patio in the sun with people eating food off pointy sticks and listening to Beach Boys music.

There's a line in the bible I learned in Sunday School. Jesus said, "Where two or more people gather in my name, there I am too, among them." Everybody at the picnic was a church member. They were there to be with Jesus. But I knew me and my mother were there because of dead babies. It made me lonely as hell. After my mother came and found me eating fruit and stuff and said, "Where've you been I looked all over for you," I'd see the people smiling and talking and feeling close to one another. I'd see Jesus glowing in their hearts like E.T. or something. I thought about them going home and hanging their shirts in the closet and brushing their teeth and watching television and I started feeling lonely all over again.

For a while after that, when I was in bed, I imagined a witch hiding outside my door, holding her hand over her mouth to stop her laughter. Then I felt safe and happy in a room so close to my parents and my sister, all of us gathered together at the end of our short hallway. My mother's baby could have been a girl, and my sister could have taught her to play with dolls and snapped barrettes in her hair, all that crap she and Sexy Lexy did to me, but I wished she could have slept in my room. I hate sleeping alone.

# The Only One In Sneakers

Kids swarmed the cabin hallway, claiming rooms, trying to keep it down to three people. It wasn't enough they got chosen for Springkill. They needed more personal friggin space, too. I made sure to have four people in my room. We planned it that way on the bus, me, Joey, Robby Morales, and Ben Croten. We'd get a room at the end of the hallway, or whatever was furthest from Brush. It was very strategic. So we'd be able to sneak out, or sneak girls in, without Brush hearing our shoes shuffling.

We didn't know where Brush was going to sleep. He'd choose at the end, filling whichever room had the least people. Meanwhile rooms were getting claimed.

Joey went to the end of the hallway, mushing three people's heads on his way, and Robby posted up near the front. Robby didn't mush anyone. He leaned against the door with his arms folded, uncrossing them now and then to move the hair off his forehead. They were two of I'd say the ten toughest guys in Finley. But in that cabin, with thirty of the nerdiest goody two shoe guys (plus me), they were the undisputed hard asses. Nobody would try to get past them. This was the real life experience Springkill was all about.

Me and Ben held it down together at a room near the middle, as a safety, so that no matter where Brush ended up the four of us would be in a room together.

In the end, Brush roomed with Chops and Moto about a quarter ways down the hall. Me, Robby, Joey and Ben were in the last room, right hand side.

We'd barely dropped our luggage and chosen bunks and taken a leak when Mrs. Ackerly hollered from the common room.

"Mr. Brush," she crowed. "Gather your children. We've got orientation in ten minutes."

Mr. Brush said, "Let's get together, *young men*," and we all loved him for it.

Hardly any girls were in the common room, just Ashley, Alicia, and a redhead I'd never seen before. Mr. Brush said, "My men have assembled Mrs. Ackerly." He smiled at us and we burst out laughing but he gave us a look.

That kind of talk between Brush and Ackerly reminded me of parents. Not mine, really. Just parents. The way they say things to each other without using words that match their feelings.

I didn't like redheads. My sister had red hair. Every redhead reminded me of my sister. But I kept staring at the one in the common room. There was something about her. She had tits, first of all. Most girls in Finley didn't. Not good ones, anyway. I should've been careful though. Ashley was practically standing on my foot. Ever since we got off the bus at Springkill Ashley held my arm. She was very affectionate when she was nervous.

Ashley always held my elbow in big groups. When we stood in line for movie tickets she'd swing from my arm like a monkey. I'd hold my hand over my chest and we'd walk the way an usher walks someone down the aisle at a wedding, very formal, our two arms hooked. It was a habit of ours. Anyway, I was holding her arm and staring at the redhead. I couldn't help it. She was like TV, glowing, every turn was something new to see. All a sudden Ashley let her hand fall away. I tried to put it back. It dangled at her side like a noodle.

You had to kick your knees high so the grass wouldn't grab your toes and trip you. You didn't feel too stylish walking that way. "Ash, c'mon. Hah? What's a matter?" She ignored me. We marched toward a building with broad wood planks, squatting on a stone and mortar foundation. The Center. It looked like a painting your grandparents hung on the wall in their dining room. The peak of the A-frame roof was crooked. It leaned to one side as if something in the mountains caught it's attention. The other schools' kids were filing into the Center or leaning against the stockade fence around it. "Hurry now. Don't dawdle." We were running late.

Soon as we saw the other schools' kids all of Finley Jr. High wandered out of line. We chatted as if we'd just shown up to a birthday party. Ackerly made us *feel* like corny little disciplined children. At least we tried to *look* good.

"Psst," Mrs. Ackerly spat. She held up her flag. So we stopped. Her face turned purple. She shook her head in disappointment, her sack sagging. She looked like a goddamn pelican. Once you saw her as a pelican you hated her a little more. If someone looks like a ridiculous animal they shouldn't get so smart and angry all the time. "You will be on your best behavior. You are representing your school. You will not enter this building like a herd of goats." Mr. Brush stared at his shoes.

The Center wasn't as spiffy on the inside as it looked from a distance. First of all there were three hundred thousand dead flies on the windowsills, mixed in with dust and other crap, like pen caps and rubber bands. There was a gross carpet on the floor, worn out, and in some spots held together by greasy silver duct tape. The worst part was the ceiling. Spider webs stretched across the beams. Some webs collapsed and dangled in the air. When I saw that I spit on the floor.

The peak in the ceiling reminded me of church, only instead of candles and crosses there were tangled webs pearled with dead flies. Kids looked at the ceiling and blinked. Tables and chairs were set in lines across the room.

The Center smelled funny, too, like our school cafeteria: frozen cardboard and pine disinfectant. The teachers were already friends. They walked their red faces over and talked to each other, smiling. They left us alone for a while.

We pooled into groups, all the schools staying together. Then little pieces tore away. Girls with girls, boys with boys, until there were chunks of three and four people spread across the place like colorful gravel. Girls folded their arms over their bellies. Boys stood with their hands in their pockets.

I felt a ball of gravity behind me. "Excuse me?" It was Ackerly, of course. "Did I just see one of my students spit? On the floor!"

"…"

"How do you suppose that will be cleaned," she pointed to the froth on the carpet. It didn't sink in or anything. It looked like bird shit, which made me feel more ashamed.

"A vacuum," I said. How the hell did I know how it would get cleaned? Nothing in the Center had been cleaned in months. The air was half dust.

"FIND someone! Find camp staff, one of these men or women in Springkill shirts, and I want you to tell them you need something to clean SPIT off the floor. I want you to tell them that you spat on the floor, and apologize!"

"I'm sorry," I said.

"Not to ME!"

I went over to the youngest looking staff I could find, leaning against the wall. His khaki shorts had about twenty pockets hanging open like fish mouths. He wore a green T-shirt with Springkill printed in white letters. Ackerly kept her eyes on me. His name was Adam. The sides of his head were shaved, and down the middle was a parting of dreads as long as your fingers folding one way or another, collecting dirt. A real hippy.

"I need something to clean with," I told him.

"Okay," he said staring into the room. His tongue dug at his molars. "See that door?" Something hard and white stuck to his tongue's tip, a sunflower seed or something. "There's a mop and rags and spray bottles in the kitchen closet." The seed came off his tongue and clung to his bottom lip. He licked it off, chewed it with his front teeth and swallowed. "It's to the right when you pass the refrigerators."

Mrs. Ackerly watched us, a frown sagging on her face. "Tell him," she mouthed.

"I spitted on the floor," I told Adam.

"Okay." He ran his hands over his dreads. He didn't give a crap if I spat on the floor. He probably did it too. He probably spat in his hair.

I went into the kitchen. I didn't go straight to the closet, though. I was thirsty. The bus ride was about ten years long and I didn't bring water or lunch like you were supposed to. Joey gave me some food but only a little because his mom made peanut butter and jelly for him, his favorite, and not a meatloaf sandwich or something I liked. So he ate most of it. I stopped at the sink and ran the tap and drank like a camel.

There were three fridges in there. I opened the one with ice cream tubs stacked on shelves and buried in steam. My favorite dessert is strawberries with cream. I eat it on my birthday. My mother whips the cream fresh and sweetens it with confectioner sugar. She dices the strawberries and chills them in a plastic wrapped bowl. By the time you're ready to eat them there's juice in the bottom of the bowl that you pour over the cream and turn it pink. The tub in front of me was called Strawberries N' Cream. I peeled back the lid. The surface was flakey and flat like a backyard covered in new snow. I scooped out a handful with my fingers, closed the lid and shut the freezer. Then I heard the kitchen door's old hinges.

I stuffed my mouth with the ice cream and wiped my hands on my jeans and ran to my left because it was further from where the hingey sound came. I found a back door, opened it, and walked into a big room with a desk and leather chair. There was a metal coat rack dripping with scarves and jackets and a daybed with a pillow sideways and crumpled. The walls were wood paneled mostly but there was wallpaper on parts, bubbling and peeling in the corners. Light streamed in from mullioned windows and rolled with slow dust. My dad's a house painter and when he brought me along on jobs what I had to do was paint the skinny wood crosses in mullioned friggin windows, finicky work that took lots of concentration. Now I hate them.

Just as I was about to leave and act all cool and surprised I'd stumbled into the wrong room and say to whoever came behind me, "Where's the closet? I gotta find some cleaner to wipe up spit," my eyes got hooked. Over in the corner were cupboards, dark wood and camouflaged against the wall panels. It sparkled with glass and syrupy liquids. A liquor cabinet.

"Uh, I beg your pardon?" A stripe of a man in the doorway said. "Who are you? Why are you in this room?" His voice was soft.

"I'm looking for the closet."

"Does this look like a closet?"

"No."

"And how long did it take you to realize you were in someone's personal space and not in a closet? Are there brooms and napkins here?"

"No."

"That's right. There are not."

"…"

"…" He had big eyes like a lizard's only his were flat and blue as wet slate.

"Can you show me where the closet is?"

"Don't play dumb with me. What's your name?"

"Larry."

"Larry?"

"Yeh. Larry Morvan."

"Which school are you with?"

"Finley."

"Ackerly?"

"Oh shit."

"Brush?"

"That'd be better," I told him.

"Come with me." He wasn't a bad guy, you could tell. He was tall and bony and weak looking. He probably felt unsafe all the time around strong men who were less careful than him.

"I really need to find a closet, sir. I spitted on the floor because a spider web got in my mouth."

He walked right through the kitchen and out into the big room where the kids were facing front. I followed him.

Adam was at the rostrum, his dreadlocks pointing all over the place. He started talking into the microphone while everyone stood around in groups but Mrs. Ackerly, listen to this, cut him off and shouted, "I think we'll seat the children before beginning our addresses." Adam was completely disgusted by her water sack and her *impudence*, which is a word she always used. Adam was a real no problem sort of guy, you could tell. Even if that goiter hanging off Ackerly's face made him want to puke he let it pass. He didn't care if we all stood while he talked. What's the difference? Your ears don't know what your ass is doing.

"We're going to take our seats now, children," Mrs. Ackerly shouted. I watched the other teachers. They were as annoyed as Adam. They probably knew Mrs. Ackerly from Board of Education meetings or something. They knew what a dick she was. "There's Brush," I said to the thin man.

"Listen to me," he said. He crouched down. He was a really tall guy. "I'm not going to put you in hot water over this. Or the ice cream you filched." He stopped for a second so I could be all impressed he knew what I'd done. Filched. What a cornball. "Just keep to the straight and narrow. There's plenty to be curious about in the mountains. Keep your mind on summer break and cute girls. Hike the paths. Learn from the counselors. It's the easiest time of your life. No need for trouble, am I right or am I right?" He swallowed hard. His Adam's Apple shot up his neck. "Find your friends."

I went to sit with Joey on one of those long, picnic type benches.

Just as we sat down Joey sees another kid. "Jimmy," he shouts, all happy. Jimmy didn't notice him at first but Joey kept smiling and going, "Jimmy. Ay yo. Jimmy!" Finally the kid sees him. He had a crew cut and wore a tank top. I'm pretty skinny, even now, but I was never as skinny as that dick. He thought he had mounds of muscles instead of the string beans hanging from his shoulders. "Oh snap. What up, nucka," Jimmy says. They punched fists and hugged.

"This is my boy, Larry," Joey introduced me.

"What up, Larry," Jimmy said. I smiled and nodded like an idiot. "Yo, I'm gonna sit with those fucksticks over there," he told Joey.

"We'll go with you," Joey said and punched me on the shoulder. "Come on over here. I know these douche nozzles," he said. I didn't know what a douche nozzle was, he never said it before. I didn't want to but I went and sat with them. They practically cheered for Joey when he got there, as if he just pitched a no hitter. They didn't even look at me. A bunch of snobby assholes from Huntington Bay. Joey knew all of them, from when he went to their school, Flower Hill, before his father got the gate from Morgan Stanley and moved out.

They took turns one-arm hugging Joey. In their vests. In Patagonia pants! In their boots, all of them. They were decked out for their hike. They didn't wear normal clothes, like sneakers and jeans. Joey, all the sudden he looked just like them. He sat next to me but we didn't talk to each other. I sat on the end of the bench, listening in. That's all it takes to feel alone, being the only one in sneakers.

# The Virgin Disease

If you want to know if Joey or me had sex with any girls in eighth grade the answer is yes, kind of. We tried like crazy. I went out with a couple of girls and so did Joey but mostly he went with a girl named Alicia, and I mostly went with Ashley.

Going out didn't mean then what it means now in high school. Where could you go? What could you do? Mostly we went to the village and watched a movie and ate pizza. You never had anywhere to go that was private.

When you wanted privacy you went to the bay. It was a long walk from the village but it was the only place you could be alone with a girl. There was a harbor there and only one building, the marina. Down the other side, away from the boats and piers, bay water swirled around the rocky shore, green-black in the trees' shadow, and moved around the algae clinging to racks as big as mailboxes. There was plenty enough room to sit and look at the water and get all meditative or read or something but people didn't come to that side of the harbor.

The reason it was private, the sewage treatment plant was just across the street. The air was made of shit. It took a long time to get used to the stink but if you didn't want to be bothered, that's where you went.

It was maybe a week before the Springkill trip. Joey and I'd been with the girls for a while, about five months. All we did was kiss and feel them up, usually at the movies or down by the bay. Nothing else. We tried of course. I'd get hour-long boners, three or four times, they felt mutilated by the end of the day. Growing pains through my pin. We'd go and whack off in the fort after hanging out with Ashley and Alicia.

I tried to tell Ashley how bad she made it hurt, and the only way to stop it was to cum. We were sitting on a rock near the stinking water.

"Come where," she asked me.

"I don't know, like, in your hand or something."

She kept making faces. She didn't know what I was talking about. I had to talk to her like it was Health class and say the most embarrassing word in the English language.

"If you touch it enough I'll, like, ejaculate." I said it as normal as I could but my voice sort of trailed off at the end. "I'll show you how."

"You want to e*jac*ulate in my hand! Gross, no. Ew, do it yourself." That's what she told me. I said I did, I whacked off practically every day, sometimes thinking about her. She kept gagging and telling me how disgusting it was.

"It isn't gross. It's normal."

"So's phlegm, Larry. So's blood. You think I want those things in my *hand*? So's cat puke..."

It went on like that for a month. Joey and I kept pushing them. I was crazy about Ashley, I really was. It's not like I only wanted to cum in her hand. I'd known her for years. She was a fireman's daughter.

Joey tried like a maniac to lose his virginity. As if it was a disease. It's all he talked about.

"This'll be my last chance maybe for three years. Minga. What's the big deal? Let me stick it in for two minutes. It's like a finger. It's only a different piece'a body."

I'd almost lost my virginity a year before to Amanda Voyage and I wasn't real *enthusiastic* about trying it again. It'd sort of been a disaster. I don't think you wanted anybody even seeing your pin when you're thirteen, it's embarrassing, especially if you have funny looking pubic hair or something.

What we did, me and Joey, we took the girls to a movie only instead of going to the bay afterwards we walked to Joey's house. It was even farther but Ashley and Alicia didn't care. In eighth grade you never minded walking.

We had to be quiet so Joey's mother wouldn't catch us. She'd've hit the roof if she caught us with girls in the fort. It was funny watching them climb up the ladder. Ashley wore loose shorts, you could see her panties. I made Joey go up first because he'd've looked up Ashley's shorts even though she was my girl. He was just like that. I looked up her shorts, though. She knew it, too. She didn't care.

One mistake we made was not taking down the nudey pictures. They weren't just naked girls, like in some artsy fashion magazine. The girls in our pictures had balloon tits. They stuffed their fingers in themselves. They even spread their assholes open. At first Alicia and Ashley laughed. They moved along the wall going, "Oh my god, look at this one. Ew, it's falling out. Is your vagina okay? Did a firecracker go off in there? So gross." They wanted to see more. When Joey pointed the light to the other wall and they saw the "meat coupons", they got quiet and it was hard to get them to kiss us.

We made out eventually, on opposite sides of the fort. Joey said, "I don't want my mom to see the light," and he flicked off the bulb. We were on the dirty floor. The wood dust got in our clothes. "I'm itchy," Ashley kept saying. She'd stop kissing me to scratch.

Ashley was one of those girls who think about how they're kissing instead of thinking about you. She'd change the way her tongue moved or turned her face to the other side. We bumped noses. Then we'd stop to wipe off our mouths.

I pulled her shorts to the side. Ashley didn't stop me. Just her underwear covered her. I ran my hand up and down her thigh. My fingers getting closer to her panties each time. When I touched her *there* she pushed my arm away. I started over, getting closer and closer. When I got to the panties again my hand stayed longer. I rubbed gentle circles on her. She was warm and damp. Then I slipped my pinky through the side. I touched her, my pinky pushing soft, sticky folds of skin around. It felt like an armpit, which surprised me. It was nothing like I'd expected, like the pictures on the wall, those shiny wet gashes. She breathed in my ear.

My hands get very dry. Sometimes my cuticles crack. I'd been peeling off the skin around my fingers at the movies that day and they were irritated and bloody. The tip of my pinky stung inside of Ashley. So I switched to my middle finger.

I should have left it alone because when I put my middle finger in her she kind of chirped and scooted away from me. She didn't stop kissing me, she just scooted her hips. I tried like crazy to get it back in her, my pinky I mean. I rubbed up and down her leg again. The whole song and dance. But it wasn't the same. I was thinking too much about sticking my finger in her and everything changed. Everything changes when you think about it.

But then Ashley started to rub *my* leg! She didn't have to, though. I'd've let her touch me anywhere she wanted. She had work herself up to it. I was patient. She went after my pin as if she were following directions, rubbing my thigh higher and higher until she touched me. I didn't push *her* hand away. She pulled it away herself, then started over.

To be honest I didn't like the rubbing. I was skinny and embarrassed about my scrawny legs. Even Ashley's legs were probably bigger than mine. I didn't feel real hot shit. We both had spit all over our faces from kissing so much. Our chins slipped around in it.

I'd just about forgot Joey and Alicia. I could've forgot the whole world but Alicia had to get all annoying and ask, "Ash, what are you doing? Are you being Trashley?"

Ashley let out a very fake laugh. You could tell she wanted Alicia to leave us the hell alone but she kept on asking, "Trashley? What're you doing?"

Joey said, "Aw, leave'm alone. C'mere," and you heard the gummy sound of kissing. All you could see was a shady pile in the back of the fort and Joey's very white sneakers.

When your friend likes a girl he becomes this whole other person. Everything stays the same but it's like there's a new owner, like a Chinese restaurant or something. You still talk about the Mets and look for dumpsters but something changed. Alicia had big, flat fingertips, like a frog climbing the window. She was pretty, a little, but she acted as bitchy and self-important as Sexy Lexy, who really *was* a knock out. I didn't tell Joey I hated Alicia.

The worst part though, about Alicia, is just because she was ten feet from Ashley she thought it was her *right* to talk to her. If we'd been in a room, Ashley and me, would Alicia walk in saying, "What are you doing,

Trashley?" Hell no, she'd mind her business. I don't blame her for being rude. She didn't know any better. Privacy is more than a door.

When Alicia stopped talking I thought it was over. Me and Ash went as far as she'd let it go. I thought we'd only kiss and drool on each other, which gets boring. But then Ashley started rubbing me again.

Rubbing legs is a big deal in eighth grade. You're sensitive about your body. You're going through puberty and you get shy. Maybe you have long, soft pubes or something if you're a boy, and girls are just starting to get periods and growing tits. You're always uncomfortable.

Ashley wasn't rubbing just my knee. Her hand went way up inside my thigh, swiping across my pin. Nobody'd ever touched me there before. When she left her hand on it, squeezing it gently, I could tell she'd never done it before because after two minutes of her touching me we'd stopped kissing and were sort of licking the corners of each other's lips. Our tongues stopped moving and just lay in each other's spitty mouths. We were both *think*ing about her hand there, as if that's all we were, hand and hard-on.

But what's crazy, while Ashley played with it I started thinking about the first time Joey met my dad.

My dad had an operation. He was sick all the time and meaner than August sun. So I didn't bring anybody around. He was on the couch all day. He didn't paint houses. My mom asked me to stay home more often and so then she told me to bring Joey over for company.

Joey comes in the house and the first thing he does is he goes over and sits next to my dad on the couch. My dad was smoking and not looking friendly *at all* but Joey sat next to him because that's what you had to do the first time you went to his house. You had to meet his father. It's a respect thing with Italians. I know Italians because one of my dad's aunt married one. By marrying one friggin Italian, I swear, I'm related to half the Italians on Long Island. I'm probably related to Joey.

My dad took a look at Joey. He didn't turn his head all the way or anything, he just eyed him. He put his cigarette out in this cup a quarter full of Coke. He was always dropping cigarettes in plastic cups and you could smell the ashes in them a week later when you got a drink of water.

They had all these melted spots. He put the cigarette in the Coke and then plopped his hand in Joey's lap. He gave Joey's balls a squeeze! "How they hanging, hah?"

Joey froze, his eyes blew open and his hands stuck to the couch like they'd been nailed down. He didn't try to stop my dad grabbing his balls because that'd be disrespectful. He just sat there, stone still, staring at me.

It was funny as hell later. We joked about it all the time. Joey told the story in a very funny way. He imitated my dad to make me laugh. Joey really liked my dad. That's what I was thinking about while Ashley held my boner.

"Hey Joey," I said. "Remember the time my dad grabbed your balls?"

"Shut the fuck up, man! What's wrong with you?"

Ashley pulled my face to hers. We started kissing again. I was pissed off though. Alicia could recite the Pledge of Allegiance for all Joey or Ashley cared but I say one thing and I get cursed!

Ashley wouldn't let me stick my finger in her anymore but I could feel her up under her shirt, finally. She still wouldn't let me pinch her nipples though. Rules.

I grinded my pin against her. It hurt a little. My skin grated against the jeans zipper. The strokes or whatever, the humps, were shorter, faster. I got the hang of it. It started to feel like whacking off.

I never came with anybody before. I'd done it with Joey in the room, sitting on a Spackle bucket in the fort, but not by being touched by anybody.

My arms and legs got light. The weight went into my body's center. It gathered like a snag around the bottom of my spine and came very close. Either Ashley would move or a groan slipped out of me and made me feel weird and it went away. I got frustrated because I wanted it to happen, wanted it very badly. I grinded harder. I pulled Ashley's shorts further to the side. Neither of us was moving our tongues anymore.

I don't think Ashley knew what to expect. She asked once, "Larry?" But I didn't answer, only kept grinding because it was close. "Larry, ouch, you're pulling." Then it was there, finally, spreading warm into my underwear, making everything slippery. "Ouch, Larry." I couldn't control my mouth. My tongue poked way into Ashley's molars. I moaned with a shaky voice. It was a Sunday afternoon. There were no cars going in the streets and it was very quiet in the fort. There was only me, moaning like an old dog scratching. My hips rocked back and forth. I couldn't stop. Usually I was quiet when I whacked off because it's sort of faggy to moan and make noises when you shoot your batch and Joey is sitting in the same room, right next to me. I couldn't help it. Ashley wiggled and scooted. She tried to say something but my mouth pressed against hers hard and I made a crazy sound like a yawn and a cough at the same time. It was embarrassing. I pretended I was laughing. As if I'd just thought of something very funny.

"Get off me," Ashley said. She scratched my neck pushing me away.

All a sudden I thought about the bay, the little harbor near the sewage plant that stinks so bad at low tide, and the boats floating around on the water. It seemed like the best place in the world. I grinded hard and slow, and each pulse of the muscle behind my balls was like a leap along the shores of heaven!

"What's so fucking funny," Joey asked, all grumpy.

"Remember that time my dad grabbed your balls," I said out of breath. I rolled to my back, finished.

"Are you fucking retarded, Larry? Seriously. You retarded or something?"

Ashley said, "Yes, and he's a pervert, too!"

We walked the girls back to the Village, thirty friggin minutes in wet, gooey underwear. I felt good. Usually, after I shot my batch on a newspaper, I'd feel guilty and gross. But with Ashley, after I shot it on her, I was happy and calm.

Me and Ashley often walked with our elbows hooked and our hands in our pocket. Walking to the village she dangled her arm all noodley. She wouldn't let me put my hook in her. The next week, too, she acted funny. We didn't have any classes together. We used to meet in the west 200's hall near a water fountain, the one boys pissed in after school because there's no bathroom nearby. I went there between classes and waited for Ashley to show up. She never did. I was late to Home Ec. twice. Ackerly gave me detention. I called Ashley's house after dinner but she wasn't home or her mother said she was busy. I didn't think it was a big deal. I'd see plenty of her in Springkill, I figured.

Alicia's mom picked up the girls at the movie theatre parking lot. Soon as the car's doors closed Joey made me smell his finger. Then, listen to what he told me, he said he dry fucked Alicia and came in *his* underwear, too! He'd been damn quiet about it, though. Just like when he nutted on the bucket. I didn't hear a thing.

"I'm definitely gonna beat that in Springkill," he said. Springkill was like ten days away. "Even before then, I bet. We gotta get them back in the fort next weekend, bro. Holy shit!"

We would have, too. But I burned it to the ground.

# Me And The Redhead

They stuck us in groups. The counselors went around picking kids at random. Didn't matter what school you were from, a boy then a girl, boy, girl until everyone was in a group. Adam, the counselor with the dredy Mohawk, picked me. A different counselor picked Joey. They told us to stand in lines. The counselors walked through asking your name and what school you were from and wrote on a clipboard.

"Joey," I called out. I stuck my tongue in my cheek and put my fist to my mouth, like to act out a blowjob. We did that all the time in school. He didn't hear me. "Yo!" He was talking across a lane to a kid in another group. Talking to Jimmy Lutani.

Jonathan was standing behind me. Our parents worshipped together and they went to group therapy at our church. Jonathan poked me in the kidney. I turned and said, "Oh shit, what up kid?" We slapped hands and one-arm hugged.

Then I figured I could get Robby Morales's attention. He could tap Joey on the shoulder or something. I needed to give Joey the finger. I don't know, just once I needed to do it. "Ay yo, Robby!" Robby was standing close by Joey. His face was flowery with red blotches. "Hey Morales!" Robby snapped around quick. He said something, just with his mouth. He wanted me to read his lips. I couldn't read them but the message was clear. Leave him the hell alone. He didn't like his name thrown around.

Great friggin start to Springkill!

A hundred yards away colored flags flapped at the trail mouths. Each trail went in a different direction, through *ecological learning zones*. You had to walk all the trails over the next three days learning about lichens and humus and mushrooms and crap, and why human consumption is bad for the environment. The counselors headed their groups into separate trails. My group didn't move right away. There was too much talking and whining but I couldn't tell you what about just then because, what was happening, Joey walked off with his group and Jimmy walked off in another and they kept yelling back and forth to each other, laughing and giving one another the finger with big smiles and red cheeks but Joey didn't once look back to give me the finger or put his tongue into his cheek and act out a blowjob. Then all the groups were gone up the trails and there was just the sound of nonsense.

Jonathan kept poking me in the back. Telling me he forgot about me. Telling me he didn't expect to see me in Springkill, and isn't weird that we're the same age and that we're *friends* and he forgot about me because I went to a different school. He kept pointing out different girls, the good looking ones, and asking if they went to my school, and did I know them.

"You see the one with the red hair," Jonathan asked. He stuck his friggin knuckle in my back again. "Check her out, nucka."

"Yeah, I see her, Jonathan, Jesus."

"She go to your school?"

"No. She was in my cabin this morning though. I don't know why she's staying with us."

"This is gonna be a fun trip," he said.

"Sure."

Everyone complained they didn't get to choose which group they were in. I did, too. I started to complain. Adam didn't stop us. He put his clipboard into his backpack then put his backpack on and stood quietly with his thumbs under the pack straps. Mrs. Ackerly was standing with her hands on her hips at the door to the Center watching, probably wanting to stomp on over and tell us all we were thoughtless and insubordinate but she couldn't. It was Adam's class now. We were his.

Adam stood with his ankles crossed, licking his molars and chewing with his front teeth. He didn't answer any questions why we couldn't choose our groups. We got bored of complaining to him and started complaining to each other. We got quieter and finally stood there not saying anything, just looking at the forest crawling up and away in every direction.

Adam said, "I'm glad you took this opportunity to bond. That's part of the Springkill experience, making new connections. With each other and nature." We all just about puked.

"Alright, so. I'll address what you seem to be agitated about. Kids here always think it's not fair to put them in a group they didn't choose. How democratic of you. Congratulations." He was sarcastic as hell. You had to watch him to know what he meant. Like with the word *congratulations*, his eyebrows bounced around his face and his eyes looked to the ground, as if that's where his congratulations were, mixed with shoe prints in the dirt. "What you need to understand is that chaos is fair. There's no thought or intention in it. What you're going to see, around us in the woods, are adaptations plants and animals made to random changes. Most species that ever lived have gone extinct. Is that fair? Who decides, you? What survives are adaptations that make proficient breeders in a changing, local environment. Is there something *good* about those species? You raised the issue before I even started asking the questions. That's one of the hardest things to get into students, one thing you can't teach: empathy. Empathy is feeling someone or some*thing*'s emotions, not just recognizing it. Okay. Now you know what random feels like. Now you feel what's fair. This isn't a democracy. This is nature. This isn't a classroom it's the wilderness. And you're going to see it."

I liked what he said about democracy. I didn't understand him, but it felt like something was happening, you know? Like we were about to do more than I'd expected, and it was exciting.

Pure bullshit! All we did, we walked around trails for hours.

The first place our trail passed was the gardens, all different sized plots and full of plants and flowers, with rows between them where wind swirled and chucked dust in your face. Each of us was due for at least six pimples.

The gardens were all together the size of four basketball courts. There were nets lying over some vegetable patches, some plants were tied to sticks. Some of the patches were viney and tangled, some stood straight up like fence posts. Adam walked the rows pointing out vegetables, telling us they came from wild plants back in the day. Europeans turned them into different shapes and sizes, mostly so they could cook them easier or carry them on hunts. And those flowers over there, where do you think they came from? From wild flowers back in the day! They've been changed, too, like the broccoli and squashes. Indians chose specific flowers for *desirable characteristics*, so they could turn them into dyes.

He asked us what it was called, changing wild flowers and vegetables so they make easier soup and brighter blankets. Someone answered it was breeding. Adam said that was right. It's the same with dogs and birds. He told us all dogs come from wolves, every one of them. He told us canaries were never yellow to begin with. Canaries were named after the Island they came from, where they used to be a bunch of shit-brown birds like you see in your back yard, back in the day.

"You thought canaries were named for their yellow color, I bet," he said. "Nope. It was a kind of selection that colored them." Then he named a million vegetables that used to be other things we wouldn't even recognize if we saw them in the wild a thousand years ago, like corn and bananas. I barely recognized any of the vegetables in the garden anyway. Adam said, "It is called breeding, you're right, but this *kind* of breeding for vegetation, and the same with dogs and birds, is called *artificial* selection."

While Adam talked, leading us from vegetable patch to flower bush, I walked with Jonathan. Not because I wanted to. There was something annoying about him. You couldn't tell exactly what. But if the whole group was a face, Jonathan was some tissue stuck in its nose. I wanted to trail along at the back of the group by myself but Jonathan kept going, "Check it out Larry," then he'd stomp on a vegetable. We walked around the gardens and he kept stepping on sprouts or cracking squashes open like pottery. I never smiled or laughed or said anything. Not that I gave a crap if he smashed vegetables. It was Jonathan I didn't like too much. If Joey done it I'd probably laugh my ass off. I wondered where Joey was.

"Why do you do this?" It was the redhead girl. Jonathan popped a baby melon. "This food is planted for you. It is for you to eat."

"Easy, red," said Jonathan. "I'm just playing around. There's a million of the things."

The redhead though, she shot her eyes through Jonathan's chest. Her shoulders hunched, her hands balled up at the ends of her arms, she looked like a vegetable herself, with a hard shell and full of spiky seeds.

"I tell you what. To make up for it? I won't eat any vegetables while I'm here. Okay," Jonathan said.

We left the gardens and followed Adam down a wider dirt trail that crossed a meadow then narrowed its way into the woods.

"Shh, sh… okay, quietly." We were breathing heavy. "Anybody know what a galliform is," Adam asked. The trail wasn't steep but it definitely went uphill. "You all eat'm I bet every week. Has feathers?" Nobody knew what a friggin galliform was, of course. "It's an order of birds. Quails, pheasants and? Cluck, cluck? Chickens." Everybody went, oh chickens, I knew that. "Shh," Adam pointed to his right. "Galliformes include turkeys, too. See him? Right there. A Tom. Big guy, there he is. A wild turkey."

We saw it, this fat, slow moving bird, looking just like Mrs. Ackerly except he was only two feet tall. He had goops of red gum hanging off his face. His head was white and blue, and bumpy. Bronze feathers shimmered across his wings. He took a quick step, all nervous.

"See the blade hanging off his chest? Nine inches long. Called a beard. He's a big ol' male. Twenty pounds, about. He's another example of breeding from a type of selection. Anyone want to guess what bred him," Adam asked, quiet.

"Oh-oh, Springkill," someone whispered. "One of you guys?"

"No, fuh…" Adam huffed. "He's wild. What coulda bred him in the wild?" Nobody knew. "*Fe*male turkeys bred him," Adam said. At first we thought he was kidding, making some weird counselor sex joke. "Females breed males for color and size. And for things like beard length. Females choose who they mate with. The males don't choose, they strut." Some of the girls laughed and said yeah boys suck or whatever because female turkeys choose who beats it up. "Shh! How do the females select? Wudda they like in a male? Look. Check out the wattles on'm, the red sacks under his beak. They're bladders. He fills them up with blood. Makes'm bright red."

"Fucking gross," Jonathan whispered.

"That's how a Tom flirts, with a faceful of blood. His feathers are iridescent. See? He fans out his tail like a wad of cash. Whatever it takes to get a female's attention, y'know? Whatever accentuates his uniqueness. That's how the females select. The colors and swelling, the shimmering, it's nature's makeup. Males wear makeup, not the females. Females are dull brown, like my boot. So the male's makeup passes on to the next Tom. Females breed sexy sons." That *was* a weird counselor sex joke. We all laughed anyway. "Sh. Anyone know what *that* kind of breeding is called?"

Nobody knew. But now, now everybody was quiet and looking at Adam, waiting to find out what kind of breeding turkeys are. "That's called sexual selection." We pretty much exploded, laughing and hell yeahing and scared the turkey. He took off, pounding his sexy wings so hard he sounded like a helicopter in the treetops.

We hiked up the mountain, everybody breathing heavy and coughing. Our faces were patchy. Adam told us about turkeys while we walked, that Ben Franklin wanted turkeys to be the national bird. He pointed out other birds and told us their names, too. He was a bird specialist. Once he pointed at some slimy crap on a tree and said, "This erumpent fungus is healthy for the tree. You can eat it, too, in a soup." Finally though, after walking along the trail and everybody breaking their ankles, breathing so heavy your throat was coated with *erumpent* slime, and all the boys hacking up and spitting, Adam dropped to his knees. He looked under a bush. His nose went in the dirt. He punched his hand into the shadow. "Ho! Check this guy out."

We practically sprinted over. Pieces of leaves stuck in Adam's dreads. Let me see, move! Everybody shoved to get a look through his dirty fingers.

It was only a mouse. But when Adam started telling us about it everyone died to hear. They prayed he'd talk about sex again.

"It's a deer mouse," Adam said. "Ouch, they bite. Lookit his color?" The mouse poked its head through Adam's fist. His eyes were drops of motor oil. "Anyone explain how mice got small?"

"Because evolution," some genius said, catching on.

"Yes, evolution did it. But how? This northeastern USA mouse is related to an Amazonian capybara. Capybaras are like fat pigs, a hundred pounds. They're both related to bats. Mice don't fly. But they're all rodents. And rodents are half the mammal species. There are only five apes, including us, human apes. And we look basically the same as the others. So how did so many rodents become so different from each other?"

"Humans are different. We're not mammals," a girl from my school said. Margaret Spinella, short and loud. She was always in trouble. But the reason she was here in Springkill, the orchestra teacher, Mrs. Jenness, made sure she came.

Margaret could play the violin, the piano, anything she wanted. She'd play the didgeridoo if you sent her to Australia. She could even sing pretty. Our school had a concert twice a year. Margaret played the violin with the orchestra. Then Mrs. Jenness would introduce "Miss Margaret Spinella," and Margaret would walk over to the piano, a spotlight following her and blinding everybody on stage. The audience clapped like crazy. Then she'd play a bunch of songs you recognized from the movies and Christmastime, but mushed together in the same song while the orchestra backed her up. When intermission finally came, you and your friends took your girls behind the groundskeeper's shed. You tried to feel them up but all they wanted to do was talk about how wonderful Margaret was and how you'd never know. She looked like such a loosery loudmouth you'd never know how *talented* she was. Might even get a makeover one day and record an album we'll all listen to on our way to a crappy job. We all should be nicer to her, my god! You never *were* nicer to her though. You saw her in school on Monday and maybe you'd want to tell her hey nice job but you didn't. The music was gone, and it was only her.

"You're not a mammal," Adam asked. Everybody knew he was a mammal for Christ sake. You learn you're a mammal in third grade. "You have hair. And a backbone. You're warm blooded. You didn't hatch from an egg, did you?"

"I know we're mammals, but not animal mammals, like real apes."

"You have the same skeleton as an orangutan."

"No I don't."

"You have the same skeleton as this mouse, too. The bones look different but they're all the same, and in the same order. You sure you're not a mammal animal?" Adam could tell she was a pain in the ass.

"Yeah, that's why I'm called hu*man*," she said sarcastic as hell.

"What's your name," Adam asked her.

"Margaret," about ten people answered for her.

"Margaret, you're related to orangutans closer than a mouse is to capybaras," Adam said. "We share a common ancestor from two million years ago. Orangutans grow longer arms and we grow bigger brains. That's the difference. Orangutan genes tell orangutan proteins to grow at a certain speed for a certain length of time. Our genes do the same. It's called heterochronic growth."

"That's not the only difference, how our bones grow. I don't come from monkeys. And I'm not an animal," Margaret said. "I don't have monkey bones."

"Who said anything about a monkey? I said you have the same *order* of bones. Like in the song. Your foot bone's connected to your leg bone. Your leg bone's connected to your hipbone." The group laughed some. "The same bones in the same order as every other mammal."

"I'm just saying, humans are different," Margaret argued. "Everyone knows that. So what we have feet connected to our legs? Duh! But we don't have mice feet, do we? Apes look the same but we don't look like them. Who cares what order my bones are in. Am I supposed to have a rib bone where my ankle goes?" That seemed right, but I didn't know why.

"If you know how the capybara got so big when bats and mice and rats stayed small you'd think different." His voice got all a sudden bigger. It stood next to him.

Margaret pouted. Her face bent around her pointy nose. She sure looked like a mouse.

But she made me think hard about something. Adam explained how little rodents turned into big fat capybaras and I was listening. But I was also thinking that if evolution worked for animals but not for us, if we're not the same thing as animals, then why are we made from the same stuff as them, from blood and cells and skin? Why aren't we made of plastic or something, or wobbly tubes of light? God could have done it easy. I didn't say anything, though. I didn't want to be the one to bring up god.

"Now, what's it called," Adam demanded when he finished explaining rodent DNA in *local populations*, "how evolution works?"

Margaret's cheeks were as red as if Adam slapped them both. You could feel the heat coming off her.

The redhead stood a bit away from the group, alone, looking bored and maybe chilly, sort of hugging herself and squeezing her boobs together.

"How's the rodent species so numerous?" Something white and hard shot off Adam's tongue. "Why are rodents the most popular, successful mammalian genera, and only five kinds of apes, *including* humans?" He asked questions like jabs and hooks. He was half out his mind. "Predation. Adaptation. The arms race between predator and prey!"

It's way more embarrassing to be wrong when you're in a group than when it's just you and another person. I think I'd rather be shot in the arm than answer wrong in front of strangers. That's what it takes to be a leader, knowing the answers and not getting nervous, or just knowing a little more than everyone else. Or even just pretending to know. I wasn't sure if Adam was right about evolution, if the only difference between me and an orangutan was that my brain grew big and his arms grew long because a gene told them to, that it's called *heterochronic* growth. Adam said the word like a spell: heterochronic, and everybody *knew* he was the leader. He could've made it up, but would you challenge a word like that? Hell no. He was the leader, and it was as good as being a celebrity. Everybody stared at him, listened and worshipped everything he said. Margaret hated him, obviously, but the rest of the group, they started kissing his ass after he finally told us what kind of selection made mice small and ape arms long and human brains big.

"Guys, it's called natural selection."

"Oh yeah, I knew that," the group babbled.

At the gardens, in the beginning, I was excited about the hikes in the woods. It was supposed to be a vacation, kind of. When we saw the turkey, Adam talked about sex. That was fun. He was tricky in the beginning. Not tricky, subtle. He was cool. It was easy to be into it, into what he was saying. But now, miles up a mountain, all I wanted to do was drop on the dirt and not do anything because I was tired. Listening to Adam pop a boner over evolution turned the hike into something worse than school. It's probably what college is like.

"Every living thing is made from chemicals and compounds that aren't alive. Your body is eighty percent water. Water isn't *alive*. The rest is carbon mostly. Coal's made of carbon. Coal's not alive. So what *is* life," Adam asked.

That's when someone had to bring up god. And I knew it would happen. Some people guessed it was your heart that made you alive and some said it was oxygen or blood or the friggin sun, but then Jonathan goes, "Yeah but so isn't your soul what makes you alive?"

"What does every living thing have in common," Adam said, ignoring Jonathan. He looked through the group carefully, like he was making his pick for a kickball team. "Genes. Every organism down to the simplest virus has instructions for copying itself. Life is information. This is where it gets trippy." That got our attention. I mean it wasn't like he was talking about sex again, but still. "Everybody's used a camera, right? You take a picture. Where does the image go?"

"It's on a memory card," some photographer said.

"Right. Can you crack open the card and see it, though?"

"No."

"So where is it?"

"Just in there, in a circuit chip. Ones and zeroes."

"How does the image exist, if it's nothing but zeroes and ones, which is what?"

"Information," a bunch of scholars replied.

Adam touched his nose with his finger and said, "Ah hah! It's information that doesn't exist without what?"

"Without a computer."

"You haven't solved the problem. It still only exists as information. It's only light shining through pixels on the screen. What else makes it real?"

"A printer." This thing went around awhile, Adam questioning, and answers tumbling over each other.

"What good's a printer," asked Adam.

"It can print the picture and then you hang it in a frame."

"And now it's ink and paper. Why's that make it real?"

"Because of people. They can see it and touch it."

"Okay, without people no one sees it. But it still exists as long as there's what?"

"Cameras!"

"What're the cameras made of?"

"Plastic and metal."

"And glass," someone added.

Adam said, "It's all material. The nonphysical information doesn't exist to begin with without physical stuff." As the wind picked up and chilled the sweat on her skin, the redhead squeezed her boobs tighter. "Just as a digital image doesn't exist without analogue parts, the human mind doesn't exist without the material brain. Your nonmaterial mind is the ultimate result of physical stuff changing. And that's what got us off the hook as prey. Before physical adaptations supercharged our nervous system we were just dreamy, insignificant apes, another animal on the African plains hiding from lions and tigers and bears, oh my."

"Oh my," most of the group said back. I didn't. I didn't say oh my.

"Wait, so then. Wait," Jonathan was confused.

"Questions," asked Adam, walking backwards.

"So like animals and plants and humans are made'a the same stuff as coal plus water."

"Right."

"But we're alive because we have information in our genes."

"I got more than that in my jeans," some kid in the back of the group said. I laughed. No one else did.

"Yeah, information to build certain proteins."

"But the difference between something alive and something like, just some coal, is more than that."

"Yeah, it's more complicated than that, for sure. The whole process is…"

"But a dead body has information in it still. Like genes and stuff. Even though it's dead."

"Ye… well, yes. A dead body still has instructions on how to build you. How to build the machine that's Jona… It's like, okay… It's like this."

"So then but wait. Isn't life really then, like when you have a soul?"

"Okay. What's that?"

"I said our souls have. No, we have a soul but coal and dead bodies don't…"

"No, I heard what you said. I'm asking what *is* that? What *is* a soul? We can describe the coal's structure and the chemicals involved in animal digestion and all that. We can demonstrate that they exist. They *are* something. What *is* a soul?"

Jonathan took a second to think about it. Maybe he was thinking Adam wasn't too bright after all. Everybody knows what a soul is. "It's nothing. Like you said our mind is. It's not made of anything. It belongs to god, it *is* god kind of. It's like a piece of chipped ice, not as big as the whole ice cube but it's just as icy as the big piece." Jonathan looked around, probably expecting us to kiss his ass for outsmarting Adam. That was pretty clever though. They get a better education in Flower Hill because they're rich.

"Our minds have no mass, you're right. It's like I said. But I can demonstrate my mind exists. Watch. I'm gonna pick my nose." Adam stuck his pinky up his nose. "See. I demonstrated my mind exists because it interacted with the real world. We do this all the time, having conversations with people, planning to remodel the kitchen, scratching our butt cheek. You can prove something that has no material properties exists when it interacts with the real world. Can you demonstrate your soul exists?"

Then the whole group started talking all at once. Some people took Jonathan's side, telling Adam that Jonathan proved the soul interacted with the real world because it made living things do what living things choose to do. But there was a smaller group of people who took Adam's side, saying no, that Jonathan was basically describing what the mind does on its own, thinking about doing things and then your brain made your muscles do it. Adam said the few asskissers on his side were right. He said, "If you're just describing things your mind does and calling it a soul, then why not keep it simple and just call it a mind? The word *soul* has too much baggage and, as a word, it's less distinct." Just me and the redhead, we didn't say anything.

And then the other side argued that, yeah, you can still be alive without a mind. People get put on life support all the time. Trees don't have minds and they're alive. That's what Jonathan was saying. It's a soul god gave you. It's a piece of him.

"Does god perform miracles," Adam yelled over the noise.

"All the time," Jonathan said. He was the spokesman for his group. He loved the attention.

"Can he lift a giant boulder?"

"Course he can. He can move a whole mountain."

"And your soul is god? A little piece."

"Yes."

"Can your soul lift a boulder? Can it even turn a stone?"

"Yeah, if I knew how to control it, it could."

Then Margaret said, "You can't control your soul. God controls your soul." She couldn't resist talking about god! "He doesn't want you lifting boulders."

"Okay, okay." Adam could tell there was going to be another argument. Everyone loves arguing over god. "If we have to talk about the soul, let's call it *the will to live*. That work?"

"No, it's different!" Jonathan, he could really be a dick.

"It's not different. Every animal has a will. Just like it has a digestive system. Every living thing is made of matter, just like people," Adam said.

Margaret goes, "But they don't go to heaven. They might *want* to live but they don't have a soul god calls to heaven."

"You better hope they go to heaven," Jonathan said to Margaret. "If it's not the same in heaven as it is down here, how you gonna recognize it when you get there? God can make animals in heaven. Why do you think god can't make an animal in heaven?"

"Listen," Adam finally said all annoyed. "We can ask questions all day. I encourage it. But we're not gonna argue about the supernatural. That's not why we're here. You can argue about what god does all you want in your cabins. But we're only talking about the real world here. Kay? You're what, fourteen years old? I know what's in your heads. You're going to high school next year with adult thoughts but your views of the world are shaped by fairy tales. Does anyone have a question about natural selection, or at least what's," he waved his hand around, "real?"

As soon as you bring up god you can't talk about anything else. People get obsessed. Even when you have a guy like Adam, even though he was kind of a dick, and he knows what every animal is called and what it's related to and how it got made, someone will tell you god knows more. The problem is nobody can ever be good enough. You can only be the smartest or fastest, or you can only sing the best song or act in the best movie, and people will like you. But a person can never be entertained enough, can never be a big enough fan, there's no limit to how impressed they can be. Talent is no match for worship.

# Eat Shit, Be Legend

We marched another hour, to the edge of the woods, to a bright open spot with skinny trees where you could see the sky pretty clear. It was chilly and hard to breathe. Purple boulders busted out of the ground. There were benches to sit on and tables. And a big green toilet box.

Everybody took chips and cookies from their backpacks. All you heard was bags crinkling, matched by the rustling sounds of breezy leaves. I didn't have anything to eat. You were supposed to bring food from home, snacks or whatever. There were refrigerators in your cabin to cool your sandwiches. My dad had locked himself in his bedroom and fought with my mom all the time. We hardly had money for anything. Nobody thought about packing me a sandwich.

I wasn't too hungry, anyway. It would have been nice to have a sandwich and everything, just so I could talk to other kids, but it was nice to sit on the edge of a boulder and not have to walk for a while. That's the first time I talked to the redhead, because just then she came and sat next to me. She only wore a dress but she sat down anyway. "You don't have anything to eat," she asked me.

The first thing I noticed was her mouth. She had very puffy round red lips. You only saw about four of her teeth when she talked, she pushed her words at you with her lips. She had an accent I didn't recognize. It was a kind of Spanish accent, maybe Mexican but I didn't ask. First off, it's impolite when someone comes over and sits beside you on a rock and all they have on is a dress while you're wearing jeans to right away wonder where the hell they're from. And also, I didn't want to assume she was from anywhere, like if she was from El Salvador or something and I asked if she was a Mexican. People get offended by things like that. To me, Italians and Jews—in my town I'm saying, not from Israel and Italy but from Long Island—they're the same thing to me. But ask an Italian if they're Jewish and they look at you like you called their mother a slut. Ask a Jew if they're Jewish they go, "Yeah! Why," all defensive. It's the same with Hispanics.

She had pale skin, red hair and green eyes. I never heard an accent from a face like that. Very little kids give me the same feeling. When a five-year-old kid speaks French, I don't know, it just sounds weird, like he's super smart or something.

"I never get hungry in the woods," I said. I don't know why I said it. I knew damn well I got ferociously hungry in the woods.

"I'm not hungry either. You are welcome to pieces of my sandwich if you like." She had a fat sandwich sitting in a plastic box on her lap. "My name is Demaris."

"Oh. Larry," I said.

"Nice to meet you."

She sounded polite. Educated. "How old are you," I asked. She sounded older than the rest of us.

"How old do you think?" She said it nicely.

"I never saw you at Finley before is why I'm asking."

"I don't go to Finley," she said.

I took a piece of her sandwich. I just reached out and grabbed it. I couldn't chew though. My mouth was dry. I wanted to put the sandwich back but I already felt rude for saying I didn't want it and then out of nowhere taking it.

I know it's corny to compare a redhead to a strawberry. My sister's got red hair and people are always calling her a strawberry. That's all you can say about Demaris, though, with her little round mouth and pale face. She was like strawberry ice cream. I don't know.

"My dad is come here to be manager for Springkill. He was a biologist in my country. He needed to come to America. So I stay in the cabins with school children."

We didn't say anything else for about five minutes. She was probably waiting for me to ask questions about her dad. He was a biologist. From another country! That's interesting. What about her mom? Where's she?

Thing is, I don't get interested in anything when I'm nervous. The food in my mouth felt funny, too. Not funny, unnatural. My back was stiff and my face was hot. I didn't know what to do with my arms. They hung all over my body, long and useless like snapped extension cords. She asked, "What does your father do?"

"Builds airplanes," I told her.

"Really! What kind of airplanes?"

"Fighter jets. Like the kind you saw in Iraq. You know the A10?"

"No. Is it a fighting airplane?"

"Yeah, it shoots up tanks in the desert. They call it the Warthog because it's so tough and ugly. He builds those." I heard about the A10 a week before. Steven Lundgren Jr. was over my house with his father. They came to say hello to my dad. Or goodbye, I guess. Anyway he told me about the friggin Warthog for like the tenth time.

"Where're you from?" I ended up asking her. Everybody probably asked her that.

"Colombia," she said.

Man, she made me nervous! I'd only eaten half the piece of sandwich I grabbed from her box with my rude hands. The bread stuck all over my teeth. When she wasn't looking I used my finger to scrape the dough off the roof of my mouth.

"What's wrong with your neck? Does it hurt you much," she asked me. I was rubbing the back of my neck and making a face like I was in pain. I do that sometimes when I'm very bored or very nervous.

Then Jonathan came and sat next to me.

"What up, nucka," he said. I had to turn all the way away from Demaris to look at him. He should've stood in front of us. Retard.

"Hello John," I said. He hates it when you call him John. My mother told me he got teased in a private school he went to. The boys in his class called the toilet *the John*. They nicknamed him P.J., which stood for Pissy John. He got bullied pretty rough and left the school for Flower Hill.

Now he only wants to be called Jonathan. But if he was going to sit practically be*hind* me I wasn't going out of my way to say his whole friggin name. "This is Demaris. She's from Colombia," I said so he wouldn't ask. He's the type of guy who'd ask where you're from right away. Demaris wouldn't look at him.

"Why didn't you bring a snack," he asked me. He didn't care Demaris hated his guts for crushing the vegetables.

"I don't get hungry. That's why I'm so skinny, ha ha." I really had a complex about being skinny. I'd started lifting weights. I got a dumbbell set for Christmas. "Anyway, Demaris gave me some of her sandwich," I told him. I opened up the bread and showed him what was in it: pork with pickles and cabbage. There was some kind of sauce, too. Colombian I guess.

"Which school are you from," Demaris asked Jonathan.

"Flower Hill," he said with this very serious face.

"Have you decided what to do for the talent show," Demaris asked.

"Talent show?" I never heard about it.

"The schools make a talent show on the last night."

"Why," I asked. My neck was burning by then. I rubbed it like crazy.

"For fun," Demari said.

"My friends and I haven't decided yet," Jonathan told her, officially. Even though she asked me.

"I sprained my ankle last week," I said. "I can't dance or anything." Pure crap. Truth is, I quit performing.

"You are walking well," Demaris said, after we started back on the hike. I forgot I told her I'd sprained my ankle.

"It's okay after I get warmed up. I hate to limp. It makes you look weak." Then I started to limp a little.

We walked together near the back of the group. Demaris knew everything Adam would say at each trail stop. When we hadn't talked a minute she'd ask about my ankle. "If you don't pull your pants up you will trip and really break your leg," she told me once. My jeans were too big.

Adam was bent over holding something, another mouse, sort of. He picked up crap with his bare hands, right off the ground. Covered in pine needles and little sticks. Totally disgusting. He wasn't just holding it though. He pulled it apart! Everybody took pictures of him picking apart a piece of shit. Inside were tiny bones and some fur.

"See the teeth," he said, pointing at a jaw. "Anyone know where this came from? I'll give you a hint. It's my favorite bird. A strigiform."

Nobody knew what a goddamn strigiform was.

"It's a bird of prey. Eagles, hawks and my favorite, owls. It's an owl pellet," he said, holding bones and fur in his palm. "Prolly from a Long Eared Owl. They're the ones you see most around here, lucky me. They're my favorite of favorites. They're also called Pussy Owls."

All the boys went hell yeah, and the girls moaned gross and turned red. Jonathan went over and stuck his hand out. "Lemme hold it," he asked.

"Sure man, here," said Adam. "There's gonna be a lot of this on our walks." He handed him the crap. "Pussy Owls fly so quietly they don't even hear themselves. They pass over fields like, I don't know, cloud shadows, listening for mice in the grass."

Then Jonathan, guess what the sick son of a bitch did. He pretended to eat it! The crap, I mean. He didn't just make faces either, like blow air in his cheeks and chomp the way you fool around with a baby. He laid the crap on his lips. It dangled from his chin, held together by mouse skin and clumpy bits of fur. He jiggled it with his friggin tongue.

Jonathan's dream is to be in a band. He has two guitars. One's black and yellow and the other's lightning blue. We played them in his room when I was at his house for a picnic.

He always talks about punk rockers he saw on the Internet. Some show from thirty years ago. After church Jonathan told me about the crazy shit they did. He didn't talk about music, or sing songs or hum guitar or anything. He talked about a guy smashing himself on the head with a guitar and knocking himself out. Or one time this guy got a blowjob on stage! And another guy who cut himself and bled all over the front row. We didn't have a computer at my house. I'd never seen the videos. Now, people do crazier things but it doesn't mean anything. They only do it to be like punk bands thirty years ago, guys who did it without knowing they'd end up on the internet, watched between homework assignments. See what I mean?

If you're doing something you think is private, or at least is just between you and a couple people, your fans or your friends or somebody, and you're bleeding on them, it means something. I can't explain it exactly. When someone who wasn't even there copies it for a bunch of people he'll never see, it doesn't mean anything.

That day at his house, when we played guitars together, Jonathan taught me how to play Smoke Over Water on the blue guitar. It was simple. It took me two seconds. I watched my hands the whole time. Jonathan drank a soda on the other side of the room and watched himself in the mirror. He drank from the can and stumbled around. He wiped his face on his forearm as if he was sweating all over the place. He made faces like he was shooting his batch. He did it over and over, drank soda and pretended he was drunk. Finally, when I thought I could get it right, that I could play part of the song, I figured we'd play it together. But he didn't want to play. He showed me videos on his computer instead.

A thousand years ago, when people lived in villages, there were one or two guys who were the strongest men. One or two guys cooked great, one or two guys told the best stories and two painted the best pictures. But now it's different. No matter what you're good at, somebody is fifty times better. Even things you thought nobody but you did, like being the fastest shoe lacer or something. And you can bet you'll find him on the Internet. You're in competition with the whole world. You even have to compete with guys from the friggin past. That drives me nuts when I think about it. It makes me not want to try.

The group snapped pictures of Jonathan knowing they'd put them on the Internet, imagining their crazy lives admired by an interested world, saving them for the future so people will look back and believe we were living so fucking carefree, a bunch of fun-loving, crazy kids, naturaler and cooler than ever. Bullshit. They're collecting moments the way bees gather pollen, mindlessly, to puke it up later and sweeten some other cocksucker's life.

Demaris didn't laugh. She didn't look away either. She plain didn't think it was funny. Because it damn well wasn't! I was glad Demaris didn't laugh. I don't know why. I just was.

By the time we climbed down the mountain and left the trail the sky was stuffed with dirty clouds. Wind poured into the field and swirled at the edges, shaking the trees, flashing leaves upside down. Globs of light rushed across the field. Everybody made faces in the wind and rushed inside the Center, its windows filled with light no brighter than the last few minutes of day. Mrs. Ackerly waited in the doorway waving us in. "Let's go, kids. Careful, careful. The rain is coming. Let's go. HEY. Don't push!"

It didn't rain though. It just kept blowing and turning colors.

# What's At The Top

Meals in the Center were pretty good. There were different stations for different kinds of food. If you wanted a hamburger and fries, you went left. If you wanted spaghetti you went to the middle, and if you wanted vegetables you went right. Spaghetti was my favorite. You could eat as much as you wanted. When you got to the end of the spaghetti bar though, Mrs. Ackerly was there. "Make sure you get your vegetables. They grow them here on premises. They're organic and delicious." You knew she'd watch and make sure you took some veggies.

Ashley and Alicia didn't even look at me and Joey. They sat on a bench packed so tight together with other Finley girls you couldn't floss between them. Joey sat with Jimmy Lutani and some Flower Hill kids. What I wanted to do was sit by myself somewhere out in the middle of the woods.

I sat with them anyway. With Joey and his old schoolmates. Soon as my tray hit the table Jimmy Lutani said, "Bro, you burned down the fuckin fort," and laughed. He had a real stupid laugh, like a cotton ball machine gun. Joey laughed too, but you could tell he didn't think it was funny. "Seriously, that fort was dope," Jimmy said.

"How'd you know about the fort," I asked him. I said it with food in my mouth, like I didn't care.

"Last winter during wrestling season, right Nailati? And the year before that prolly around wrestling season, too. After our brothers' matches we'd go chill up in the fort."

"Were the pictures on the wall," I asked.

"Hells yeah," Jimmy said.

"You and your brother came over after meets for dinner," Joey said.

"Your mother can cook. Real Italian food, not like these crap noodles here, eh? And why do I give a shit about organic broccoli," Jimmy said.

"You Italian, Jimmy," I asked him with four pounds of noodles in my mouth.

"Hells yes. Jimmy fucking Lutani, bitch!"

"Oh!" went Joey.

"That dude goes to your school, right," Jimmy asked Joey and me.

"Who?"

"The one with the Finley Falcons T-shirt."

"That's Robby Morales," Joey said. "Yo, Robby!" Robby didn't look up from his plate. He sat at the end of a table. Other people were at the table but he sat at the end, alone. "He rooms with us in the cabin."

"Why's he sit over there then? Not here?"

"He's always in a bad mood. He's weird."

"He started shit with Chad and them. You remember them, Nailati, right?"

"The soccer fags?"

"Your boy Robby started with them."

Then Jonathan sat down all heavy. He dumped his tray on the table. Food fell off. He didn't even clean it up. He left it there. A few strands of spaghetti and like two pieces of organic broccoli. "What up Jimmy," he said. Jimmy nodded. They went to Flower Hill together. "Dude, Demaris is super hot," Jonathan said to me.

"Yeah, she's hot, Jonathan."

"Who's Demaris," Jimmy asked.

"The redhead. There," Jonathan pointed over my shoulder with his spaghetti saucy fork.

"Oh shit. Yeah, I saw her this morning," Jimmy said. "She goes to your school, Joe-Joe?"

Joe-Joe. What a dickhead.

"I've never seen her," Joey said.

"Her father's the manger here or someshit," I said.

"You talked to her the whole hike," Jonathan said. "What was she saying to you?"

I wished he'd leave me the hell alone. What did she say! I hate it when someone asks what a person said. Especially after your first conversation.

"I don't remember every-friggin-thing, Jonathan. Jesus." He wanted me to remember everything. "We talked about you the whole time. What a funny guy you are, eating owl shit."

"Really? That's what you said?"

"Sure, PJ, that's all we talked about."

"What the hell's your problem?" He was offended. He looked at Joey and Jimmy and shrugged his shoulders.

"Nothing. I don't have a problem. I'm just not gonna sit here and enter*tain* you with my private conversation. Want me to show you my dick, too?"

"Hey, relax!"

Relax! That's another one that pisses me off. When someone tells me to relax.

"Sure, no problem. Now that you ask me. I'll just kick back and re*lax*." I shoveled the spaghetti in. I wasn't even hungry anymore. The food stuck in my chest. It hurt like hell. I drank water to flush it down.

"What'd I do? Make you angry like that?" Jonathan wouldn't let it drop. He was one of those guys who thinks everything is about him. If someone's pissed off at anything, he thinks they're pissed off at him. He'd like it, too, if you were pissed at him. He wants all the extras out of life. Good or bad. He wants it. The attention. The thrill! He'll get it, too. He deserves it. If you're mad at him he thinks he's special for in*citing* your passion. He's in your head permanently, tagging the walls.

I didn't finish my spaghetti. I cleared my plate into the garbage. I figured I'd head back to the cabin. What I really wanted was a cigarette. Thinking about sitting alone in the room drove me nuts for a smoke.

I walked to the front door. Mr. Brush came over and asked where I was going and I told him. We had to leave together, he said, as a group. He wasn't mean about it. Like Mrs. Ackerly would've been. She'd've been thrilled to say no. If a genie granted her three wishes, one of them would be the power to say *no* to everything.

I could've left if I wanted. There were about twelve doors in the Center you could sneak out. Nobody would know.

Walking around the cafeteria, looking at people and things, I checked the doors. Which ones were guarded and which I'd be able to sneak out. Just in case. Not even with Ashley, but just to be alone somewhere. I was walking, swinging my arms around and I bumped into Robby Morales.

"Oh. Robby," I said when I saw who it was. You don't apologize when you bump into someone you know. You just say their name. Robby gave me a stinker of a look.

You didn't want to be on Robby's bad side. Not because he was a mean guy or a bad guy, he wasn't. He just got offended easily. The thing about him was, when he took offense, he called you out. Take your average person, not a mean guy or a weakling, someone in between, and insult them. Just a joke. Nothing serious. Your average guy will brush it off even if he was offended. He won't insult you back he'll just brush it right off and probably never think about it again. Say you're riding your bike along with an average guy. There's a mound of dirt and a bunch of plywood outside a foundry near the railroad tracks. You and the average guy lay the plywood over the dirt mound and make a ramp to jump your bikes. You take the first jump and go about six feet. The average guy goes next. He peddles real hard, making faces and everything, with his tongue hanging out the side of his mouth and his eyes squinting, and when he hits the ramp the plywood buckles and his head snaps forward and the bike goes crooked through the air. This average guy jumps the ramp maybe three feet landing hard and his hair goes flying all over the place like he'd got donkey kicked in the face. You'd laugh your ass off and say to the average guy, "Holy shit! You nailed that, man." Something sarcastic, not even mean. The average guy'll say back, "I'm Evil fucking Knievel! Next I'll jump it backwards!" He'll be a little embarrassed, then let it drop.

Not Robby. Robby'll say, "I don't know why the hell you're laughing, Larry. I could a got hurt." He'd go, "I wouldn't laugh if you'd a got hurt. I don't think people getting hurt is funny. I'm not a dick like that. Everybody laughs when someone falls and hurts himself. Or embarrasses himself. It just shows what assholes people are."

He wouldn't do it either. He wouldn't laugh if you fell off a ramp. He didn't have a sense of humor. He was always that way, confronting people about things. He was used to it. You get used to confronting people. That's why you didn't want to be on his bad side. He'd bring up the past. He'd keep confronting you about it until you finally apologized. The thing is, I probably shouldn't have laughed at him when he nearly killed himself jumping the ramp. Laughter probably is some kind of cruelty.

When I bumped Robby in the cafeteria and said his name and he gave me that nasty look, I knew he was going to confront me about something. I couldn't think of what the hell I'd done wrong but I was ready to apologize. I felt bad enough already.

"Why'd you call my name out before the hike today? You don't just call someone's name out in a crowd like that. What's wrong with you? You don't go yelling out to somebody in front of a crowd a people they don't know."

"You're right, Robby. I don't know what I was thinking. I should've waited until you introduced yourself," I was joking with him.

"You don't know if I had a problem with one a them guys, Larry. What happens if my uncle's in business with one a them guys's father and they got beef? You don't know. You don't go throwing a guy's name out, callin'm out in front of a bunch a guys."

I didn't waste my breath on Robby. I apologized five times and beat it. I had to sleep in the same room with him for three nights, I didn't need him preaching to me at dinner. Robby and me were only friends because we lived close to each other. He was around the corner, the last house on a dead end street.

I went over where the Finley girls were sitting, figuring to say hello to Ashley. There was a piece of paper on the table about in the middle of them. They leaned over, butts lifted off the bench so they could see the paper better.

"You can tie it to a shoelace and swing it against the wall!"

"That's 43."

"Did you write the last one down, Rebecca?"

"Yes."

"You stick an eraser in its butt and feed it till it pops!" Ten girls squealed.

None of them realized I was standing there. Not even Ashley, and I was practically breathing in her face. They kept talking and laughing. Then Ashley goes, "You can pitch it to someone and they hit it with a bat."

"Yeah, I like that one," Alicia said.

"T'cha doin," I said in Ashley's ear. She practically jumped off the bench.

"Jeez Larry. You scared the crap out of me."

"Sorry. What'cha guys doing?"

"Oh, oh. Glue it to a car tire and drive to the mall."

"That's gross. Put that down, Rebecca!"

"I'm trying. You guys are talking so fast."

"We're making a list of ways to kill a hamster," Ashley told me.

"Cool. What for? I'm just asking," I said.

"I don't know," Ashley said.

"Wrap it in tin foil and bake it in the oven."

"Ew, like a potato!"

"You want to sneak out, Ash? There's an open door by the kitchen. The cooks or whoever, they go out with garbage bags. Me'n you could go one at a time and meet…"

"What're you talking about? I'm not sneaking out. Are you serious?"

"Yes. I'm totally serious. What we'd do is go to this clearing in the woods we ate our snacks in today. There's purple rocks all over the place."

"Oh, nasty," the girls cried out.

"It's kind of far but if we go fast…"

"I'm missing what's happening," Ashley said. "What was the last one," she asked the table.

"Suck its guts out with a vacuum," Alicia told her.

"We don't have to do anything. We could just. I don't know. Just go and sit or whatever." She probably thought I'd try and beat that. Everyone heard the rumors about Springkill.

She wouldn't go with me. Wouldn't even face me. She put a leg under her ass and stuck her head over the table. I kept talking to her. She blocked me out. She pulled a smile across her face and listened to the ways you could kill a hamster. There aren't many. It's all the same thing. Crush it, stab holes in it, burn it, suffocate or poison it. Destroy the material! That's how to kill a hamster. The rest is art.

I went to the door by the kitchen. I could've walked right out. There was a fence with a gate in it where they kept the garbage. The cooks dumped carrot peels and chicken bones and crap from plastic bags onto a heap. The fence had mesh wiring over it and a mesh roof I guess to keep animals out. All that garbage stunk like hell. You could walk out the garbage door and go around the Center to the trails. All I wanted was to go to the rest area and smoke a cigarette. I could forget about Jonathan and Joey's twerpy friend Jimmy. And Ashley, too. I could imagine the rest area, a little bit of emptiness to fill with thoughts and dreams, just like a home is a hole in the air filled with furniture and television. All I needed was a cigarette to make my home in Springkill. I could make a fishing pole out of saplings and underwear string and find mushrooms and weeds to eat. Like Steven Lundgren taught me. Maybe I'd slip into the forest and disappear. I imagined Finley and Flower Hill, Demaris and her father, all of them spending the next three days looking for me. I'd be gone. I'd be living by a lake or something.

All a sudden I started thinking about Demaris. She'd been a real sweet kid sharing her sandwich and not laughing at Jonathan. I figured I'd go find her. Maybe sit with her for the rest of dinnertime. She was over the other side of the cafeteria with the counselors.

I didn't walk right up to her. She sat by the hamburgers so I went and looked at the burgers and fries like maybe I'd have a second dinner. Then I walked over to the window and looked out. You couldn't see a damn thing. The night held its hand over the window. Then I walked over to Demaris and acted like I'd just noticed her.

"Hey," I said smiling. My face was red as hell.

"Hello Larry. Would you care to sit with us?" Her legs were crossed, an arm on the table like a trickle of milk.

"Me? Nah. I'm just walking around. I like to walk around after I eat. Food gives me a lot of energy." What a retard.

"Come sit here." She moved over. "It's alright." There was plenty of room. I went and sat next to her. "This is Pasqual, this is Theo, and you know Adam already." She introduced me to some of the counselors.

"You guys are all from Long Island," Adam said right away, motioning over the cafeteria.

"Yeh," I said. I felt very uncomfortable.

"Me too," he said. "Syosset."

"That's the next town over from me. I'm from Huntington Station."

"My aunt lives there," he said. "Norma Aliperto."

"Aliperto? That's your last name?"

"Uh huh."

"My aunt is Bettie Giavanni," I said. "The Giavanni's are related to the Aliperto's by my cousin Nancy. She married the guy who's got the cesspool company with the trucks that say, 'We're number one in the number two business.'"

"That's my cousin Frank!"

Italians from Long Island, I'm telling you, they're all related.

"Holy shit," I said. "You don't have a cigarette do you?"

"You smoke?"

"Sometimes," I said.

"I can't give you a cigarette."

"It's okay," I said. "I only smoke a little. My dad lets me sometimes."

"I'm not even supposed to smoke. Not on the grounds, at least. We're supposed to go down to the service road."

"I wouldn't say anything. It's just nice once in a while."

"Can't do it. Sorry."

"You guys aren't eating," I asked. None of them had trays in front of them.

"We eat in our cabins. We're vegan. Well, most of us are, at least."

"I eat eggs," the counselor named Theo said. "I'll put milk in my coffee, rarely, if it's organic. I don't eat anything that died screaming." His Adam's apple bumped over every syllable. "Are you staying out of trouble," he asked me. He's the one who caught me in the office that morning.

"He's alright," Adam said for me. "Got'm in my group. He's just quiet."

"Why didn't *you* eat," I asked Demaris. She didn't have a tray.

"I'll eat later with my father. He cooks vegan in his cabin."

"Vegans don't eat meat," I said.

"I don't use animals for anything," she said.

"You had a pork sandwich today. I ate it."

"Larry, it was tofu," Demaris said.

"You couldn't tell the difference," Adam chimed in right away. "But people still eat meat, man. It's part of this nutritious breakfast. You got your frozen vegetables, some processed starchy shit and a slice of carcass. Ding. Dinner."

"Slice of carcass," I said.

"It's what it is. You call it steak and pork chops. Not cow and pig. You tell yourself it's a glass'a milk, not puss and mucus secreted from infected mammary glands."

"Jesus."

"The mind of an American," Adam said.

"You're from Long Island," I reminded him. Sometimes Italians forget they're American. "Anyway, I don't think a French guy thinks his milk is puss. A Chinese don't think he's eating a cow. Maybe it's a cat though, ha ha." Nobody laughed at my Chinese joke.

"Take it easy," Theo said to Adam.

"I'm not gonna rant. I'm just saying, people think it's a natural right to kill and eat animals. They think eating animals makes you strong and smart! Especially Americans think that." He was saying this to me. "I was that way before I started thinking for myself. Not letting the beef industry pay to legislate until my thoughts were as manufactured as sausage. We're trained to think we're the top, the fittest, the best, the smartest blah blah blah, because that's what politicians and commercials and the military and shit tell us. We're the best and everyone else is garbage. That's American as fuck. We're the top of the food chain. Meanwhile, the *real* top of the food chain is bacteria, not Americans."

"Adam," Theo said, "you're ranting."

"No I know, but look at that pile of burgers. It all gets thrown out. Tonight! Pronto! A pile of ground up animals, rotting before you take your first bite. Vegetables don't rot that quick. They're still alive when you bite into'm. When you eat a carrot you eat one carrot. No autolysis. No anaerobic bacteria and bloat. When you eat a burger you're eating fuck-knows how many animals' muscles and guts and hearts and feces—

literally shit, as in poopoo, is mixed into it! Plus like ammonia to kill the bacteria that would make your burger stink. It's a shitball on a bun. I wouldn't eat it. Not in a million years." He asked me, "What do you think's at the top of the food chain?"

"Ranting, Adam."

"Human beings," I told him. I spent that very day listening to him talk about our nervous system and how evolution saved us, as in the human animal, from being prey. I knew Americans aren't top on the food chain. Humans were. He wasn't making any sense.

"See. He thinks humans are the food chain's top. I mean, you're right but you're wrong. It's a good, American answer: you, a human being, are *created* to kill and consume animals. Specifically cows and chickens. The meat industry has inculcated you with total certainty. You don't even have to think."

"Adam," Demaris said.

"Those burgers there?" Adam ignored her. "It's an ambush. A hundred million bacteria beat you to the first bite. They get into your guts and start pump toxins into your blood. Bacteria are in *you*. Waiting for the day *you* die. And then, bing! You're the burger now. Apples and carrots'll be on the table for days and don't rot. No fridge, no unnecessary energy. I'm not even gonna start on energy policy in this fucked up country. It takes more fossil fuel to store your food in the fridge than it does to grow it. Death hides in the fridge, man. Everyone talks about TV is where American culture goes to die. I think it's the fridge, just as much. Our minds are made by television, our bodies by the freezer." He'd rolled his napkin into a tube. He pointed it at the burger table. "When you die, the first place you start to rot is your guts. Remember that. Think you're top of the food chain. Yeah okay, tell that to your ass hole."

"Don't worry," Theo said. "He's not upset with you, Larry."

"My father next will change the food at Springkill," Demaris said quickly. "He already since last year brought more local meat and uses as many organic as he can. But if he doesn't put the burgers the schools won't come."

"He's doing everything right, Dee," Theo said to Demaris.

The other counselor, Pasqual, didn't say anything, just smiled. He was older than the others, like 30.

"All this food talk is making me hungry," Adam said smiling. Just before he stood up, he pointed at me with that napkin he was fooling with. "Roll your own," he said, and placed it very carefully on the table. The counselors got up and left.

Me and Demaris didn't talk for about five minutes. I was uncomfortable from meeting the counselors. Feeling uncomfortable lasts a while, like when you get a splinter. You pull it out and it goes on hurting for an hour. Same thing. Demaris took my hand. It surprised the hell out of me. She curled my fingers around the edge of her palm and stared at them the way women look at a necklace.

"They are good," she said. She was talking about my fingernails. "They're dirty and the cuticles need to be pushed back. They look bad but they are really good nails. Strong nails." She scraped around the edges of my fingers, at the cuticles, pushing them with her thumbnail. Waxy looking skin rolled up. "I saw your hands when you took my sandwich today. You have good hands. Dirty but good." I could feel my ears get hot. I wanted her to stop but it would've been rude to pull my hand away from her.

"Ouch," she dug too deep. A sliver of blood shined at the torn edge of my pointer. I kept looking over at Ashley while Demaris held my hand. She was laughing over that list. They must've had a hundred ways to kill a hamster by then.

Number 101: rip its cuticles off.

I switched seats. I didn't do it rude or anything. I stayed next to Demaris for a while admiring how much better my nails looked. I said I'd try taking better care of them now that I saw what a big difference she made. Then I moved.

I went to where Adam had been sitting on the other side of the table. We didn't talk for a little while but it was okay. I don't know, I just knew she didn't care if we talked. I kept looking at my fingers, though. Not to compliment her or anything, I just looked. The napkin Adam left had unrolled a bit and I went to use it to wipe my bleeding cuticle. There was something in it. Adam Aliperto, my cousin for all I knew, left me a smoke!

# Back Home Bullet

I stuck the cigarette in my breast pocket. I was wearing a button up plaid shirt with a breast pocket my got me for my birthday. I mostly wore white T-shirts in the warm weather and when it got cold I wore sweaters. My legs are very skinny and my knees are knobby. My calves are ash white with a million red dots. I'm very shy about my legs. So I don't wear shorts. My mother packed my bag for Springkill and she only put one T-shirt in the duffle bag and no snacks. I don't blame her because my dad locked himself in the bedroom with a gallon of vodka. She wasn't thinking straight. The other thing I had in my breast pocket was a bullet I'd taken from the top of our refrigerator. I don't know why, I just liked it. I'd probably get in trouble if one of the counselors or Mrs. Ackerly saw it but I didn't care. It's not like I was going to shoot somebody. Bullets don't go off for no reason. They're safe. You can knock them around or drop them on the floor.

One thing about cigarettes, they almost make me crap my pants! Just the thought of smoking a cigarette, like alone in a room or when I used to smoke in the fort, makes me want to crap. Just the thought.

When we got to the cabin though, Mrs. Ackerly had to make a speech. She was always giving speeches just when we were happy to do something else, like choose our rooms or take craps. She should've waited until we were bored or something, then maybe we would've listened to her.

"Attention children," she said, standing in front of the pot-bellied stove. "I want to congratulate you all on your first day at Springkill. You behaved like young men and women and represented your school admirably." She paused, probably so we'd applaud ourselves. People always stop their speeches to let you clap. We didn't do it, though. "I'm sure you're aware about the talent show." She paused again. She wanted us to participate in her speech. "It's tradition at Springkill that the final night of our stay the schools participate in a talent show. It's only fun. It is not a competition. However," again a friggin pause, "I want each of you tonight to meditate before lights-out on a skit, a routine, a song, even a comedy sketch, some sort of performance because tomorrow," one more friggin pause! I thought I'd crap my pants. A fart grew in my guts but I was afraid if I let it go I'd pop like a champagne cork. "Tomorrow you will form groups and perform your skits here in the common room. Your performances *will be* a competition as the best three, judged by myself, Mr. Brush, and your classmates, will be our representation at the show. Good luck."

I sprinted to the bathroom.

There were only two stalls, no urinals. Who knows why? There were showers next door, about six of them, so if you had to pee and the stalls were occupied and the door was locked you just went and pissed in the shower. Nobody cared. It all ends up in the same place. When you went to take a shower there was a back-of-your-balls smell.

I was in a stall by myself and started thinking about Demaris. She had red hair a bit like my sister's only Demaris's was darker. Anything that reminds me of someone in my family turns me off. This one time I went to the movies with Ashley. We were watching some movie only a girl would like and I kept touching Ashley's leg and rubbing my head against hers. Not *rubbing* my head, just touching her. I was trying to make out with her. She really liked the movie so she'd only turn to me for a second. Her eyes wouldn't leave the screen or anything. She'd leave a bit of spit on my lips that I'd lick off. I was palming her thigh and all that and trying to get her to make out with me and she all of a sudden said, "Good lord, Larry, just let me see this part."

Good lord. That's exactly what my mom would say. Man that turned me off. I didn't even want to make out with her after that. I mean I had this hard on. It was really painful, all bent up in my lap. I thought it would never go away. Sometimes I carried the same boner around for hours. It'd go a little limp and lazy but then it came back hot and pulsing until I took it to the fort. As soon as Ashley said *good lord* my boner dropped out of the sky and I didn't even try making out with her for about a half hour.

Maybe it was her skin or her accent or the way her hair was darker or her tiny mouth. Demaris didn't remind me too much of my sister. She was just very pretty and nice. I thought about the way she held my hand and how I'd eaten her sandwich, and walking in the back of the group with her on the hike. This very weird thing started to happen.

All day I'd felt like I was skin, like that's all I was, just a surface. I felt like I was out in front of myself, this flat deflated thing, greasy and cold. A pole was jammed in my back and on the other end of the pole was something heavy pushing me, sticking me in peoples' faces, pushing me along the trails.

Now I was alone in the bathroom getting warm. Warm blood was soaking into me, filling me with liquid weight. I got ideas that were recognizable. They were my thoughts, remembered. I wasn't flat anymore.

People are like sponges, I think. The real person is the warm, heavy liquid soaked into the pulp. I felt that way in the bathroom. I was held firm, pulpy, and sort of restrained. It was a good, solid feeling. There was no pole or heavy driving thing, just me. I thought about Demaris. And then I had a boner.

The door to the bathroom opened slowly. Someone checked under the stalls if they could see feet. Some guys can't shit with other people in the room. I took a squint under my door to check the shoes. I recognized them. They were clean white. Joey'd put his sneakers on.

"Joey. It's me, man. Close the door."

"Larry, oh shit."

"Yeah, close the door. There's a lock on it, too."

I heard the door close and the lock click.

"You shitting," Joey asked me.

"Yeah, I did but. Yeah. You gotta take a shit?"

"Nah."

"The door's locked, right?"

"Yes, I locked it."

"You sure," I asked.

"I'm sure, dick." He went into the stall next to mine. "It smells like the back of my balls in here."

# Full Moon And Stars

There are three ways you can insult a person with your ass. The moon, the full moon, and the full moon and stars. The moon is showing your ass. Just the cheeks, that's it. The full moon is when you spread your cheeks and show your asshole. Then there's the full moon and stars. That's when you pull your pants down around your ankles, bend all the way over, spread your cheeks and part your thighs so your balls are visibly dangling.

You had a hard time getting the story straight, why Robby got sent home, because all the teachers and counselors would tell you was that he got sick. Bullshit. Eventually you got the story from the *student population.* You had to pick true pieces out of the gossip. Everybody screwed around with a rumor to make it more personal and involve himself.

There were three boys in Robby's group who were from Flower Hill. Everybody said that, three boys. What they all said was Robby got himself into a fight with the boys over pubic hair. Robby was like Joey. He had a bush between his legs. He changed his clothes right in front of you. Like if he'd just gotten back from the shower or something. He'd drop his towel and have a conversation with his pin pointed straight out from his shriveled cold balls. Joey did the same thing. It's because they had so much hair around their pins, I'm telling you. They were proud.

Robby lived a couple blocks from me, on a dead end street not far from a cement foundry that makes septic tanks and roadblocks. Robby's lawn was clumpy, and after it rained his red house was streaked grey. We'd been friends since we were little kids and I remember asking him once, "Is your pecker tan?" I had a tan pecker, much darker than the rest of my body. It still is dark but now I know that's normal. Anyway, I asked Robby and he said he didn't know. We were about eight years old. I pulled mine out and showed him. I wasn't shy about it yet. We were hanging out in the backyard kicking the soccer ball around and he went behind the shed and checked his pecker for a tan. He was shy about it. When he came back he told me yes, it was tan. He had a smile on his face, too, like he'd just discovered something hilarious about himself. He laughed and laughed. There was a time when Robby was shy about it. But not anymore, not in Springkill with his hairy pin.

On the first day, on the hike our different groups took around the woods, the Flower Hill boys, I saw them, they were wearing the same clothes. Not a uniform or anything, just the same *kind* of clothes. Shorts above the knee. Brown wool socks and old-looking leather boots. They weren't beat up, the boots, not like Robby's Reebok's with the hole in the toe and broken laces. Theirs were aged or something. They wore fleece vests over button-up cotton shirts. You didn't know where the hell they shopped. It wasn't at the mall. They shopped at stores with futzy window displays, like on the small streets in the village, with canoes hanging from the ceiling, and skis nailed to the wall's wood planks, and you can't afford even a keychain there, literally. The way they dressed, it sort of was a uniform. It gave them some kind of authority that made you respect and hate them. The thing about the way they dressed was you could tell they weren't trying to be like you. They looked like each other. I'm not saying they were unique or something, it just looked as though they belonged in those clothes, you didn't, and it was natural.

What else you heard from everybody was that it was all Robby's fault. But I didn't believe it because Robby, I knew him, he didn't start trouble. He got mad easily and sometimes when he was mad you didn't know why. It seemed like he was upset over nothing at all, that he'd made it up. But he didn't *start* trouble.

Sometimes I rode my bike to Robby's house. I had this piece of junk bike I'd gotten for Christmas one year. I didn't feel hot shit riding around the neighborhood but Robby lived on a dead end street with only three other houses, plus a foundry. It was a good place to ride. There was a loading dock at the foundry with a steep drop, fifty yards long. You could build good speed on the dock. I loved the feeling, going fast. You pedal as hard as your legs will go and duck your head and speed down the hill like a bullet. The little worms in your guts curl up so tiny they're not even there. You're weightless for a second. You scream, "Motherfuckin motherfucker," and it's done. There were trashed wooden forms we used to build jumps. It was a fun spot.

I went there pretty often and rode around with Robby. But the last time I went he wouldn't come out of his house. He was sick or something. He was always getting sick, probably from the cement dust in the air. When you left the dead end you always had grit in your teeth and your hair felt like straw. He wouldn't come out so I rode around doing the tricks, flying down the dock, circling around the cul-de-sac, just fooling around on my bike.

Fifteen minutes later Robby came out of the house. He didn't have his bike. He stood in the middle of the road. I went over to him. He's got his usual stinker face.

"You got some hair on your balls riding here," he said to me. That's how Robby talked.

"I always ride here," I told him.

"No you don't. You don't always ride here alone."

"So?"

"So go ride on your own street."

"I live two blocks away. This is my street."

"No it isn't. No it isn't," he said it twice.

"What's the difference," I asked him. I didn't know what the hell he was upset about. 2nd Avenue was strictly off limits to me, and like a week earlier, some asshole got shot on West 4th Street. So my dad made me stay in the neighborhood. "I'm not allowed to ride anywhere else."

"You only come here when you want to ride that crappy bike," he said.

"It isn't crappy," I told him, even though it was a clunker.

"You only come here to ride bikes. You don't come any other time. Even when I go to your house, you don't want to do anything except ride bikes over here. It rubs me the wrong way, that's all."

He was right, though. I only went to his house to ride bikes. He wasn't much fun for anything else. I wanted to tell him that, to say, "Bro, you gotta admit, you aren't much fun." I didn't have enough hair on my balls, though. Robby always had the hair to say what he wanted to say.

They climbed the hills together and around paths marked with colored arrows. Everybody had water bottles you were forced to buy for the trip. That was part of the hundred dollars it cost to go to Springkill, and they were drinking from them. Thing was, you weren't supposed to relieve yourself anywhere along the path. There was one rest stop the trails ran past and you were supposed to hold your waste until you got to the porta-potties. There were ten million animals in the forest relieving themselves wherever they wanted, crapping mice bones, but people had to wait to pee in a box.

Finally they made it to the rest area. There are picnic tables, and a clearing behind them. The mountain is made of grey and purple rock and covered with ten million years of decay. *Humus*, Adam called it. The wind and rain peeled some humus off the mountain's corners where no trees or anything grow, just little weeds in the cracks trying to break pieces off the boulder. They have, too. You find little stones lying around and you throw them off the mountainside. It's quite steep at the clearing. There's a wire strung from post to post to keep the students back. At the bottom of the cliff is a river and on the other side of that is another mountain's cliff. If you follow the river you see Connecticut and Massachusetts. They come together with New York. It's supposed to be a big deal, seeing all three states together, but there's no difference between them. It's the same trees, same river, same clouds.

The trails' different lengths meant groups made it to the rest area at different times. We weren't supposed see each other. You weren't supposed to leave any waste behind. Everything you came with you left with.

You weren't supposed to know anyone had ever been there. The tables and the wires, the green plastic huts, they've sprung up like ferns and lichens and wrinkled brown mushrooms and china jutes. The only clue that people came before you is the waste they left in the porta-potties and the fog inside them. Walking into the potties was like walking into a warm kitchen where soup has been boiling. You wanted to hold your nose and breathe through your mouth but you're afraid you'd taste it. That's where the trouble started for Robby.

One by one the kids went into the potties to empty their waste, then came out panting and gagging.

"It reeks in there."

"Spray some Glade. Damn!"

"Don't eat so much sugar and processed food, and drink more water. Your waste won't stink. My waste hardly smells at all," the counselor says, all proud.

"There's like a hundred pounds of crap in there."

"There's no way for crap not to stink. It needs spray! How often them things get cleaned?"

And then it happened. I wasn't there or anything. I heard about it. Everyone said the same thing. Someone asked when the toilets get cleaned and then one boy from Flower Hill said, "We need to call Mr. Morales up here!"

"Yeah get Mr. Morales to clean that crap out. He *loves* it. He doesn't use a plunger either. He uses a fishing pole." That cracked the three Flower Hill boys up.

Mr. Morales was a janitor at Flower Hill. Mr. Morales is Robby's father.

"He has a collection of turds mounted on his wall."

"The prize winner over the fireplace. Length and weight written out, ha ha."

I'd never been in a fistfight. But if I had to get into one I wouldn't have wanted to fight Robby!

Each of Robby's thighs is as big as my chest. He grabs you around the hips and tackles you. That's his style. No matter how much you wiggle or try to flip him off he stays on his toes and arches his body, his big legs driving his hard shoulders into you.

One time I watched him wrestle around with Joey in Robby's clumpy front lawn. Joey and me became best friends a week before, behind the foundry by Robby's house.

Robby told me he didn't like me riding my bike around his street. I started taking Joey with me. We'd only bring Joey's bike though. I didn't let Joey know I had a bike because it was such an embarrassing piece of crap. Joey could ride anywhere he wanted on account of he had an older brother who's a wrestling stud and he knew all the older guys in the neighborhood. And because Joey was a pretty tough guy, too. I knew it from the wrestling he did to me, the moves his brother taught him so he could be a wrestling stud when he got to high school. He kicked my ass.

We took turns on Joey's bike riding down the loading dock. His bike was way smoother than mine. It was solid and so light and quiet that it felt like there was no bike under you at all. You breezed along, hunched over, with the wind going down your neck and your shirt flapping against your skin. You pedaled your ass off. At the right speed it felt like the bike evaporated. When you reached the dock's drop the bike was gone, you floated. *My* bike fell away, rattling and vibrating so much you might as well have been riding a beer cooler.

Every time I turned back up from the dock Joey waved me off. He let me take another turn. I got about five rides in a row. When I came up from the dock one time, Robby was talking to Joey by the curb. I took another turn down the hill because I thought Robby'd tell us to get off his street in a very persuasive way. I came around again and they were still standing there, just talking, so I walked the bike over.

"What up, Rob," I said. Robby nodded at me. Not mean or anything. "You gonna get your bike," I asked him.

Joey looked at me and said, "This guy thinks wrestling don't work in a real fight."

"What if you get punched in the eye? That's all I'm saying." That's what Robby said.

"A real wrestler wouldn't, though. He'd stay away and circle. He'd keep circling, looking for angles and when the other guy's off balance he'd shoot in and take him to the ground. You can't get punched when you're on an angle."

"That only works in a match. With rules. In a high school gym. There aint'ny rules in the street. You don't shake hands with a guy and start circling around on angles. It happens fast. Like this." Robby flicked his fingers against Joey's chin, and when Joey flinched in surprise, Robby shot in, bear-hugged him. His big thighs lifted them both off the ground. Robby jumped a foot and a half. They came down hard with Robby on top. Robby wrapped Joey up, pinning Joey's arm against his chest. Robby was out to the side of him, driving with his legs. They made a squirmy T shape in jeans and T-shirts. Joey bridged his back the way wrestlers do, using his neck and kicking his feet, grey dust rising around them.

"I got you pinned," Robby kept yelling. He didn't though because Joey kept bridging, the back of his head pressed into the clumpy lawn. "I got you pinned."

"No you don't," I sort of screamed. "His shoulders aren't down." That was a cheap shot Robby took. I wanted to grab him by the hair and pull him off. I was very upset, seeing Joey stuck like that. When Joey wrestled me it was so impossible to escape I couldn't imagine anyone controlling him the way Robby did. My heart beat against my belly button.

Finally Joey flopped to his stomach. He had this confused look on his face, like a dog gets when his leash wraps around his paws. The dirt turned his sweat brown. Robby grunted and breathed like a madman. Joey wasn't pinned but he was beat. Robby proved how friggin strong he was.

"You give? You give?" Robby kept asking Joey if he'd give up. One of Joey's arms was trapped and Robby slid it higher up his back like a chicken's wing. That can really hurt your shoulder. If you've never felt it before don't try it. It hurts like hell.

"Don't give, Joey," I said. I would have gived. Anytime I was trapped, like when Joey pinned me in the fort, or when his brother wrestled me, I'd fake an injury. "Ouch, man. I got bad ribs, let me up," I'd say something like that. Or I'd start coughing like crazy and say I inhaled my gum. A guy will let you up if you start coughing all over the place.

But Joey's clever. What he did, he started to make things worse for himself. Robby had a chicken wing hold and cinched Joey's arm higher and higher up his back. If Joey had a day's growth on his fingernails he could scrape the back of his own head. Robby's red face was close to Joey's going, "Give! Give it up," and then but Joey said, "Your breath stinks," and turned his nose away. "Oh no, not the breath torture. Anything but the breath torture," Joey says. Robby forgets all about the arm. He starts hacking in Joey's face. He lets the arm go to get a better angle. "Hhhhhha! Hhhhha," he's blowing his breath right up Joey's nose and Joey's going, "Ah man, the breath torture," and laughing his ass off. He goes, "I can't stand it, you garlicy bastard."

He made a big joke of it! I would've never thought of that, planting ideas in someone's head to torture you in a different way. I would have faked paralysis or something. Robby kept breathing until he got light headed and bored and let Joey up.

The Flower Hill boys didn't know Robby was a Morales. They hadn't heard me call Robby's name out a few hours before when we were in lines at the Center. And nobody knew them, the Flower Hill boys. They wore anonymity the way they wore their uniforms, and the inside joke, they figured, wore a uniform, too. They didn't know Robby was, in a way, a part of them, and that their inside joke was as obvious as Robby's dad's coveralls. Robby was very tough, but he was caught by surprise.

What everybody said is this. The group went through the rest of the hike, down the other part of the mountainside looking at animal bones and finding where deer scraped their antlers against trees and wondering why moss only grows on one side of stones and all that crap. Then Robby said, "I gotta take a leak. And it can't wait. I'm going behind that tree. I'm just another animal in the forest."

"No. You're going to stay… Hey!" The counselor tried to stop Robby. "What's that boy's name," he asked the group. "We're not far from camp. Don't leave the group. What's his name?"

"Morales." He called it over his shoulder. Then he stopped. "I'm'a piss right behind this tree and if you don't like it send one of those dipshits to clean it up." He pointed right at the Flower Hill boys. "One a you wanna clean it up? You got nothing to say now, huh? You got no hair on your balls."

"Hair on my balls? What's this fruit loop talking about? Why's he talking about my balls?"

"You're a bunch a cowards. Got no hair on your balls!"

"Hey! Cut the crap," the counselor said, probably. "What's your name? Get back over here!"

"Morales," Robby kept shouting, pretty much everybody said. "Roberto Morales Junior."

He peed while the entire group waited and practically watched. You couldn't see him because he was behind a tree, but still. I can't even pee if I'm on the phone with somebody.

The next day his group took the second trail. My group had been on it the first day, with the mouse and the turkey. They alternate. Anyway, the group was near the rest area again. Nobody'd said a word, not Robby, not the Flower Hill boys. They were getting closer to the rest area when one of the three boys—everybody said this—started screwing with Robby. "I hope some nice gentleman cleaned those porta-potties." Nothing too controversial. Nobody *had* to say anything, but one boy did. It was like the breath torture trick. And Robby fell for it, again. "Maybe you should get a straw and suck it dry," Robby said.

"That's enough. Stop now. I won't allow this to regress into immature histrionics. We're together here. Survivors in the forest. You must learn to be team players," the counselor probably said some survivor crap like that.

"I bought my fishing pole," one of the Flower Hill boys said. "I want the record catch."

"Whoa, Chad, you must'a grown some hair on your balls talking like that."

Flower Hill boys, I don't what it is, have no fear. It's maybe because they don't have day laborers ready to kick their asses when they're digging through dumpsters. There are no 2nd Avenues in their neighborhoods, no West 4th Streets where people get shot and they're not allowed to cross it on their bikes. They've never met anyone who *wanted* to hurt them.

The whole group laughed at the Flower Hill boys' jokes, at Robby.

And what did Robby do?

He walked away, to the rest area over the hill. People bet what Robby would do to retaliate. They said he'd push the porta-potties over in anger and pack shit like snowballs to lob at the three boys' faces. The group walked after him. They were dying to know how Robby would retaliate. To get even. To get rid of his anger. The Flower Hill boys didn't hurry. They stayed back a little.

Robby's group climbed the last part of the hill and turned the last trail corner where it emptied into the clearing with their counselor chasing them saying, "Stay together now."

There were the picnic tables, the outcroppings, the wire strung from post to post and the odor of piss and crap that had just been dumped from bodies, from my group there before them.

Robby climbed a porta-potty. His feet banged like drums. High above the rest area he bent over, dropped his pants around his ankles, and saluted the group at the third level. The full moon and stars.

# Name That Color

When me and Joey came out of the bathroom that first night after dinner, we went to our room and changed into sweatpants and T-shirts, then went to the common room. The stove was lit. Mr. Brush and Mrs. Ackerly were going around asking what the groups were planning for the talent show. Mrs. Ackerly kept saying, "Oh I love it. Such a good idea. Love, love, love it! But..." She'd bend over low, her green and brown skirt stretched so tight you could count the divots on her ass, and whisper her own ideas.

"Oh shit, the talent show," Joey said. "I forgot about it." We were looking for Ashley and Alicia.

"I don't think you have to do it. Do you want to do it?"

"Nah, I don't want to do some gay ass show in front of everybody."

"Me neither," I said.

"Fuck for?"

"It's supposed to be for like fun."

"Fucking retarded."

"Yeh."

"Look at'm." The girls were sitting on the floor. The same group they'd been in, floss-tight.

"I know."

"Springkill sucks, bro."

"Two more nights. And Ashley's in your group. Didn't you even talk to her? She's Alicia's best friend if you don't at least…"

"Pshh."

"You didn't even talk to Alicia at dinnertime. At least I tried to talk to Ashley. You talked to friggin Jimmy the whole…"

"Pshh." He closed his eyes and huffed.

"You're the one talking about it all year. How you're *definitely* going to bang Alicia."

"We gotta get some beers."

"Are you retarded, Joey? How we gonna get beer? I think that's bull-shit, anyway. Sneaking out and getting drunk. I don't believe it."

"It's not bullshit. Everybody does it. My brother told me. I bet they got beer in the Center somewhere."

"Wait. You know what? I just thought of? The talent show. It's in the Center."

"Fuckin talent show."

"No. I know, lame ass talent show, but there's like ten doors in the building."

"Oh shit."

"Yeah and you know they're gonna turn down the lights and light up the stage."

"Word."

"Word."

"Yeah and we can try to find beers in the kitch…"

"Nah man, forget the beer." I didn't tell Joey about the liquor I found in the Center, in that wooden room behind the kitchen. If I told him about it, I knew what would happen. He'd make me steal it. I couldn't do it, but that would be The Excuse. If we didn't bang the girls forget it, Joey would hold it against me for not getting them drunk. It would be *my* fault. "We'll sneak them out. The talent show'll go on for two hours. Think about the fort the other time? If it goes like that again, we're all good. Forget about the beer. Okay yeah it'd be better if there was beer but then why didn't your brother leave some behind in a river or something?"

"A fucking river?"

"The talent show."

"Yeah but you gotta talk to Ashley. I don't want to chance it and wait till the show. I want to try'n sneak out at night if we can. That's the right way. Tomorrow, bro."

"I guess we can try." I took a look the girls, and then everyone else working on their skits. "Let's go to the bunks," I said.

"Yeah, fuck these guys."

Ben Croton wouldn't stop moaning. He got a cold or something and he tossed and turned. I was waiting for everyone to fall asleep so I could smoke the cigarette Adam left me. Ben kept everyone up. Finally I just opened the window.

It wouldn't open easy. I got on my knees and pulled hard. It came unstuck and flew open but only about three inches. Someone screwed metal braces into the frame and the window banged against them.

"What the hell are you doing?" Robby, of course, was the first to get upset. "I'm tryin a sleep."

"Okay, Jesus. The window got stuck."

"What are you opening a window for? You sneaking out?" He was on the top bunk dangling his head over me with his hair falling and a vein swelling in his forehead.

"Look at this. The windows don't open wide enough even to fit your arm through," I said. Everybody was awake. "Joey, you see that?"

Then Ben goes, "What're you opening the window for anyway? It gets cold at night and you get condensation on your sheets and I've got this stuffed nose already."

"Alright Ben, I get it. You're a pussy."

"I'm not a pussy, Larry, it's true. If you leave the window open…"

"I wasn't going to leave it open. I'm just gonna smoke a cigarette. Then I'll shut it."

"Are you retarded, Larry? You can't smoke in here," Joey said.

"Calm down, I'll make sure it's out this time."

There was a weird minute when we were all quiet. Ben and Robby's eardrums swelled to hear what Joey'd say. Everybody knew I burned the fort down. Joey probably wondered if I was kidding or if I blamed him for blowing the fire all around the fort instead of smothering it with a shirt or something. I didn't blame him for being weird and quiet because even I didn't know if I was kidding or *what* I meant *if* I meant anything. We never talked about it, about the fire. The only time either of us mentioned the fort was one time at the train tracks.

There weren't any windows at the back of the foundry and you couldn't see us from the road. It was very private by the tracks. We hung around there a lot for a few days after the fort burned down. We were sitting on the track rail talking about girls when Joey asked, "What color are Ashley's nipples?"

"I don't know," I said. "I didn't see them. Aren't girls' nipples the same color as their lips? Isn't it made of the same kind of skin?"

"I don't think so."

"What color are Alicia's? Same as her lips?"

"I didn't get to see'm either. Girls are fucked up. You can finger them but they won't let you see their tits."

"I think nipples are the same as lips. They're both wrinkly and bumpy and red."

We both were thinking about the fort then because we could have checked the pictures, looked at the girls' nipples and see if they matched their lips. But then I remembered the girls in the pictures always wore lipstick and we wouldn't be able to tell. I knew Joey was trying to remember the pictures, if the girls had matching lips and nipples. I wanted to tell him it didn't matter because of the lipstick. We wouldn't have been able to check anyway.

"Know how we could'a found out," Joey said.

"I already thought about it," I said. "But they always had lipstick on."

"In the pictures?"

"Yeh."

"Yeah, but what about inside their pussies? That's got to be the same skin, I bet even more than face lips."

I didn't think of that.

"I should've kept some magazines hidden somewhere else. Sucks not having those pictures." Joey said.

"What was your favorite? The one with the cut in half shirt, right, cut above her tits and she's got see through underwear on? You can see her asshole. You put Alicia's school picture on it."

"Nah, my favorite is the girl blowing a guy on a ping pong table and her ass is all red from getting paddled and she's got the paddle handle up her pussy."

"Gross, man. She got a guy's pin in her mouth."

"Yeah but you hardly notice the guy. It's more realistic. I don't care just seeing a girl naked and not doing anything, just looking at you. It'd be awesome to be the photographer and have a boner the whole time you take the picture and probably get to beat it up after you take her picture. But I like to see what they look like while they're fucking for real."

"I guess you're right, Joey."

"I got the biggest boner right now."

"Me too."

We got quiet because we both were thinking about the fort and if we wanted to whack off we'd have to go home or something.

"I'll do it here," I said. "I don't care. No one can see us."

"Yeah, no one can see us, right?"

Joey sat on a track rail and I was on the other, back to back. We didn't need tissues or newspapers because we were outside.

"You want to pass out," I asked after. I liked to pass out after.

"I don't know, man. It was fucked up last time. I should'a known something bad was gonna happen. That was a sign from you-know-fuckin-who."

That was the most we said about the fort. After that it popped up in sentences like a stutter, you heard it and pretended not to notice.

Insurance men came to Joey's house one day and said they'd build a new garage. The burned up wood and ruined weed whacker and trimmers and old radios and junk went into a dumpster in front of Joey's house. We looked for nudey magazines everywhere, in recycling bins and regular garbage even. People don't throw that stuff out too often. And there's no insurance for porn.

"You'll get us in major shit if Brush finds out, Larry," Robby said. "He's gonna smell it and he'll ask who's smoking and none of us'll say anything. We'll all get in major shit."

"I'll say something," Ben said. "Shut the hell up! It's hard enough to sleep with my nose all plugged up and you assholes talking all night doesn't help."

"Yo Robby. What's going on with you and those Flower Hill assholes," I asked.

"Nothing. What a you talking about?"

"I heard you got in a fight with some soccer fags Joey used to hang out with."

"I never hung out with them," Joey said.

"It's lights out, Larry. If there's something I was dying to talk about, d'you think I'd wait here and pray for you to ask me about it?"

"Right. I guess not, darling," I said, sarcastic as hell.

I'd already taken the cigarette and matches out of my sneaker. We were way up in the mountains where there were no street lamps or lights from other houses and no noises besides the wind in the trees. When I struck the match the room lit up orange and the sulfur flared with the tearing sound of notebook paper.

"Fuck, Larry. Wud'ja light, a road flare," Robby said.

The tip of a flame is the hottest part. My dad taught me that. He said the tip of the flame is like the point of a knife. He'd just barely touch the end of a cigarette with the flame's tip. Some people, you see them poking at the bottom and sucking like they're drowned and snuffing out the flame before the cigarette lights. They put a black smudge on the white cigarette paper. It just looks bad, I don't know. You don't want to inhale the fuel from a lighter or the smoke from a match. That's what gives you cancer, my dad said.

It was windy in the morning and looked about to rain. Me and Joey hadn't talked to Ashley or Alicia. Joey bothered me about it.

"We gotta get'm to sneak out to*night*," Joey said. He always made me do the talking.

We were in the common room waiting to go to breakfast while Mrs. Ackerly went through the girls' rooms making sure they'd made their beds and left things neat. Mr. Brush didn't bother. The boys didn't make their beds or anything. I walked towards Ashley but Demaris touched my arm. She was sitting on this love seat near the stove and I had to squat down to talk to her.

"Don't forget a snack for the hike this morning. I know you don't have food from home but you can take a fruit from the cafeteria."

"Thanks for reminding me, Demaris. You should wear some jeans or something today. It'll probably rain and you're only in a dress." She was wearing a dress again. It was yellow with thin brown and purple swirls.

"It won't rain," she said. "I know this mountain."

I walked towards Ashley again but Robby stopped me. "Two people told me I smell like cigarettes. How much did you smoke last night?"

"Just one. I blew it all out the window." Who the hell cared if he smelled like smoke?

"I don't need a be breathing that shit all night while I'm freaking sleeping. Go to the bathroom next time. There's a window in there, too."

"Okay, Jesus. I don't even have another cigarette."

Finally I got to Ashley. She was standing with five other girls. They got quiet. Every one of the girls looked at me except Ashley.

"Ash. Hey come on over there. I want to talk to you a minute. Hah? You coming?"

She came, finally. She made a big deal about it, though, as if I was dragging her away from Thanksgiving dinner. Her chin stuck out so far she couldn't keep her lips together. You could hear her breathing while she sulked.

"How you feeling? I mean about the whole Springkill trip," I asked her.

"It's fine, I mean. Yeah, it's okay I guess." Her crossed arms were like a rifle strapped to her chest.

"Me and Joey are going up the mountain tonight. We're gonna take a trail to the rest area. You know the rest area right, with all the purple rocks and porta-potties? We want to go over to the clearing back there. We want to go tonight and hang out over the cliff. You and Alicia could meet us here in the common room after Ackerly and Brush and everybody goes to sleep. Then what we should do is…"

"Are you serious, Larry? No. No way, out of the question."

That pissed me off. "Why the hell not? I mean, why wouldn't you want to do that?"

"It's not that I don't want to. It's impossible."

"It's easy. You got two feet on your legs. It's just walking. You got to be quiet, that's all. Did Ackerly do a bed check on you guys?"

"I don't know. I was sleeping, obviously."

"I wasn't. I didn't sleep at all hardly last night. I know Brush didn't check on us."

Ashley unfolded and refolded her arms.

"I mean everyone'll be sleeping, Ash. It's like time travel. You know, when someone gets taken into a spaceship or something and goes to a wormhole and they're gone for about twenty years but only two seconds pass on earth? That's what it's like. Everyone'll be asleep and when they wake up you, me, Joey and Alicia will be back in our beds with everyone only we'll have been up the mountain over the cliff."

"Lame, Larry."

"It's not lame."

"Yeah it is. And actually? No. I don't want to climb up a mountain. I want to sleep. You can go get abducted by aliens if you want."

"What the hell are you talking about? No one said anything about aliens. All I said, it's like time travel. Everyone'll be snoring their stupid friggin heads off and we'll be doing something. You don't have to do, like, *it* with me. And neither does Alicia. How's that lame?"

"…"

"Okay, well, then one more thing."

"What?"

"I can get alcohol."

She didn't say anything when she left. She walked out the door with everyone else. Ever since that day in the fort she wasn't the same.

"It's you being lame," I yelled after her, so Joey could hear it and not ask me, all excited, if the girls would sneak out.

# Dumb Long When You're Hungry

Breakfast was the same deal. Three stations. The cafeteria mostly smelled like bacon and the blue flames' chemicals and the hot aluminum serving trays filled with scrambled eggs, sautéed mushrooms, spinach, and tomatoes, fried potatoes and sausage. It made you hungry to see the stacked white plates, the orange juice pitchers, the flatware bins, the bowls. There were cereal boxes and jugs of soy milk and regular milk with the plastic wrap over them peeled back where you pour. The other schools were there first, naturally, because Ackerly had to do her god-damn room check then get us all *in order* before we walked to the Center, following the red flag above her head.

The other schools lined up at the stations, especially at the pancake and waffle table. Me and Joey walked fast to get ahead of our school's kids.

"Fucking Ackerly, man," Joey said. We were way at the end of the pancake line. Then Jimmy Lutani, he was sort of near the front, stepped out. He was wearing another tank top and a stupid looking wool cap and he held a tray. He called us to come up, cut in.

"Yo, the line is dumb long when you're hungry, right," Jimmy said. Him and Joey punched fists. Somebody behind us, it was a girl, said, "You guys can't cut me. No cuts."

Jimmy goes, "Why don't you shut your gob? Nobody asked you."

"That's right, you didn't ask me or anybody else. We're all waiting."

I didn't feel too hungry anymore.

"We just came to say what up to Jimmy. We're not cutting. Let's go, Joey," I suggested that we go back to our spot. But all the other kids from our school had made it to the line by then. We'd have to go all the way the hell to the end and we'd be the last to get pancakes.

"No fucking way," Joey said, and turned his back to me. The tall counselor, Theo, came over. I knew him because Demaris introduced us the night before.

"Jimmy just let these guys cut," the girl said. Her name is Alison. I didn't know her then because she went to another school. I know her now though, in high school.

"Why don't you mind your business, flatface," Jimmy said. He called her flatface because her nose was sort of pressed in and she had wide cheeks on account of she was Japanese.

"Ew, Jimmy. You're such an asshole," she said.

"Okay, whoever got here first, stays. Anyone else goes to the end of the line," Theo said with his tired voice. You could tell he didn't give a crap if anyone cut.

"Joey was behind me the whole time," Jimmy said. "I don't know what she's talking about."

"You let him cut, too," Alison said, chucking a thumb at me.

"You know your face is flatter than your chest? Did you know that?" Jimmy was giving her shit about her flat chest and being Japanese.

"Whoever cut in line, okay, just go back where you were," Theo said. "It's not like you aren't going to be fed. What's an extra minute's wait?"

I punched Joey in the back. Not hard or anything, just to tell him we should go. He wouldn't look at me. "Nobody cut," he said. He gave me a look, not in my face but at my chest. He stared at my chest like he was guarding me in basketball or something. I don't know what it meant, even now, but then. Then, what I thought, he was telling me to get lost. He looked at me like I was a retard with gum in my hair. You look at dogs that way sometimes, like one that's even being walked on a leash. It's clean and it has a family but you just don't like it and you wouldn't mind if died.

"Joey's with me the whole time," Jimmy said again.

I beat it. All the way to the end of the friggin line, further back than where I was to begin with. Joey stayed with Jimmy. I watched them while they got their pancakes. I wasn't even hungry anymore. I swear to god.

# Lame Prudes

I had my plate of pancakes but I couldn't eat. I felt nauseas, sitting with some Woodhall guys, part of my group. A bunch of assholes. Ashley and Alicia sat at the table behind me is why I sat there.

Ashley's plate was all fruit. That's practically all she ever ate. She was crazy about fruit. Her favorite was pineapple. When we camped, her parents brought about ten Tupperware's filled with chopped pineapple. She'd eat it plain, or in cottage cheese, or on honey rolls with ham and some other stuff in a sandwich. The juice ran down her hands and dripped from her elbows. There wasn't any pineapple in Springkill. They had every fruit except pineapple.

"You want some pancakes, Ash? I'm not hungry. You can have mine if you want." I was talking to the back of her head. All morning that's all I did, look at the back of people's heads.

"I think I see some pineapple in the fruit bowl. You can put it on the pancakes." I was only teasing her. One thing about Ashley, she could be stubborn but as soon as you made her laugh she was your best friend. She never faked a laugh either. You had to learn that about her because her real laugh sounded fake as a three-dollar bill. She doesn't double over and fling her hair around or anything. Some girls fling their hair around. She puts a hand over her mouth and wrinkles up her nose.

She's got a gap in her teeth. It's no big deal but she covers her mouth when she smiles or laughs. She shouldn't do it, though. Even though people teased her about it, like they asked how many quarters can she fit in there and does she floss with a shoelace. I think it's nice, the gap. When she talks you can see her tongue through it, shaping words. It's not a secret, but she gets self-conscious when she's happy.

I kept messing with her about the pineapple, trying to make her laugh. She wouldn't listen to me.

"Hey, you guys still making up ways to kill a hamster? How long's the list," I asked later. I still hadn't eaten anything and everybody was putting their trays up and getting ready for the hike. What we were going to do in the woods that day was called *orienteering*, which basically means getting lost.

"I know another way to kill a hamster. You never thought of this. Want to hear it or not? Hah? A new way to kill a hamster." Finally Alicia turned around.

"What, annoy it to death?" Some of the girls laughed. Ashley didn't though. I couldn't hear if she laughed or not but she didn't put her hand up to her mouth.

"You trap it in a room where the windows don't open," I said. "Then you burn the building down."

Kids were getting up and dumping their trays, and hanging out in groups. Joey and Jimmy talked to their counselors. They were in different groups but they all talked to each other. The counselors had pens and everything and I could see them marking their clipboards and nodding their heads. Joey and Jimmy punched fists and one arm hugged.

Then all the counselors went outside to start roll call and when they opened the doors a gust of wind ripped through the Center. The wind tangled in your clothes and blew the girls' hair around. Everyone cheered like something was happening. It was the same when you were in class and the teacher turned the lights out to play a video or something. Everybody cheered when something unusual happened. Retards. The wind *did* feel exciting, though. The building was very big, so a lot of wind came in to fill the room and all a sudden it started to snow! It wasn't really snow. It was the cobwebs and wrapped-up flies, grey as dead berries, falling from the rafters, landing on the tables and plates.

Outside, the sky was packed with clouds, grey and black as pit ash. I never had a break-up before. It was pretty easy. Ashley just pretended I wasn't there for two weeks.

I followed her out the door. "Ashley. Hey. You want to sneak off now? Hah? We can go down to that river. The one between three states."

"Leave her alone, Larry." Alicia said. She put her arm around Ashley as if she were about to die from grief. It was pretty dumb. It was acting. Nobody gave a crap if Ashley and I broke up. Not even me or Ashley.

"Hey Ash. Remember when you followed me and Steven in the woods? We've spent more time in the woods together than anywhere else."

"Oh my god, is he still talking?" That was Ashley.

"Yeh. I'm talking. We thought you were annoying. C'mon Ash. Let's go to the river. Let's make out."

"Shut up, Larry. Is your brain okay? You're embarrassing yourself."

"You're annoying, too, Alicia. You wouldn't shut up in the fort."

"Larry!" Ashley spun around so quickly her hair flew across her face. She tore herself from Alicia's arms. "What's your problem? Leave me alone. If you want to bother someone, go bother the redhead. Grab *her* by the hair! Remember *that* from the fort?"

"Sure I will. I'll go do that, Ash. But don't you want to go down to the river? You want to hunt for dead animals? Got any firecrackers?" I wouldn't stop. I wanted to make everything disgusting. I wanted it really to be over and terrible, so when I looked back at our memories, they'd be wrapped in film, oily and speckled, with fur and bone stuck in the wrinkles. It wouldn't look like something I'd want.

"You're both lame prudes," I said as they walked away. Alicia shot me the finger.

The counselors read names and made checks with their pens. I watched Joey because he was only ten feet away. Jimmy Lutani stood beside him, even though Jimmy's group was over on the other side. He didn't move while Joey's counselor called the roll. I listened very closely.

Remember I was telling you about the liquid? The way I could sometimes feel it suck into my body all warm and dense, and then I'd feel like myself? Like the liquid was me and my body was a sponge, just some pulp holding it in? I felt that liquid then, going cold. The color of the sponge turned milky blue. I listened to Joey's counselor read his list. I felt the liquid drain and leave sludge in my guts the way sink water does after you wash the dishes. Then Joey's counselor said it, the name I was listening for. "Jimmy Lutani."

"Here!"

They made a switcheroo. Jimmy and Joey were now in the same group. The sludge balled up in my belly and the worms went at it. I stood there like a dried out corn husk with a drop of puke in it, and when the wind gusted, I swear to god, I thought I was blowing away.

# A Rose With A Fever

When we got to the rest area I finally felt hungry. I hadn't eaten anything since dinner the night before and we'd just hiked halfway across the friggin state.

"You forgot to bring a fruit, didn't you?" It was Demaris. The wind wasn't strong in the woods but she was only wearing a dress. It flapped all over the place. Her hair was blowing across her mouth. She'd get a ribbon of hair in her mouth, then run her fingers across her cheek to pull it out. I tried not to miss a moment of it. If it were possible to eat movement, I'd choose tossed hair over fruit.

"Here, take this." Demaris handed me half her sandwich. "I know how much you love tofu but today you get almond butter and pear with agave nectar." I didn't pretend not to want it. I practically swallowed my hand. I finished it in two bites. I knew it was rude to house a sandwich like that without having a conversation or whatever. It didn't bother Demaris. She sat beside me eating small bites and gazing over the cliff.

"You don't talk much today," Demaris said.

"Yeah because Adam kept getting us lost and making us find our way back to the trails. I was concentrating."

"You did very well finding a way back. The whole group followed you. How did you learn orienteering?"

"This kid Steven. Well, kid. He's not really a kid. He's older than me and he's an Eagle Scout, which is kind of like a counselor. We used to camp all the time. He showed me how to turn my watch into a compass, and to look at which way the like prevailing wind is bending the tree tops, and to notice which side of the rocks moss grows on."

"You're not wearing a watch."

"No, I know. But you can make your watch a compass if you're in the northern hemisphere." It's true you can, but I forgot how to do it. Anyway, it wasn't hard to find our way back to the trails. Adam barely lost us. We walked a hundred yards into the woods and all I did, I bent branches in the direction we came from. Every twenty feet I pointed a branch.

"You are going to be a scout," she said, surprised.

"I don't scout. We camped with the fire department. Our fathers were firemen and we camped probably somewhere near here. The campsites looked a lot like this. I sort of feel like I already know where we are, y'know? Getting lost is mostly feeling uncomfortable where you're at. I don't feel more uncomfortable here than anywhere else."

"Your father is Mr. All American Hero," Demaris said chewing.

"That guy's no hero."

"No? He builds warplanes and fights fires. Firemen are heroes, especially in New York? Did he go to nine eleven?"

I forgot I told her that my dad built A-10's instead of just painting houses.

"He wasn't at nine eleven. He's a volunteer in my town. Huntington Manor. There was a guy named Peter who was a real fireman, like a professional one in New York City, who also volunteered at Manor. *He* was at nine eleven and he got killed! There's a plaque for him in the game room in the Station One firehouse. My dad has a plaque on the wall, too. He was the first fireman to win two first-place trophies in the Bucket Brigade and The Fireman's Carry in a single tournament." He did have a plaque, my dad. That's true. Still does.

"You talk about him like a hero."

"No I don't. These are just things he did. How else can you talk but to just explain them plain. I don't lose my breath about him."

"I see," she said.

"He's not a fireman anymore. He doesn't build warplanes. He's sick."

"He will get better. He will be a fireman again."

"No he won't. He can't get better."

"Of course he can get better. Anyone who is sick can heal," she demanded.

"Maybe you're right Demaris." I didn't feel like explaining it to her.

Adam was eating seeds and spitting the shells into his palms. Everyone talked and laughed and took pictures.

"What do people call your hair," I asked. "They call you a strawberry or something?"

She didn't answer me right away. She was sulking. "Yes. They call me like I'm a strawberry in America."

"Do you hate it? My sister hates when people call her a strawberry."

"I don't hate it. It's nice sometimes when people acknowledge something that makes you different. It's like a second hello. One to you, another to your qualities."

"Right."

"The best I heard?" She smiled with some kind of sneaky happiness. "It was a day like today, with clouds. It was the same, gloomy dark, but colder. I was in the woods with a boy, looking for mushrooms that grow at summer's end. The clouds opened and the sun came through the trees. Do you know this word, *crepuscular*? I think you have the same in English. When the sunlight comes down like fingers? We turned to each other. The light touched him. It was beautiful. I felt the light on me, warm, you know? We say nothing about the moment. It was too good, too much itself. It didn't need us to make it be." Her eyes were half closed. Her voice was soft and quiet. That kind of stuff, it makes me uncomfortable as hell. I was sorry I asked. I'd rather talk about my dad.

"Later we made lunch with the mushrooms we found," she said. "While we ate he told me how he saw it. We were separated by grey cold when the light found me. He said the light showed him the most beautiful thing in the forest. Me. 'Like a rose with a fever.' That is the best I heard." The wind flipped her dress up her thighs and she flattened it out. "Strawberries are stupid."

"They are stupid. That's what I'm saying," I said. "I think it's lame to compare a girl to a strawberry."

She wouldn't listen to me anymore. She was staring at Adam.

Near the wire that keeps you back from the cliff's edge, Adam pointed across the valley. I thought maybe something was happening, like a forest fire.

"What's everyone looking at," I asked.

"Right there," Jonathan said. You can't see that? It's freaking moving, dumb ass. Look straight. See it?"

An eagle hung in the air, drifting from one side of the valley to the other. It was hard to see at first it was so slim and dark, the way a knife looks from a certain angle. It was directly across from us, a dark blade in the air, high above the river. She was big and moved slowly, the opposite of little birds and their mid-air seizures. Everybody stood around and watched. We were quiet for once.

"It's a Golden Eagle," Adam said. "They're rarer now, because humans, but they survive all over the world. Goldens are apex predators. She's out to hunt. See she doesn't flap her wings? The sun is heating the ground and the air over it warms and rises. She's surfing the air current as it rises up the mountainside."

Everybody was just electrified by that, the surfing bird.

"She's looking for leporids or sciurids. Remember what a leporid is? I said it yesterday. It's a rabbit or a hare. And a sciurid? Remember the owl pellets? Jonathan, you remember." Nobody remembered what the hell those things were. "Mice and squirrels."

Adam sure knew his nature. He went on and on about the eagle. It could fly 150 miles per hour, he told us. The turns it made, the G-force its body withstood while she was hunting other birds, were, "Incomparable to any modern technology. There's not a jet in the world that can imitate what a Golden Eagle does. Nature-made machines are astronomically more sophisticated than anything man-made." Shit like that.

We stood around watching the eagle for ten minutes, hoping she'd jump on a rabbit or something. Adam told us Goldens could hunt deer if they're small deer and not the ones with branches growing off their heads. People kept saying she looked beautiful and how cool she was and wouldn't it be great to jump off a cliff and be able to fly! To dive through the air 150 miles an hour! Not me, though. I mean, yeah, it would be cool to fly and jump on deers and all that crap. But I don't know. The bird depressed me. She looked bored and she was all alone. She probably had three eggs hidden away in a nest somewhere only a snake could get to. The snake will eat one of them. Then after the other eggs hatched the big chick will push the littler chick from the nest to splatter on a rock where bugs will eat its eyes. When the big chick learned to fly it'll wind up hunting at a truck stop and eating a poisoned rat.

We stayed at the rest area longer than we were supposed to. Adam kept stressing the Golden Eagle's rarity. So we watched it surf the mountainside, making circles from New York to Connecticut to Massachusetts. If the bird only twitched its head everybody went, "Oh!" and expected it to tear after an animal and rip out its guts. It got a little higher and after a while we were looking up at it.

"When the hell's it gonna hunt," Jonathan finally asked. Just as he said it there was a pounding, like drums. It was getting windy and the trees going crazy over our heads sounded like a faraway football stadium cheering. It was another group, Robby Morales's group, coming up behind us.

# The Pass Out Game

It smelled strongly like pine in the Center while we ate dinner. Dust and dead flies and crap got blown out of the rafters and the staff had to clean the place. They used natural cleaner made with pine extract and lemon acid. You weren't supposed to talk about Robby Morales. He was getting sent home for mooning his group. Mrs. Ackerly kept sticking her face in everyone's conversation and telling them, "You are not to spread calumnies. There are more important things to discuss." As soon as she walked away though, everyone went back to talking about Robby's asshole.

I didn't know where to sit. Everywhere I went there was either someone I didn't like or nobody I knew. I'm not trying to sound sorry for myself. I wasn't. I could've sat with Joey and Jimmy and Jonathan, with a bunch of Flower Hill kids, or even with Ashley and her friends. The thing is, sometimes I want to be alone. But when I'm by myself I get so depressed I could commit suicide. Not really commit suicide but I think about it very seriously. After ten minutes feeling lonely and wanting to die I usually want to be around people again. Not with them, I want to be near them, to hear them. What I really want is to watch them smile and talk and be happy and hate them for it. I know it's unhealthy or whatever. I can't help it.

I've thought quite a lot about it. How I'd do it depends on my mood. When I'm angry I think about shooting myself in the heart, like with my dad's .45. When I'm bored I think about another way.

There's this game Joey and I played. You put your head between your knees and take deep breaths until you're dizzy. Then you hold your breath and lie on your back.

Joey pushed into my stomach. "I can feel your fuckin spine," he'd say. I don't know how it works but you pass out. It's a strange sleep with dark, smeary dreams. I can't explain it. You always have a dream though.

Sometimes when I passed Joey out his legs jerked around and I knew he was dreaming about running. You wake up by getting slapped in the face. You're not supposed to let a person sleep longer than a minute. We played that game for a month by pushing into our stomachs. Then we learned a new way from Joey's brother. What you did, you pressed your palms against the sides of the other guy's neck. They can still breath. You don't choke their windpipe or anything. You shut off your arteries. Blood can't get to your brain. Your head gets solid and heavy. Your eyeballs feel like they're going to pop out of your face. Then you pass out. Me and Joey told each other about our dreams. I told mine quick because the details fell out of memory like pebbles through my fingers. Joey told me he talked to the Devil, every friggin time.

Joey's mom and dad were Catholics. They were always telling him he'd go to hell for lying or for giving them shit when he was supposed clean his room. "You burn forever and you don't get used to the pain. And the smell," Mrs. Nailati told him. "You can have the dry heaves for a hundred years. It stinks in hell from sulfur and brimstone. You know what that smells like? Your father's farts. Don't you laugh at me! It's true. You can go to hell for laughing at your mother!"

One time I was lying under Joey in the fort's dust. His lips curled over his teeth and his eyebrows crunched together while he strangled the hell out of me. That was the last thing I saw. I got a headache. I had a dream where I was looking for it, for the headache. There was this pain that I was looking for all over the place. I can't describe the place. I was inside somewhere big with lots of corridors. It was dark. When I found the pain it was a geometric animal, with skin like pantyhose, and it was filled with vapor. The animal's flat sides came together at points that it used to spring itself at my face, but I kicked it away. It crawled up my jeans, scurried into my shirt and emerged wiggling at my neck. It flashed across my face and crawled into my eyes. Then my arms were too heavy to move them. The pain went into my head, it got stuck in my eye sockets. It kicked against my face like a trapped rabbit.

"You were asleep for five minutes, bro. Holy shit," Joey was slapping my face. "I thought you were dead. I was about to run in my house and call 911."

The pain stayed for a week. Headaches woke me up at night. We never played the game again. We found out you really could die from it. Actually, that's what the sleep was, a waiting room outside death's door. Joey learned all about the room, but maybe I should wait to tell you how it works.

That's what I thought about sometimes, when I thought about suicide. I figured I'd hang myself. It's just like the game. You go to sleep. You have a dream. Any pain, like a headache or someone slapping your face, stays in your body. Your soul or whatever, it slips into heaven if there is one, or this waiting room under the mall Joey's always talking about, the place the devil showed him. Anyway, hanging wouldn't hurt too much.

"Bah!"

It was Ashley. I damn near dropped my tray when she startled me. She was always scaring me. She liked to hide behind doors or around a corner. She crouched low the way cats do. Then she'd pounce at you.

"Jesus, you scared the crap out of me." I was thinking about hanging myself. Stupid, I know.

"Sorry. I didn't mean to," she lied.

"And?" She just stared at me. "What do you want?"

"We need you," she said.

"For what?"

"For the talent show tonight."

"Who needs me?"

"Me and Alicia and Megan." She pointed to her table. They weren't looking at us or anything. They were sitting with their legs tucked under them, leaning over paper. "You know that Will Smith song? Parents Just Don't Understand?"

There's this song by Will Smith, the actor, he used to be a rapper before I was born, called Parents Just Don't Understand. It's about being a kid in high school and the crappy things parents do, like buy you the wrong clothes, or grounding you all the time. I knew the song. There's one part when Will Smith steals his parents' Porsche. He takes it for a spin around the neighborhood, like me and James did with Amanda's parents' Cadillac.

"We want you to be the girl he picks up in the song," Ashley said. "It's funnier that way." She smiled and put her hand over her mouth. "Larry!" All a sudden we were friends again. Not boyfriend and girlfriend or anything, just normal. The way I felt, it was like the first morning after your flu has gone away.

# Magic Dance

It wasn't my choice to dress up at Springkill. It just happened.

At every camp there's a talent show. The schools performs skits in their cabin and they vote on which are best. It's lame but you have to do it. On the final night there are three performances from each school on the stage in the Center.

I'm shy about my boney legs, even now. I'm too skinny. In eighth grade I worked out with dumbbells my father took off a firemen who got a new weight set. I did five hundred curls a week plus shoulder presses and lunges. I gained a little weight, naturally, just from growing. I didn't get big muscles. All I got were swollen veins pumping in my arms, and deep, sharper shadows in my legs. I ate potatoes and cheese by the plateful. My mom said it would make me fat. I drank three glasses of whole milk every day. Fat was fine by me! Joey was fat, sort of. It wasn't all rolly and gross, like Jonathan's. Joey was athletic. I'd have probably looked more like Joey if I gained fifteen pounds. That didn't happen. You could see every one of my ribs.

The girls dressed me in a skirt halfway up my thighs, it showed my knobby knees, and my guts squirmed with embarrassment. I acted like I didn't care I was skinny. A guy's lame if he's embarrassed about his body. The skirt was slutty though. They put a purple blouse on me, made from silk I think.

Moto and David, two nerdy dicks, did their routine before ours. It was supposed to be a comedy but all they did was imitate teachers from

Finley. They didn't care that nobody laughed. They cracked each other up. Ackerly and Brush gave them some courtesy laughs. That's what Alicia called it, courtesy. While they stunk up the place Ashley, Alicia, Megan and me were in a closet with a cot and brooms and huge stacks of toilet paper wrapped in plastic and some bottles of starter fluid for fires in the stove. It smelled like horseshit in there. Alicia put eyeshadow on me and Ashley put lipstick on my mouth. They didn't do anything with my hair, the way my sister and Lexy did. It was shorter, less curly, and darker. "Wow, Larry," Ashley said, "you'd be the prettiest girl in school if you wanted to be."

"Seriously," Megan said.

"I got no tits," I said. You can't look like a girl without tits.

"You don't need them. Does he need them?" Alicia thought it over.

"Course he needs them," Megan said. Megan was one of Ashley's friends. Her monster teeth barely fit in her mouth. They leaned against each other. "He needs big ol' boobers," Megan said. "Who's got the biggest boobers?"

They looked at each other's pickle tops.

"What about that girl? The Mexican one," Megan said.

"Who, Larry's girlfriend," Ashley said, not mean or anything.

"She's from Colombia, retard," I said.

"She got mazoongas." Megan held her hands out in front of her. She had brown freckles splattered across her hands and her knuckles were white and smooth as cream cheese.

"You ask her," Ashley told Megan. "I'm not gonna to talk to her!"

Then I was in the closet with all four of them. The smell of horseshit disappeared, or I'd gotten used to it, which meant it wasn't hell, and what I smelled was soap and lotion on the girls' skin. Maybe it was heaven.

Demaris put her hands behind her back and up her shirt. She'd changed out of her yellow dress and wore a grey T-shirt and cutoff jeans. The shirt stretched over her chest and I could see the outline of her bra beneath it and a knot at the end of each boob. Then it sort of popped. Her bra popped, I mean. She pulled a bra strap down one arm and then the whole thing came off the other. It was a magic dance. Even the girls were watching. I popped a major boner. When I put the bra on it was still warm, which was sort of like swapping gum on the bus.

On the bus ride to Springkill, boys and girls swapped gum. You took the gum from someone you liked, straight from her mouth, and chewed it. You didn't make a big deal of it. As long as you didn't make it a big deal nobody got nervous or jealous or anything. The gum had no flavor. The point is you're eating the other person's spit. It's close to kissing. There was this one girl though, Barbara Dunne. She kept trying to give away her gum. She'd take a wad out of her mouth and go, "I don't want this anymore. Here Ben, you want it?" Nobody wanted to chew Barbara's gum. She offered it to me once. I told her I was carsick and might puke. After a while she stopped offering. Every half hour a girl would say, "I'm tired'a chewing this. D'ya wannit?" Robby or Brad Pepron would go, "Yeah awright," and pop it in his mouth. Each time it happened Barbara lifted her big round head, her hair dull-brown and curly, and she'd sulk as the gum went from mouth to mouth.

We sung a dirty variation of The Kinks' song All Day And All Of The Night. It was pretty far into the ride. We were close to Springkill when a Filipino girl named Tala, she was sitting next to Barbara, put two fingers in her mouth and pulled out a purple wad. We were singing quietly so Ackerly couldn't hear us.

four and four
we closed the door
to my bedroom
all day and all of the night

Tala calls out, "Anyone want my gum?" The song kept going but Barbara stopped singing. Ben Croton said, "Right here," and opened his gob. Tala stuck her gum in his mouth and then they kept singing:

six and six
she sucked my dick
in the bedroom
all day and all of the night

Barbara though, she slumped into her seat the way people on television do when they get shot. I watched the whole thing. It made me feel awful. She had this old hunk of gum in her mouth she'd been chewing for six hours. I hated to do it but I went and asked her, "You got'ny gum, Barb?" Her face lit up like a Christmas tree rammed through her ears. "I got the piece I'm chewing," she said. "I'm tired of it." A grey blob squeezed through her teeth. I put out my hand. It dropped into my palm like a turd. Barbara stared at me all happy. After a few chomps I jumped back to my seat.

The gum was so old and hard it wouldn't stick under the seat. I dropped it on the floor. I didn't let Barbara see me trash it. I didn't want her to act like she'd been shot again.

Demaris's bra felt even nicer when I thought about that nasty gum. The girls stuffed my bra with tissue from a toilet paper pile. All their hands were up my shirt, stuffing. Their faces were close together. Their hair mixed. I felt dizzy, like after passing out. Then it was our turn to perform.

# Drive Fast Speed Turns Me On

Megan played Will Smith's part and did all the rapping. I waited in the closet with my boner stuck behind my leg. But then I got nervous about performing and it went limp.

Everyone laughed their ass off when I came out with my lumpy tits. Even Mrs. Ackerly cracked a smile. And not as a courtesy. I pranced all sexy over to a chair Ashley and Alicia had set up and pretended to sit in a Porsche with Megan. I pulled ribbons of imaginary hair out of my mouth and threw it over my shoulder. I scrunched my mouth up small and puffy and tried to let my front teeth show.

I was so nervous that the room, the people and the chairs they sat on, the books, the window blinds and rugs looked the way things do when you pass them on a train. I saw Demaris in the crowd. I saw Ackerly smiling. And I saw Joey. I remember because he was the only one who wasn't laughing. He didn't even grin. He stared at me with one cheek raised practically over his eye. I had one line: "Drive fast, speed turns me on."

Then I opened a couple buttons on my blouse. Megan was the lead but I was the star. Joey shook his head and stared at his shoes.

It was pretty faggy, I get it, to dress up like a girl and flutter my stupid eyelashes all over the place. It's not like I enjoyed it or it was something I'd do in my spare friggin time. All I was trying to do was make people laugh. You can do anything if it makes people laugh. Embarrassing yourself is probably the best way. People laugh if someone hurts themselves or gets embarrassed, like by crapping their pants or falling off a stage.

People laugh at jokes about dead babies or Chinese people. You don't laugh at handfuls of flowers. Not unless you hid a piece of dog shit in it and you're tricking your sister into smelling it. I did that once. It was funny, trust me. When you see a group of people laughing you can be pretty sure something bad happened to someone. Laughter is what cruelty feels like to bad guys.

When the performances were over Mrs. Ackerly handed out flash cards. We wrote what group we thought had the best skit. She wrote our names on the top of the card in red pen. That way you couldn't vote for yourself. Ashley, Megan, Alicia and me won the election. Joey came up to me after the vote. He had a stinker on his face. "You seriously gonna dress up like a slut in front of everybody at Springkill?"

I laughed at first. Sluts. That's what Joey called the girls in the fort, the pictures. "My little sluts," he said. And then there was Amanda Voyage. He called her a slut, too. You don't call a boy a slut. It sounded funny. But he wasn't kidding.

We were standing at the entrance to the hallway. Boys passed between us on the way to their rooms.

"It's a joke, Joey. Jesus."

"You think prancing around with big titties is a joke? It's not even funny. What's funny about it?"

I didn't know what was funny about it. People laughed, that's all. "You can't explain why something's funny," I told him. It's worse to have an argument when you're wearing makeup than when you look normal.

While I worried about the makeup Ben Croton walked by. "Hey sexy," he said and pinched my tits. I wanted to punch his friggin face in.

"Don't touch me," I said. I wish I hadn't, either. That's exactly what a girl would've said.

"I don't know why it's funny," I told Joey. "It's just a joke. Nobody's gonna…I don't know."

"Gonna think you're a fucking fag? Yeah right." Then he got all calm. He talked to me like he was a grown man who'd just met me and wanted to give me advice. "Look. I don't care what you do. If you want to dress like a slut, that's up to you. That's all I'm saying, man. You do what you want. Everybody took pictures and ten years from now people can watch you act like a faggy little slut."

"I didn't do it for pictures." Joey walked down the hall. "I'm just trying to make you idiots laugh." He wouldn't listen. He went to our room.

I went to the bathroom to wash my face. There was no mirror over the sink, so I didn't look at myself, thank god, and reflect about my choices or whatever. I knew it was a dumb thing to do, dressing like a girl, and I didn't need to look at my face to hate it.

I washed as hard as I could but every time I wiped my face there were black mascara stains on the towel. I couldn't get it off. Finally I stopped trying because my face burned and felt like it was shrinking.

While everyone was in their rooms changing into sweat suits or whatever, clothes to sleep in, I sat in the common room in my baggy jeans and sneakers. There were two couches to sit on, plus beanbag cushions for people to lay all over.

I was the only person in the room when the cabin door opened and a man came in, wind chased leaf crumbs around his feet. His boots thumped the floor. Whiskers as course and grey as steel wool clung to his cheeks. He moved slowly around the cabin collecting split wood and stacking it in the stove. He wore a heavy black sweater. He didn't look at me. He probably couldn't see me through the black hair hanging over his eyes.

He dumped the stove's ash pan into a paper bag. Then he took a bottle of starter fluid from a shelf in the closet and sprayed it on the kindling. He slammed the iron door shut and adjusted the damper slide. He fished a match from his pocket and scraped it across the cook lid. He dropped it through a hole and the fluid whooshed to life. Heat flashed across my face and stung my eyes. I rubbed them with my knuckles. When I looked again the man was gone.

He didn't disappear, I just couldn't see him for a second because he was standing at the entrance to the girls hallway. It was pretty dark there. He clogged the entrance with his stuffy sweater but I could see the pale face and red hair he was talking to. They were close together and what I was thinking was, "Man, that guy looks like he stinks." Demaris smelled clean and sweet in the closet. Now that old dirt bag was showering his odor on her. When he hugged her I knew who he was. The biologist, Springkill's manager, her father.

Demaris stepped from the hallway. Some kids walked into the common room. She looked at them all squinty until she saw me. She smiled but with pressed together, pale lips.

"Mr. Brush," her father's voice was gravel and black pepper. He and Brush talked a couple seconds, then all three looked at me.

Brush walked over. He's about ten feet tall, standing there, leaning, looking down at me. I could see into his mouth. "Larry," he said, "you need to call your mother."

# Daddy Don't Leave Me

We walked outside together, me and Demaris's dad. His boots drummed on the deck. We stood in the field between the cabins, their porch lights ballooning into the night. He took a cell phone from his pocket and handed it to me.

"Here?" I was surprised. I thought we'd go to an office.

"I'll wait," he told me, and walked away.

I dialed. My mother answered the first ring.

She didn't tell me he died she just said, "Larry," and sobbed. I didn't know what to say. I had to say *some*thing, though.

"I don't know what to do. What do I do, Larry?"

I held the phone to my ear and just didn't say anything. I'm not a crybaby. I'm not. I never cry. I told you about the time in the subway station when it smelled like horse shit and my mom cried because she couldn't smell. I felt like it then, but I didn't do it. If you start crying when your mom does, what happens next? I knew I couldn't make a mistake, like telling her, "I don't care he died. I don't care!" But something awful happened. I did care. I looked all over the place, at the cabins, at Demaris's father. Up at the sky. I still didn't say anything because I couldn't make a mistake, but my throat tightened and my eyes burned and I wanted to scream, "Daddy don't leave me, don't leave me daddy!" I felt panicked, and horribly sad and angry.

Finally, I said something. Not because my mom was sobbing but because Demaris's father was standing a little way off, not walking around or anything, probably listening.

"Has the car been going crazy," I asked her.

When my father was too sick to work, my mom got a second job. It wasn't a real job, like with eight-hour days and lunch breaks, but she got paid for it.

Once a month she drove to a squat brick building by the railroad tracks, between a lumberyard and a drain pipe factory. She brought me along. The building spooked me. Its narrow windows were covered with steel strainer plates. Someone painted a Playboy bunny with a dick in its mouth on the wall. You couldn't park close to the building. Cement pilings surrounded it. They were there to protect the building from something. Terrorists maybe, thieves. The parking lot's yellow lines were faded, and weeds grew in the cracks. I wasn't allowed inside. I had to wait in the car.

"I'm leaving the keys so you can listen to the radio," my mom told me. "But don't turn the engine on. I mean it. Last time the car was slantways when I came out."

Nearby, trucks groaned under their loads and there was the quick, hard talk of the lumberyard boss. "Let me see your ears," my mother said. I laid my head in her lap. She stuck her pinky in my ear and scraped out some wax. "Other side." Her pinky went in and scraped. Sometimes it hurt. I didn't complain. I liked to lay my head on her.

"Why can't I go inside with you?"

"Children aren't allowed. This ear is full of potatoes. Use Q-tips like I showed you."

"Dr. Orlin said the only thing I should stick in my ear is my elbow. What's wrong with children?"

"There's nothing wrong with children. It's just against the rules."

"But they have rules for a reason. Even stupid rules have stupid reasons."

"There are dangerous things inside. And sensitive things that children touch and get dirty."

"I won't touch anything."

"I'll be back in ten minutes. Don't turn the car on. I'm serious. I'll be watching."

"You can't see me through the windows."

"There are cameras. Look. I'll be right back. Sit up."

She hung her bag on her shoulder and walked to a grey door. She pressed a button. The door buzzed and she pulled hard on the handle.

I waited in the car listening to music while the sun came in and heated the air. The warmth made me sleepy and impatient.

I started the car and turned on the windshield wipers. I pulled the emergency break, switched on the hazard lights, turned the air conditioner fan on high. Just before switching off the ignition I cranked the radio. Then I pushed the seat way back and turned the mirrors in different directions.

All those things waited with me and it wasn't bad. Fifteen minutes later the building's door opened a foot and my mother squeezed out.

When she got into the car she looked surprised. "What'd I shrink? I don't remember the seat being so far back. Oh, and the mirrors! What was I looking at?" She turned the key. Music came on loud and the air conditioner's fan blew her hair around and the wipers flapped back and forth. "What happened to the car," she said. I raised my eyebrows and shrugged my shoulders.

"I don't know," I said.

I played the same prank every month. Once in a while, like before she went to church or something, I'd ask, "Has the car been acting crazy?"

She'd say, "Nope. Strange, isn't it?"

A few days after going to the building her back would start itching. She liked her back scratched anytime but after visiting the building scratching became an emergency. Like if I was watching television, she'd plop down on the floor in front of the couch and say, "Scratch!" She'd pull her shirt over her shoulders.

I spread my fingers and made my hands wide like leaf rakes. I scratched her back in rows up and down, then in lanes across. I used my thumb. That was my trick, to scratch with all ten fingers.

"Mmm, magic fingers."

"You said dad has magic fingers," I said.

"Daddy is the best back scratcher," she said, "but more than one person can have magic fingers."

The bandage was on her right shoulder blade, about the size of a postcard. That was the itch that made her crazy, this Band-Aid with twelve lumps. I couldn't scratch the Band-Aid because it could affect the study. I scratched around it while she moaned and rocked back and forth. She couldn't get the bandage wet or get sun on it. She took baths instead of showers to keep it dry. She washed her hair in the kitchen sink.

"What's in it this time," I asked her.

"I don't think about it."

"I bet it's cat pee and WD-40."

"Gross, you little monster."

"Maybe it's hair growing chemicals. You'll have to shave your back!"

The patch stayed on for ten days. Then we went back to the building. My mother left me in the car and I played with the controls, waiting in the heat. She came out after twenty minutes and aimed her back to me, lifted her shirt up to her neck and showed me the pale, wrinkled patch on her shoulder blade.

"No marks, ma. You weren't allergic to any of it. What was it this time," I asked her. They wouldn't tell her what the products were until after the test.

"They said it was makeup. Or something that goes into makeup, I don't know. I don't like to even think about it. Now scratch!" I scratched the pale rectangle on her back where the patch had been. Scraps of waxy skin rolled under my nails.

"Do they pay you more if you're allergic?"

"No, but they do more tests if you're allergic and those pay a little better."

The doctors (or scientists or whatever) paid cash. I don't know how much they gave her. It was enough to buy groceries for the week. That's what we did next, drove to Waldbaum's and bought groceries with the money.

She turned on the ignition and when the wipers flapped and the air conditioner blew her hair around she pretended the car had gone nuts. I shrugged my shoulders and rolled my eyes.

"There it goes again," she said.

"Crazy."

She didn't answer me right away. About the car, I mean. She sobbed. I asked her again, though, "How's the car, ma? Going crazy?"

"No. It's been acting fine."

"Yeah? That right? No flapping wipers and stuff?" She stopped sobbing. She sniffed and took a deep breath. "Oh, lord," she said. She did that after work sometimes. Sometimes she had homework from Don's office. She sat at the dining room table typing. When she finished she'd straighten her back and go, "Oh, lord," in a yawny voice.

"You sound tie-yud," I said. "I theenk you need me to pomp you op!"

She whispered a laugh. "What would I do without you, son?" Then she said another good lord. "You can come home tomorrow morning. There's a van that can drive you, they told me. Or you can stay with your friends another day. There's nothing for you to do here, Larry. Don't feel pressured."

"What should I do, ma?"

"What do you feel, son? Pray about it, and do what you feel."

When I hung up the phone Demaris's father walked over to me. I thanked the nosy bastard and went in the cabin and sat on the couch. Mr. Brush sat beside me. He was very tall and skinny. He had a scraggy beard, trimmed along the cheeks without a mustache. He had a mole on his cheek. He reminded me of someone but I couldn't think of who. "This is going to be a hard for you," he said.

"Yeh," I said.

We stared at the floor. It was uncomfortable.

Joey came into the room. Not all the way. He stopped at the end of the hallway and leaned against the wall. His eyes were projectors. They flared across the room then fell on me. I burned. I wore women's clothes and held a dick in each hand. Then the projector snapped off. Joey turned and walked down the hallway.

"It's going to be hard without him for a while," Brush said. "But time is good to pain."

"He's just mad," I said. "We're best friends, though. It'll be alright back home."

"I mean your father." He smiled at me the same way when he handed back a paper with a bad grade.

'. . .'

"Your parents alive," I asked.

"Yes," he said after a pause. You could tell he was debating how personal he should get with a student. "Divorced. My mother lives in Northport with her husband. My father's in Rhode Island." He rubbed his palms along his thighs. Calluses sounded like Velcro on his pants. It was my turn to talk but I didn't feel like it. I wanted to tell him it was okay. He didn't have to sit with me or wait for the right-thing-to-say to make its way from his guts to his head. I wanted to be alone, like near people, listening to them and maybe hating them for being happy, but from right there on the couch, by myself. He rubbed his thighs and crackled his calluses a minute. "How do you feel," he asked me. Just like my mother. Why did they want to know how I felt? Would that change anything? It's not like I had a splinter they could pull out. What I felt was inside my stomach and connected to my cold, oily face by a silver thread. I wanted to tell him, no offense, I wish he'd leave me the hell alone. The way you feel isn't a thing with colors and shapes. It doesn't do anything. It sits there like a couch or something heavy in your way. And talking doesn't help. Talking isn't a tweezers you pick a feeling out with, or a tube to drain it. What if I screamed at him? Called him a cocksucker? That would help! What if I smacked him in the face! I scared myself thinking that way, and ended up saying something stupid.

"I feel like there's a giant kneeling over our cabin. She's bounced me around for days. She has this friend she told, 'Okay, so now Larry's father dies and we're gonna dress him up all *dar*ling and make him sing.' And in two seconds she's going to open up the cabin like a briefcase and start something new. She'll get a dumb new idea and make me do it. I hate that! I want a man to stand outside and tell me, 'A bad thing is coming. Here's your gun. I'll grab him first. He won't get you. When I have him down, shoot! Shoot until he don't move anymore!'"

Mr. Brush put his elbows on his knees and when he put his chin in his hands his beard sizzled like a bitten apple.

"I can't imagine how you feel." Then why'd you ask! "Life isn't always fair." Good lord! "No one is in control," he told me. No fucking shit! "I wish there were laws, like in physics, and you could expect life to deliver known results. There are in ways, like death and birth and struggles of various sorts, but va*riety* makes life what it is, the arrangements of the constants. It's this thing rather than that thing that sets up the possibility of reflection, of consciousness, of a personal reality. Does that make sense?" Hell no! "One day, and this is what I wish for you Larry, and what I know will happen: this thing will be a constant for you. Death is certain but how it affects us, when and where it comes, is uncertain.

"In quantum physics there's the fine-structure constant. It's a number, an equation, actually, that's formless. Don't worry. You won't be quizzed on this," all smiley. "It's like one of those letters with square brackets around it. Remember the letter *M* for distance, but we put it in brackets so it doesn't represent meters or feet or miles but just the *idea* of distance of some measurability? You're a very good science student. You remember the brackets, right?" Nodding yes. "The fine-structure constant is a number that's always the same no matter where you look. Just like the speed of light is always the same no matter where you see it, from any vantage point, always going the same speed. Red light moves as fast as blue light and as fast as radio waves. It all moves the same speed. Nothing can go faster. Why? You don't have to tell me, Larry. When something speeds up its mass increases. And so to increase speed you need more energy. The more mass increases the more energy you need. You understand. You do don't you? You're a smart boy. You get it. The faster something moves, the closer it gets to the speed of light the more its mass increases. Until what? Can mass keep increasing? Can it? Is there a limit? Now don't get fidgety there's a point I'm making, Larry. Stop breathing heavy. Should I stop? You don't want to hear this. I'll stop. Yeah, you want to hear it? You sure? I'll keep going? Okay well, I will. No, it's just. You look like you want me to leave you the hell alone. No?"

I wanted him to keep talking for a bit. Just for now. Sitting on the couch like it was home base, so none of the kids walking into the room would come over and ask me to hang out on a beanbag and play a game.

"So relative mass gets bigger as it approaches the speed of light and with it the amount of energy it takes to increase speed expands until it reaches the speed of light which is oh, a hundred and eighty-something-*thou*sand miles a second, and relative mass reaches infinity. How much energy would it take to increase the speed of something with infinite mass? You know. I know you do you just don't feel like talking. You feel like listening, don't you? You shook your head yes. Okay well then it takes an infinite amount of energy to increase its speed even a millimeter per second. So and you see that you… y'know… you can't go faster than the speed of light. Ah, but you can slow light down. Did you know you can slow down light? Just send it through something. The speed of light is only constant in a vacuum so now it moves slower through water. In water other particles move faster than the light in water. You can cheat!"

He was a very excitable guy. He was practically a kid. That's why we liked him. He was like one of the students, just very tall and bearded. He taught Physical Science and another kind of Science, too. Chemistry maybe. Everybody got good grades in his class because he helped you cheat. Not cheat, have an advantage. Like his room number was 206, for example. One test we took had to do with the bones in a human body. How many have we? The answer, he told us, was 205, one less than his classroom number. On the day of the test, this is what he did. He left the door open, pulled into the room, and he'd taped a sign next to the door number. "Minus one," it said. He did things like that to help you remember answers. It worked, too. I still remember how many bones I have.

"Radioisotopes move faster than light through water and makes the water glow blue. That's why in comic books radioactive waste always glows, because of the way it makes water glow. But, anyway, the particles don't go faster than light travels in a vacuum. The law still applies in a vacuum, a lifeless, empty, static, sum-of-nothings, cold vacuum. Laws are applied in the real world, Larry, this one that we both know and talk about. And when they get bent, whew, reality happens! Without bending laws there is no difference, there is no reality. One thing's got to be different from ānothēr. There's got to be at least two possibilities for some kind of reality to exist. The fine-structure constant is a perfect example; its formlessness, like life, like reality, is bent through the universe. From one side to the other it's not uniform in time like it was *known* to be for a century. In¯time, in different quarters of the universe, the fine-structure constant ain't so constant. It fluctuates. It bends. When a cosmologist looks at a galaxy he's seeing light from the past, from 8 billion years ago. Just recently we, quantum physicists I mean, observed a variation in the fine structure constant across billions of years. But a law it remains! If the constant were different by just four percent, stellar fusion wouldn't be possible. If the fine structure bent too far there wouldn't be enough heat to make stars. Carbon couldn't come into existence! Carbon, as you and I know, is what life is made of. It's every earthly organism's brick and mortar. As far as laws go, can it get more important, at least concerning us, you and me as actual physical beings, than the fine structure constant! And but it bends from one side of the universe to the other, Larry, from the past to the present. The law fluctuates in time as light's speed does in place. In that… that… *flex*, you don't see just life's vulnerability, but existence and reality's, too. Your father is a constant, Larry. And he'll take on many realities in different times and places, informing you and shaping you. That's a law, a certainty. It's one of many laws that bend, that you can cheat. This is how you'll make your own reality, make your water glow, from your past to your future, and mark your presence."

Jesus H. Christ! He wasn't going to be outdone by my giant story. He finally dumped the wise old teacher crap he felt the circumstance demanded. His own private laws.

He sat next to me, touching his beard and fidgeting. Then he said, "I recommended you for this trip."

"*You* did? Why'd you do that? I mean, why'd you do that?"

"You're a good student. Your grades should be better. Would be, if you did your homework."

"We don't need to do homework."

"No, *you* don't need to. Your test grades are the top two or three in the class and that's without doing any of the homework. But homework is 25 percent of your final..." He squinted and shook his hand in front of his face. "That's not the point. The point is you're interested. That's what science is about. I thought you'd get something out of Springkill other students wouldn't."

I could picture him, Mr. Brush, sitting home at the dinner table, his wife bringing out the food and dropping pots on coasters, and he's thinking hard about who he'll invite to Springkill. Really thinking it over hard, thinking about his students. None of his students are thinking about him. They're playing video games and imagining who they want to hook up with, whose tits they want to squeeze.

"I wanted to come here. I really did. It's not your fault what happened. I don't care anyway. I don't care he died," I said.

He sat up straight. Sucked his lower lip.

"When my parents divorced, and my dad moved to Rhode Island, the *reason* for the divorce was very hurtful to me. I acted out, got in trouble. I blamed my father. To some extent he was responsible. But how can he help it if his compulsion hurt other people? The thing is, you're not *people* when you are young. You're a child. Someone's child. A son. But you grow up. You become a man. That means no one is responsible for your actions but you. I forgave my father as a way to take responsibility for myself. To claim my manhood. But I'd done things I wasn't proud of in my great anger. Things that were way more abusive to myself than anything my father had done. You live with the scars from your boyhood and find that, in the words of William Wordsworth, the child is father of the man. The way for you to become a man is to forgive your father," he said rubbing his calluses on my knee. "If you need to talk." He walked away feeling pretty terrific, I bet.

All a sudden I realized what he looked like. Mr. Brush looked like Abe Lincoln. That's what I was thinking as the news of my dead father spread through Huntington Manor. Mr. Brush looked like Abe Lincoln. There's something wrong with me. Seriously.

# These Goggles I Get

I couldn't stop thinking about my dad. Just like on the bus. He's all I could think about. I'd look through the slits in the black stove door, at the fire wiggling inside, or I'd noticed the orange peel scent missing from the fire's smoke, and I thought of him. Kids kept coming into the common room wearing comfy clothes. I prayed to god he'd stop me thinking about him, but when something's in my head it stays there. It becomes like goggles locked on my face, and I see everything through them.

Kids came into the room to hang out around the stove. They flopped down on the couches, and sat on the beanbag cushions stuck around the room like gum wads. There were board games and books that nobody played or read, even though there was no television and no video games.

You weren't forced to hang out in the common room. You could stay in your own room if you wanted, but you couldn't go into the girls' rooms. A lot of rules were changed since Ben's or Joey's brother or my sister went to Springkill, to try and make kids read and play games instead of sneaking out to fuck each other. For example, there was no way to sneak a girl into your room. The windows were screwed shut so you couldn't get in or out if you tried.

Maybe the stories about parties in the woods and everyone drinking and banging each other were bullshit. They never happened, just like the hazing nightmares you hear about in school or the stories about Amanda Voyage. People, I think, make up stories to scare you or to make you believe they had a better time, or a harder time, than you had. It's a trick.

Imagination contests. Even that idea reminded me of my father because him and the firemen were always telling stories about when they were Your Age and everything was better. They shouldn't do it. It makes guys like me think we should be having a better time, and that now everything sucks. You get mad and frustrated when you can't sneak out and girls won't let you fuck them. You switch friends so the things you used to do, like whacking off and passing out, seem fun again. It ruins your mood, and it can ruin your life. Those old timers probably truly believe they were better off thirty years ago because they were kids then, like us, and not old assholes with credit card bills, calling people cocksucker on the phone. They don't want you to have a good time or even to think you *can* have a good time and I know why. It would erase their youth, and their lame stories about when they were Your Age would sound like what they are: the fantasies of old men!

These goggles I get do something. They turn people into little kids. Light shines from their little kid eyes onto each other's little kid faces and all over the room. Wherever they look the thing they look at changes. It doesn't change, it's covered by the projection, and my goggles let me see it.

I was really watching Ashley. She sat on a beanbag with Alicia, not doing anything, and I was thinking maybe I'd go and tell her what happened. My dad died. Her father was a fireman and they knew him. We were friends again, not boyfriend and girlfriend at all, just friends.

Ashley picked bits of skin off her lips. She always had red marks on her lips from biting them and peeling off skin with her fingernails. She was a little kid sitting there. Her butt sunk into the beanbag and her feet, in yellow socks with stars on them, wedged under the bag. She wore an oversized Huntington Manor Fire Department sweatshirt. I got up to go tell her about my dad, but Megan went over to her and started talking quickly. She was excited about something. Megan's projector flared bright as headlights.

Ashley put her elbows on her knees and rested her mouth on her fists. Her knuckles pushed her lips sideways, wrinkling her cheek. When she straightened out her face her mouth slid across her knuckles. Ashley's light fluttered like it was about to die and I knew she wasn't listening to

Megan. She smelled her knuckles where her lips wiped spit on them. Every few seconds she rubbed her lips on her knuckles and smelled them as her light flickered. I couldn't tell her about my dad while she smelled her knuckles and didn't even pay attention to Megan's bright lights. That's the type of thing the goggles showed.

I wanted to tell somebody about my dad. Demaris's father knew, and Mr. Brush, too, and Demaris probably knew and I hadn't told any of them. They knew before I did. I went looking for Joey. First I checked our room. He wasn't there. I went to the bathroom and tried the door. It was locked.

"Joey. It's me. Open the door. There's something I gotta tell you. Yo, open the friggin door."

I knocked and shook the handle but the bastard didn't answer me. He was whacking off, probably. I quit trying to open the door. I walked back to the common room, saw all the kids with their stupid projector eyes and kept going right out the cabin. I saw Mrs. Ackerly stand up ready to gobble at me, but Mr. Brush shook his hand at her. "Larry," he called. I stopped to let him catch up. He looked like one of those dolls on strings, marionettes or whatever. His clothes twitched all over the place. His knees stuck out to the sides as he jogged. I stood about where I'd been talking to my mother on the phone, in the middle of the cabins.

"I know you need space, Larry," he said out of breath from sprinting ten feet. "You need to be alone. I understand." What the hell did he understand? The reason I was walking out the door, it wasn't because of my dad. It was Joey. I knew I wouldn't get in trouble for doing it though, for walking out of the cabin, on account of my dad being dead. "I can't let you wander around the grounds. I'm sorry." He looked at me. "I'm really sorry."

I went and sat on the porch outside the cabin. I had to promise I'd stay there. He kept checking on me. He wanted to make sure I didn't sneak away. Every now and again he poked his head out the door and shot me one of those bad grade smiles.

If you want to know how my father died I'll tell you. It's pretty gross. I didn't know it then, while I was sitting on the porch in Springkill. I learned about it later bit by bit, mostly from the firemen.

My dad had prostate cancer. Prostate cancer isn't that bad if you catch it early. He waited too long to see a doctor. They had to cut his prostate out. After that, after his cancer was gone and he didn't have a prostate anymore, he slept on the couch and stayed angry. He never went for check-ups. He was busy painting houses and wallpapering and always saying *ah fuck them*. The doctors, I mean. His insurance dumped him. The bills were high, and they kept coming. We figured the cancer was gone anyway, all cut out with his prostate. Then he got sick again. Pains in his stomach. He couldn't eat. He threw up all the time. Finally he went and got checked.

It was in his liver. Liver cancer is one of the worst kinds to get. They say that about a lot of them, like brain cancer and bone cancer, which is what my neighbor Cookie would die from, and especially pancreatic cancer. I don't know, liver cancer seems as bad as any of them. Anyway, my dad didn't die from cancer.

*His* father died from cancer before I was even born. He was a painter, too. He had five kids, my aunts and uncles. He couldn't afford to stop working, to get treatment. There wasn't much they could do back then. My grandfather kept working until he got too sick. Then the cancer killed him. It happened much faster with my grandfather than with my dad because there wasn't any science back then. I think that's why my dad bought the .45. He figured he'd shoot a dog, sure, but then he'd shoot himself when the sickness was too strong.

It was Sunday, and my mom came home from church. She went to the bedroom to check on my father. The door was locked. He'd been locking her out because she tried to take away his booze and cigarettes. She talked to him through the door but he didn't answer her. She went to the kitchen for coffee. She made the coffee and got the milk from the fridge. She slammed the fridge door shut. Everybody slammed the fridge door. I did it and so did my sister. Whenever someone was angry the fridge door got slammed shut. And every time, for the last six months, after you slammed the door there was a little tap when the bullet fell. Sometimes the bullet rolled off of the refrigerator and dropped to the floor. You'd pick it up and put it back on top of the fridge. You didn't even think about it.

There wasn't any tap when my mom slammed the door this time. The bullet was gone. It was in my shirt pocket in Springkill but she didn't know that. When she finally kicked the bedroom door open he was covered in blood. She couldn't smell there was no gunpowder in the air. She couldn't smell the blood on him, on the sheets and pillows, was mixed with the alcohol he'd puked. She lifted his head off the pillow and felt it all over for a bullet hole. She checked his chest and everything. I wish I didn't know about that. Anyway, she couldn't find the hole she thought the bullet made, like he *said* would happen.

All he'd been eating for two weeks was Vodka and coke. It burned ulcers through his stomach. They were like perforations in notebook paper. Puking tore his guts open. The more he bled the more he puked. That's what killed him.

I stood near the coffin while people waited on line to pay their respect. Mom sat. She stared straight ahead, at the coffin, the whole time. Gil was a fireman and an EMT. He was the first responder when my mom called 911. He went and put his hand on my mom's shoulder and said something in her ear. Everybody said things real quiet in her ear while she stared. She'd only move her lips. She didn't say anything.

Then Gil came and stood next to me. I had to stand by the coffin with Uncle Lloyd and shake people's hands and thank them for coming. "You're the man of the house, Larry. You got to look after your family. Your mother and sister. You know that."

Pretty much every fireman and cop said that to me. I was a man and had to look after my mother. Gil wasn't the first, though. I remember the first person that called me a man.

I liked Gil. He let me sleep in an ambulance, on the gurney, after the fireman's fairs, while the game booths and rides shut down and the firemen drank cold ones in the station. There was a game room in the firehouse. There was a trophy case, full. There were plaques on the wall for men who died after long careers with the department. There were plaques for men who'd done something brave. There were framed letters from mayors and governors. There was a plaque on the wall for my dad, for being the only man to win a first place trophy in both the Bucket Brigade and the Fireman's Carry in a single tournament. It was next to a plaque for Pete, who died in the Towers on 9-11.

"My father died when I was about your age. Heart attack. He was at work. *Monday morning at the bank*, it's like a diagnosis. Middle of processing a loan. Didn't take a minute." Gil was bonding with me.

I wanted to cry. I only cried once after my father died. Once. I'm not sure why, like if it was because he died or from something else that was happening. When Gil told me about his father's heart attack I felt cold and dry and oily and this burning went through my eyes. I said, "My dad killed himself. It's not the same. He's an asshole." That stopped it.

"Maybe. Maybe not," Gil said sort of leading me off to the side. It sounded like he had a cobweb in his throat. It was a permanent gluey fixture. You always cleared your own throat when you talked with Gil. Fat, purple bags piled up under his eyes and crackled with red threads. "I see loads'a checkouts. Only difference to me how a man goes, if he done it himself, it's communication."

I remember he was wearing brown shorts and white socks. It wasn't hot that day, and the funeral home was air-conditioned. Gil's legs were pale, hairless and shiny. He had bumps on his shin blade and there were tangled veins all over. He chewed gum. "I corner MMA matches. You know that? Local stuff. I'm a cut man."

No, I didn't know that. I didn't say it, just shook my head. I watched the people in line shuffle up the side of the room toward the coffin. They looked around trying to spot someone crying or just searched for someone they know. The people up front talked less, and quietly. It was louder towards the back. There were smiles and sometimes laughter even. The line went down the hall and out the funeral home doors onto a slate porch. They probably had a blast out there. There were fire trucks in the parking lot, and police cars. It was like the fair came to town. I bet half the people who showed were just passing by, on their way to the mall or something, and saw the trucks and uniforms and hats and came to see who the hell was so important. They don't know firemen are like family, like brothers, and the police are their cousins. This was just a normal funeral for them, not a special service for a Mayor or a Judge or somebody important. And afterwards, the firemen will drive the trucks back to the firehouse, sit in the game room and unbutton their shirts and drink Coors Light and smoke and curse while they joke. People I never met waited in line and looked up front where my mom was hunched over, shivering. They pointed and said to the person behind them, "That must be the widow," I guess.

"I'm a big MMA fan. Sports in general. But I have passion for the fights. Y'know why?" I stared at the people. "There's no ball or sticks between the athletes. Nothing abstracts the sport. It's pure, unalloyed competition. It gets accused'a being too violent. It ain't no more violent than any other sport is, it just looks that way because it ain't hiding behind layers. All sports is violence minus death. That might turn some people off. But if you want the truth, not just talk about what's right, you need that kind'a action, you gotta *do* sump'n. Deep down everybody knows that might makes right. Follow me?

"That's why people watch fights. Okay, for blood and violence. And to bet. I'll give you that. For the whole show, y'know. There's all the *talk* about who's the better fighter, who's got the skill-set to be the champ. But when the fighters get together they gotta *do* sump'n. Exchange. And you can see it. The momentum builds around one of'm. In the end one guy gets knocked out. He gets choked, His arm gets bent back. He has to tap out. The other fighter gets his arm raised."

He was speaking too loud for a funeral. He chewed gum the whole time.

"The winner. He's the truth. No treaties signed. Nobody reformed the tax code. But the truth was in the building and it was good enough. That's why people watch. To *see* the truth. Not to *hear* about who's right. You follow me?"

His lips frowned around his purple and yellow chin.

"There's sump'n to be said about a guy in a fight. Y'know he's beat. His technique's exposed. He's weak. And but he hangs in there exhausted and bleeding. Convinced that heart and toughness and even sometimes *naivety* can hang him on, outlast the other guy, beat him for one second, and that one second he's winning could beat it all. There's definitely sump'n to be said. Life is a fight, yeah okay. But has it gotta be so damn hard fought to the end? The man who takes his time, feels his, I don't know, *joyousness* slipping away. Says, shit, I'm gonna check myself out when this *joy* is gone. And without fighting chooses his own way. Says, 'That's it I had enough. I'm not hanging in no more to have my nerves plucked. And fall into bloody, degraded, permanent defeat.'"

He kept his hand on my shoulder the whole time. "D'you think a heart attack is noble? You should see one, kid. Or ten years' worth'a bone cancer? Have a look at the end of that! Shit. Hooked up to machines and stuffed with medicines don't make a champ. I'm talking to you as a man, now. You know how many times we heard your father complain about what he got?" He shook his head. "That many. Some kinds'a checkouts is communication. Says I was in control and I chose my opponent. I beat the fight itself. The whole world can be good and determined, and it can be healthy and happy. It can be successful and watch movies and hope to be rich one day. It can elect people and make laws. But all together the world knows shit about one man's suffering. And they don't give a damn about one man's life. And the whole world'll sit around that man. And he rejects it, totally, its goodness or its terribleness and the man says to it, 'Hey, fuck you. I'm not part of it. I'm not gonna be your insignificance no more because you, the whole world of things and people, are less significant than my pain.' And he says fuck you because that's the truth. How it's always been. From each of us to the rest'a them. And any man who can say it and show he means it. Really show it like your old man always showed he was significant enough to himself and to who he loved. I respect that. Follow?" We were standing side by side but he stepped in front of me and tapped a finger under my chin so I'd look into his face.

"I don't want to say anything bad at the funeral. And because when I was your age I was here, too. But I know I was a man then, like you are now, so I'm going to tell you this like a man. We knew Otis, your father, and we loved him. Watch your mouth how you talk about him. Follow?"

See! Everybody loved him! No matter what he did, even puking his guts out in the bedroom, everyone thought it was just the right thing to do! He was such a *joy*ous fucking guy!

The windstorm blew leaves all over the porch and against the cabin. There were piles under the windows. I got off the porch and kicked them around. I kept bringing my fingers to my mouth, taking drags off an imaginary cigarette. I really wanted a smoke.

Some of the lights in the rooms were on. I looked through the window into my room. Joey laid on his bunk. He had one hand down his pants and the other under his head. His eyes projected against the ceiling, a dinner with Jimmy Lutani at Joey's house. They were sitting at the table with their parents and both their brothers. They laughed and talked about the wrestling season and ate Italian food. I saw the whole show through my goggles.

# Let's Go

Lights in the cabin windows, ours and the others, started blinking on. Everyone was going to their rooms, getting ready for bed. I sat on the porch bench and leaned against the cabin wall. The wall itched my back. It was covered with thick hair, like shredded wheat or something. I didn't hear Mrs. Ackerly's voice gobbling inside telling the kids to get ready for bed. They just went on their own. When you don't have TV or video games or anything, when you don't have the same routine anymore and you have to start making things up, you get tired pretty quick.

I didn't want to go back in the cabin. Everybody would ask what my problem was and why I sat outside on the porch. The last person I wanted to see was Joey and he'd be sleeping right next to me. What I wanted to do was wait until everyone was asleep. When all the lights were off I'd wait twenty minutes more, then sneak into my bunk. Nobody would see me. Mr. Brush though, he'd probably come out in two seconds and sit down next to me with his pointy knees. He'd give me advice or tell me about some lesson I should be learning. My stomach turned when I thought about Brush walking around inside, getting his words together so he could talk to me again.

There's no way to avoid it. They'd want to know and I couldn't tell them. They'd get sore about it and the imagination contests would start again. If I explained the whole thing they'd all feel bad for asking but they'd spread it all around anyway, trying to be the first to give the story to someone else, as if it was gold, but multiplying the more you gave it away. You can't make it up and you can't make it stop. Everybody has to be an asshole sometimes.

When I went to move my legs though, to stand up, they were stuck. I don't know why. They wouldn't move. They weren't numb or anything. They could have moved but I didn't want them to. You have to want to move your legs. Most of the time you don't think about it. You just stand up and go brush your teeth or something. It was a very peculiar thing happening with my legs. I would've liked to be in my room on my bunk with the lights out and Joey sleeping and Ben snoring. There was all the stuff I had to do in between. I had to brush my teeth, change into sweatpants, and get my clothes together for the next day. Worst of all was Joey. I had to do something with him. I didn't have to talk to him if I didn't want to but even not talking was *doing* something. It's even harder not to talk to someone.

Before any of that happened, I had to want to move my legs. I tried, they wouldn't move. The cabin door opened.

It was Demaris. She sat down on the hard bench and rubbed my back. It was nice. It wasn't sexual or anything, just nice. I asked her, "Will you scratch?"

"Your back is itchy?"

"Yes."

Her hand went up my shirt. Her fingers spread like a rake. Her nails went up and down in columns, then across in rows.

"Magic fingers," I said.

Joey pretended he was sleeping when I came into the room, thank god, even though the light was on and Ben was looking at a dirt bike magazine. I knew Joey was awake. I didn't care, though. It made things easier. He was damn clever.

"Where you been," Ben asked. He didn't look at me.

"I'm tired, Ben. Mind if we turn the lights off?"

"It's lights-out in two minutes anyway. Where've you been," he asked again.

"I don't know, Ben." I cut the lights. "Goodnight," I said.

"D'you need some private time after your stellar performance?"

"Probably," I said to shut him up. Ben's magazine flopped to the floor and then his head smacked against the pillow. I undressed in the darkness. I hadn't brushed my teeth or anything. I didn't get all the way undressed, though. I only took off my shirt and shoes. Then I climbed onto my bunk.

Mr. Brush walked down the hallway. One foot hit the wood floor, the world spun, and then another foot dropped. He was checking we all had our lights out.

Joey and Ben were asleep in two seconds. I know how Joey sounds when he sleeps. He does this thing where he chews. You can hear his teeth pop together and all this gummy noise. He twitches like crazy, too, like he's dancing. Ben had a cold and was snoring.

For something not burning, the moon was very bright, you could see the room pretty clear. The bunks, the little chair in the corner, the luggage, everything took on a brown, grey-greenish color and looked dead, which made them seem like they'd once been alive and could come to life again. For a few long minutes I stared at things, my wide eyes stinging, waiting for something to happen, like for a pair of sneakers to twitch. I saw a carpenter ant, fat as a blueberry. Joey was doing his sleepy dance and popping his teeth. In the stillness the ant seemed to dash across the wall, quick as an ostrich, and just as out of place. He followed a groove in the wall's planks, climbing towards the ceiling.

What sense did a straight line make to an ant? Why should it follow a groove the way I would, like if I was lost in the desert, knowing it was man made and would lead somewhere? At the top of the wall it crawled along the ceiling's edge. I watched it follow a crack in the ceiling awhile. Then I had to piss.

I pee at least four times a night. Even if it's an ounce, I'll fixate on it, the concentration adding heft until, blind with sleep, I'd toss off the sheets and creep down the hall to the toilet.

If you want to be really quiet and not make the floor squeak, you walk along the edge of the hall, hugging the wall. At home, after my parents were in bed, I'd sneak to the bathroom, my back rubbing along the wall. There was a dark streak on the paint from years of built up skin oil. I'd piss against the toilet wall so there wasn't any splashing noise. Sometimes, in the dark, I missed the toilet and splashed my feet. The radiator beside the toilet was corroded with urine.

The night swept across the mountain, through the forest. I could almost hear the darkness, silk wrapped, slipping along the walls. My skin tingled.

"Larry?" A haze at the end of the hallway. Pale and wobbly like spit in a puddle. It was only Demaris.

"What are you doing out of bed," she asked, standing in the common room. The stove was still hot. Embers glowed through the slits.

"I was going to the bathroom," I told her.

"With your sneakers on?" She said, smiling.

I felt very nervous talking to her. Not nervous, insubordinate, which is what teachers always gave you detention for. I told her my plan. "I'm gonna go for a walk or something. I think I'll go up one'a the trails, to the rest area. Go see those purple rocks and..."

"Shh!" Demaris put her hand to my face. "Come," she whispered. We snuck into the closet and closed the door. We didn't shut it all the way, though, so that the latch wouldn't knock against the strike plate. The floorboards creaked, and sticky footsteps came into the common room.

In her nightgown Mrs. Ackerly was white and round and goose eggy. Me and Demaris pressed our faces together looking through the crack, watching Ackerly peek down the boys hallway, then the girls. There were two couches by the front window. Their arms touched but Ackerly moved them a little further apart. Then she went and checked the hallways again. She looked suspicious as hell, with her hand on her chin and her head swiveling back and forth.

Demaris's body pressed against mine. When Ackerly walked back to the couches I practically knocked Demaris over trying to see through the crack in the door. I felt her body sort of flex against my fingers.

"Tickles," she whispered. Her eyes were wide open.

Ackerly climbed onto one couch's arm. Her nightgown slipped up her thigh while she hopped her other knee onto the other couch's arm. She lost her balance and fell on her shoulder, spilling a tit on the floor. Demaris smothered a laugh on my neck. Her fingernails dug into my back. She smelled like vanilla.

Finally Ackerly found her balance. Her spilled tit hung out. Her gown was way up over her belly, and she squatted into the space between the couches. She was surprisingly flexible. Her hand went between her thighs and moved in quick, jerky circles. She twisted her tit, stretching out a nipple like a wad of purple gum.

We bit each other, me and Demaris, to keep from laughing. I got a major hard on. It bent double in my jeans. Demaris bumped it with her hip or brushed her thigh on it I think on purpose. And I swear by my aching pin if she touched me, if she reached out a finger and tapped my zipper, I'd have gone off like a firecracker. We kept hugging and moving around and then, bang, my heel knocked over a mop.

Everything froze. Ackerly pulled up her gown straight. She climbed off the couch nimble as a rabbit and thundered towards the door.

Demaris yanked my shirt as she tucked herself behind the toilet paper stack. "Larry," she whispered, waving me in.

Ackerly was coming for me. And I waited, smiling. My cheeks were up to my ears. I let my teeth fly. I saw her through the crack in the door, the bitch, her head haloed with frizz in the moonlight, getting closer. She peered in through the door's crack. Her eyes were level with mine. She couldn't see me, it was too dark in the closet, but my smile was waiting. *I* was waiting for her, for her threats, her vituperation. Brush would come climbing into the room with his spider legs asking what was going on for god's sake it's after midnight! And man did I have an explanation. Go ahead! Open the fucking door!

Her hand was on the knob. It gave an inch. She paused, then turned and hurried away. The girls hallway swallowed her, long tits and all.

"Come out Demaris," I said. I didn't even whisper. I wanted Ackerly to hear me. I knew her eardrums were swelling out of her head.

"Did she see you? Did she?"

"She knows *some*one saw her."

"What should we do?"

"…"

"Let's go," she said. She grabbed my wrist and pulled me out the door.

The moon was high and bright. Our shadows flung against the grass, hysterical shadows that fluttered at the edges. Demaris's dress whipped around her knees. A hundred yards into the forest she said, "This is where the staff go," down a narrow path weaved with branches.

Demaris pushed past branches and let them snap back at me. "Sorry," she said every time. She was doing it on purpose, you could tell. I kept close. The moon may have been bright, but under the big trees the night swarmed the trail from turn to turn. In some spots the trail was too narrow for a rabbit to squeeze through and I'd call out, "Demaris."

"Right here, Larry."

Her arm stuck through bushes and I grabbed her hand. "Don't pull me so hard, Larry. I keep slipping." Fat roots sewed through the ground and you tripped if you weren't careful. Waves of solid rock busted your kneecaps when you fell.

"Where the hell are we going," I kept asking.

"You'll see. Don't be scared, little boy."

"I'm not scared," I said. I was a little, though. We held hands for about a quarter mile. The forest floor was so wobbly, there were so many roots to trip on, holes to fall in, hills to slide who knows where to, and so many dead trees laid flat or leaning on the one beside it and ready to fall on your head that it seemed like the forest was drunk. When the ground flattened out Demaris let my hand go. There were fewer trees and more light. "I hear something," I said.

"Oh really?"

We walked toward the noise. Orange light wobbled in the space between trees. I didn't know where we were going, but with Demaris I couldn't wait to get there.

# Devil In The Shoe Store

But then, what was there, it was Adam, plus Theo and Pasqual, the two other counselors I met at the dinner table with Demaris, sitting around a fire. It wasn't very big. You could jump over it. It made a bright hole in the night and released a more solid darkness around them. They sat on brick and mortar, pieces of a wall or something. I hid behind a tree. Demaris though, she walked into the firelight as if she were walking into her house. I didn't know what she thought she was doing but all of them, Adam, Pasqual and Theo went, "Oi, oi! Demaris!" They'd been expecting her.

"Where'd you go? Larry! Come here," Demaris squinted all over the place.

"Whoa, wait. What the hell, Demaris? You bring someone?"

"Yes, don't worry, Adam," Demaris said. She called me again. If you think I was comfortable coming out of the darkness and setting up a broken brick wall to sit with the counselors you're out of your mind.

"Larry from Finley," Adam asked. His dreds crawled in the firelight. He was wearing cutoff Dickies, frayed. He had tattoos on his calves, black and splattered looking. One tattoo was a capital A in a circle that didn't quite fit around it.

"Yes. Larry from our group," Demaris said. "Come out, little boy."

I didn't know what to do with my hands. They seemed to be saying something. I stuck them in my pockets. Should I look at the counselors, or into the fire? Jesus, I felt like a moron. Demaris came and grabbed my arm and pulled me to the bonfire's edge. "Sit down. It's okay," she said.

Everybody was quiet. I dried up like an old pinecone and a shiver jumped into my hips. It wasn't cold or anything, especially with that fire going. I could feel the heat with my eyeballs. My hip joints just jiggled a little.

"He should really be in the cabin," Adam said. "This isn't cool."

"It's okay. He needs to be here. It's fine, guys." Demaris rubbed my back again, like on the porch.

"I wouldn't be sleeping anyway," I said quickly into the fire.

"His father died," she said into the fire, too.

She could've told them I'd just eaten watermelon, it made no difference to me. It didn't mean anything. The thing is, my dad was already a memory. I hated spending time with him. I never wanted to be around him. All I ever thought about were things we'd done together, never what we *would* do. Ben Croton or Joey, they thought about doing things with their dads all the time. Opening businesses or going to wrestling matches. They wanted to do those things. Once in a while my dad took me to estimate a job. He was a house painter. He was always driving to people's houses to tell them what it would cost to rip off old wallpaper or skim coat their ceiling or something. Along the way he pointed out the places he grew up around.

"See those houses, how they sit up on a ridge, and all the trees below with the scummy pond? When it rained it flooded. This whole street would be a lake. Me, Wesley Erickson, and Tommy Gerardi went swimming in it. They put drainage in years ago. This Home Depot? Used to be a farm. That's where the goats and chickens were, over in the corner of the parking lot. They had a donkey I used to feed apples. One day the son of a bitch bit me. Right on the tit he bit me. I punched him in the jaw nearly broke my fist, the motherfucker! That house there, the guy used to make plaster dinosaurs, six foot tall. Kept them on the side of his driveway. I wonder what happened to them dinosaurs."

That's all we ever did together, drive around while he pointed out his memories.

After the estimates we went to the firehouse. There was a big pot of coffee and someone brought cookies from the bakery down the street. There were always four or five guys in there, like Steve Lundgren and

Eddie Bird. There'd be cops hanging around, too. "How's it going, Larry." They all knew me. "Your boy's looking good, Otis. Be careful, they get big fast. Trust me. My boy's nineteen, the son of a bitch is built like a brick shithouse. I can't take him no more."

"Yeah, well he'll have to go to sleep sometime, ha ha," my dad said.

"Your old man bust your balls, Larry? Crazy old bastard."

"He's a good boy," Steven Lundgren defended me.

"He goddamn better be. He knows better. Right, Larry?" dad said.

I wouldn't say a thing.

"Shit," dad said, "my old man catch me doing the things I let *him* get away with! Jesus, I'd be black and blue three days. And if he didn't catch me, he beat me once a week in case he missed something. Right Steve?" The firemen laughed. The cops laughed, too. That's why he brought me around there, to show off.

A plainclothes cop tells us, "I remember this one time I hit my sister with a tennis racket." His ears are gnarled like cauliflower. Detective Brunetti, that's his name. "I barely even touched her. My father saw me, though. He goes and gets a paperweight. You know them brass ones? I had a Camaro I was fixing up that I bought with my high school graduation money parked at the curb. He goes out to the porch and launches the paperweight across the sidewalk. Hits my quarter panel. He goes, 'You touch something of mine, I touch something of yours.'"

They all had stories about their fathers being assholes.

I went out to the fire trucks. It smelled like tires and car polish in the hangar. There were about ten trucks in there, mostly Tankers and Pumpers. I messed around with Bonkers a little. Then I climbed on the trucks.

I liked the black and red Tower Ladder. It's got more technology than the last rocket to the moon. Eddie Bird always said that. You'd believe it if you saw. There're TVs and navigation and computers and digital equipment to measure water pressure and keep the truck balanced when the ladder booms and tilts or swings. I climbed up the truck and crawled along the ladder and sat inside the bucket. That's where my father was during fires, on the Quint ladder, in the bucket.

"I'm sorry to hear zis," Pasqual said. "How did your fazzer die, if you don't mind I ask?"

Another friggin accent, I thought. I wasn't going to ask where the hell Pasqual was from. He sounded like a French cartoon, replacing every *th* with a *z*, saying *ziss* and *zat* instead of this or that, as if his tongue was allergic to his teeth or something. He was funny looking, too, with dense shadows on his face. His skinny body parts looked assembled, like his arms and legs were individual pieces, folded and leaning against his body. His head was small but his face was big. He had a butt-chin. The crack in his chin was so deep he couldn't shave it. There was black stubble inside so the crack was darker than regular shadow and even deeper looking and butt cracky. You could hang posters on his forehead.

"He had cancer," I told him. I thought he died from cancer. "He got sick again last year, I guess. But the past few weeks. Like the past few weeks he's been pretty bad. Just sleeping on the couch." Pasqual rolled a cigarette slowly, pinching a filter with his lips. "I wasn't supposed to come to Springkill because he was sick and my mom works. But then I was allowed to come anyway." Pasqual took the filter from his mouth—I saw it was a corner torn from a matchbook—and wrapped the cigarette paper around it.

"He knew he was going to die," Pasqual said. He had this very serious look on his face. He was pretty interested in the story. "This is why he sent you to Springkill."

"No, not that. We had a fight. Then what happened was I was in a fire. And my mom took it as a sign from the Lord or something. She's very sensitive to the Lord now. She figured it was his way of telling her I should be here, I guess. I don't know."

"What was it, why you should come? Something was wrong, no?"

"No, man. It was good. I had my best friend. My girlfriend. Everything was okay."

"But it is not okay anymore. Pourquois? Why?"

Pasqual was better at helping you tell a story than Joey or Amanda Voyage. He didn't care about violence or fucking. The problem was, I didn't know why things were not okay. I knew what was wrong, but it was hard to know why. That's the problem with telling stories. There are a thousand ways to tell how things happened. But there's no way to know *why*. You have to pick a reason out of thin air. Then you have to explain it with the same words you use to talk about your shoe. *Why* should be like a yawn, something everyone understands immediately.

"Pasqual," Demaris moaned. "His father died today. Of course things are not okay anymore. That's why, if you need a reason."

"No. He says his best friend. His girl. It is more than his father, no?"

"Pasqual, let it go. You're right, there's always more to a story," Adam sort of calmed him down, as if Pasqual was a horse or something.

"It's okay. I don't mind. Seriously," I said. I didn't either.

"Pasqual's a writer. He asks loads of questions," Theo said. A branch laid across his lap, and there were bark strips around his boots mixed with curled slices of wood. I saw he had a knife.

Pasqual picked up a bark strip from the ground and held it to the flames then lit the cigarette with the burning bark. He turned his whole body to me, the cigarette between his thumb and middle finger, and pointed the filter at my face.

I never smoked a roll-up before. It tasted totally different. The smoke didn't burn my lungs right away. It only made me cough after Pasqual said, "Hold it a little longer." I took three drags. Pasqual motioned to pass it to Demaris. "I am curious about people," he said. "What makes them go. Americans are religious people. They like to go, but they also like very much to stop. Religion makes them stop. This is their use for god. He's the wall the bus crashes against along the road. They call this the truth."

"…"

"Your mother, she is getting comfort by this. To not have to go. That's what religion is for her, no? Not to look forever. To be shown the truth?"

"I guess so," I said.

I never thought about the truth, like critically. I mean, now though, now I think it's like Gil says. It's something that can't be argued about because it's obvious. You can be right, but it's different from knowing the truth. The truth is a thing, and being right is what you do. The difference is that one's a noun and the other is a verb.

"Do you believe god sent you here, to Springkill, like your mother says?"

Pasqual, there was a mean streak in him. I know a bastard when I see one.

"I don't know," I said. "I don't know what god does."

"But you are Christian."

"Of course I am. I'm baptized, and I went to confirmation classes for three years and everything. I hate going to church, but still."

"You believe scripture? Everything the bible says?"

"Yeah. I mean, I never read all of it, to be honest. My mother tells me about it. All the time. She studied it hard, in a bible school called Diacania, I think. There's stuff in it you have to be smart about because it was written for goat herders with rotten teeth who didn't even have toilet paper. My mother says you're not supposed to believe everything in it, like that the world and the plants were created *before* the sun, or that it only took six days to do it. If there wasn't a sun, who knows how long a day was? See? You have to think about it. You can't believe everything."

"What about slaves? People can own other people?"

He thought I liked slavery because I was American and we had slaves and churches.

"The bible doesn't say you can own slaves," I said.

"It does. It sets the price, and allows you to beat them as long as they do not die before two days."

Demaris passed the cigarette to Theo. We were all sharing it. That's just how they did it.

"That's probably in the Old Testament, before Jesus changed it," I told Pasqual. "You have to use your head at least. I just said that. You can't believe exactly what it says. Christians know you can't have slaves. Look at it, god hated almost everybody before Jesus. He was always making the people he liked kill the people he didn't. Jesus forgave everyone instead, so now it's different."

"But before Jesus, in the Old Testament, there was no hell. You say god stopped telling us to kill people, but if you do not follow Jesus now you go to hell forever."

I happened to know that I'd go to heaven no matter what, Jesus or not, because my mother was going there. What's heaven if a mother can't have her son? I didn't say anything for a minute though because I was wondering if that also counted for my dad.

"What do you think god is," Pasqual asked and took a drag off the cigarette.

See? Everyone can talk about god for hours. I hate talking about him. I answered the question anyway. Only because saying nothing made me feel more self-conscious than talking. Maybe Brush was right. Maybe talking helps.

"My mother once told me god could be a man living on another planet, like an alien or something," I said. "We were on a bus to Vermont, me and my sister and my parents. My mom was very interested about getting us saved. My dad didn't believe in it. He kept saying, 'How do you know there even was a guy called Jesus.' And, 'How come god likes war so much, and letting children starve all over the place? Why'd he make diseases and retards?'

"My mom was quiet for a while, just pressing her thumbnails into her fingertips one by one. Then she said to me and my sister, 'It's foolish to try and understand the Lord.' We were on the other side of the aisle and my mother had to lean over. 'But do you know what I think he could be? God could be an old civilization, from another galaxy.' She told us that could be what all the *glowing clouds* and *booming voices* in the bible verses were about. That's what the spaceship thing in the Old Testament means, when it says the sons of god saw the daughters of men were beautiful and they took them for wives and all. The sons of god were different from men, my mother said she thinks." The counselors were very still, and really listening, I could tell. "Maybe that's why it says Jesus was *sent* here, and that's how he *ascended* into heaven. And now, look at now, you can be a virgin and get pregnant. People get brought back to life after they die all the time. People ascend into the air and you don't even think about, it's just a spaceship. It's not impossible, all the miracles Jesus did."

Pasqual let his teeth fly. "Larry! Your muzzer is an atheist!"

"No. She's Lutheran. I just told you!" He thought my mother was a friggin atheist! I know my mom. She has faith. Trust me.

"She believe god is from another planet! An astronaut, maybe. But not an omnipotent nebula in the firmament, listening to your thoughts and answering your prayers. Here, take your turn," he said, and shoved the cigarette in my face. It was a centimeter long and shiny black.

"Or it could be the Bible's account of evolution," Adam said. "The sons of god were human males leaving Africa. They met the daughters of men, which could be female cave dwellers in Asia. The modern female is eighty-thousand years older than modern males."

"Mitochondrial Eve," Theo said.

"Exactly. So maybe a modern human male with the same brain we have today left Africa into Asia, or from Asia into Europe or somewhere…"

This is where it's hard to remember exactly how things went. I felt tired and there was something else. I felt funny.

Everybody talked about what god was. Pasqual insisted god wasn't anything. He said you could study, "What effect the god myth had, but that is all. He is a fixture of historical theory. As a thing, he is nothing."

Adam said, "Okay but. *But*, Pasqual, laws are nothing. Beauty is nothing. There are, listen, stop for a second and listen, Pas, I'm agreeing with you but I have to add this. No you don't know what I'm going to say. I agree, there is no such thing as god as a being, okay you're right, but what I'm saying is that a collective conscience created and refreshes this thing. You know, the whole social drift thing."

Every now and again, Theo would add a point of fact to Pasqual and Adam's conversation. When Adam said social drift, for example, Theo said, "You're talking about memes. The genetics of society and culture." He was like a referee or something.

"Yeah, memes," Adam said. "I don't believe in a god. But I still I love Christmas and church weddings, and when I pass Holy Trinity in the car with my family we cross ourselves. I love that shit. Call them Catholic memes. What I'm saying is god is as much a part of the collective conscience in America as patriotism, which isn't a thing either. It's got no material substance. So even nowadays with the benefits of science, god is still as *real* as five thousand years ago."

And Pasqual said okay he understood, it was the same where came from in Quebec, but, "That means god will eventually drift away and become nothing. If he is nothing tomorrow, why is he something today?"

"Evolutionary psychology," Theo said.

"Yes, it is this," Pasqual said. "As the fear of ghosts is the left over feeling from being hunted, when our ancestors were prey. Fearing ghosts is a fear of nothing. Even the words are similar. Hunted and haunted." Pasqual, you could tell, never stepped foot in church. What the hell did he know!

When Demaris finally got a word in she said what a lot of people say: she didn't believe in a white bearded man in the sky, but god was *something*, like a kind of energy. And if you had the right sense, like faith or something, you picked it up clear as a radio station. Theo didn't talk about god. All he did was dig into the stick with his knife and play referee.

Pasqual and Adam talked more about religion than my mother did! They were real god snobs. I was sick of talking about it so what I did, I told them about this game me and Joey used to play.

# A True Story

I told you about the game, when Me and Joey put our elbows on our knees and huffed until we were dizzy then held our breath and lay on our backs. One of us pushed his hands into the other's stomach. I was pretty skinny. Joey was always telling me he could feel my backbone. That's how hard he pushed.

When I passed out I had dreams. When I woke up they vanished like a breath in winter. Joey told me I forgot them because I wasn't really dreaming. What it was, he said my conscience, like my mind or whatever, left my body. He said when your mind leaves your body you're basically dead. You could talk to spirits or go places, like to shoe stores for example, where you can see living people. You can do that for hours in death but in the living world you're actually gone for twenty seconds.

After I was dead for twenty seconds my mind came back into my body because it wasn't my time to die yet, Joey told me. Not only that, it wasn't even my last life. He said my brain wasn't allowed to remember death because I wasn't ready to be dead forever, and I'd probably have to live three more lives or something before I could remember my dead walks and all the lives I had before this one. He said most people aren't ready to be dead permanently. They can be dead for a long time between lives until they're ready for the final death. That's why the world population keeps growing, Joey says, because people live over and over, and meanwhile new minds are getting made and born into babies all the time. I don't know where he got it, but it seemed right.

Joey's parents are Catholic. They make him go to church twice a year, but it was the pass-out game that made him believe, I told the counselors. Pasqual rolled another cigarette and we were all sharing it again, coughing.

I told them Joey and me played the game one afternoon, passing each other out in the fort. He dreamed quite a lot about the devil and when he woke up he'd say, "I saw him again," which sort of creeped me out.

It never worked the first time. I don't know why. You passed out on the second or third try. Anyway, we'd been playing for a while this one day, both of us passing out twice already. The third time Joey passed out he started shaking, and kicking his legs. The thing was, he was shaking too much. He was kicking too hard. I thought he was joking, he played around like that sometimes. I kept saying, "C'mon, stop playing. It's my turn." You sort of get addicted. He stopped shaking and laid there, not doing anything, just sleeping. "Joey. Alright man, enough with that shit," I told him. Something was wrong.

How you know a guy is faking, you flick his eyelids. If he isn't sleeping his head will jerk, or he'll slap your hand away or something. I popped Joey on the eye but it only twitched. I knew he was passed out for real.

You aren't supposed to let a guy sleep more than thirty seconds. I think your brain gets damaged after that. I shook him hard and yelled in his ear and slapped his head. "Joey," I screamed. I wanted to cry. I didn't tell *them* that though, the counselors. I told them I screamed and rubbed his head and smacked him until he finally woke up. He stared at me until he realized where the hell he was, just like my father used to do.

Passing out will give you headaches, like when you eat ice cream too fast. It hurts as bad but it lasts longer. Joey got one of those headaches and crawled to a corner. I didn't say anything because I've had them. You won't listen to anybody.

Joey curled up in a corner and rubbed his temples. Then he told me about the shoe store.

He was with the devil, he told me, and they went to the Footlocker in the Walt Whitman Mall. He said his mother was there, Joey's, not the devil's, but she couldn't see him because she was living and he was a dead mind. She was sitting on a Footlocker bench, trying on sandals. The devil lead Joey through a door at the back of the Footlocker to a staircase. Joey climbed down the stairs, into a cave as big as the mall. Halfway down the steps something scared him, so he turned back. But the door shut.

The stairs hung off wet, solid rock, with the friggin Footlocker door at the top shut and locked. Then he sees all these normal looking people down there, like men wearing suits or jeans, and women in dresses, walking around the cave. They carried brown paper bags in their hands. All along the cave walls were other doors, and the normal-looking people went in and out of them with paper bags. Joey said he knew, the devil didn't tell him or anything, he *knew* those doors went into living people's minds. The people in the cave were demons doing the devil's work. He said it was like a job or something, and one day he'd carry a paper bag and haunt someone's mind. He said haunting was the funnest job he could think of.

Joey didn't know what was in the paper bags, though. He figured they were filled with things to make people crazy, like tools or nightmares. I guessed there were memories in them, which the normal looking people stole so the devil could watch them the way we watch television.

"Weren't you scared you'd be dead forever down there, Joey," I asked.

"I won't die until I want to. I've lived enough lives," he told me.

The stairs ended twelve feet above the cave's floor and if he jumped off he couldn't get back up. That's how he would die permanently, he told me. One day he'd have a heart attack, or a car would hit him. The devil would take him to the Footlocker and he'd jump off the stairs and become a demon in some crazy person's mind.

I must've been talking for fifteen minutes. The counselors gave me looks and I felt all a sudden extremely embarrassed.

"This was just dreams. Some people remember them, some don't," Pasqual said.

"They weren't dreams, Pasqual. I know. Joey told me."

"Okay," he cut me off. "If your mind goes out of your body," he said, pointing his finger at me, "you are saying the mind is distinct from the brain. But if a mind goes out of a body and it has experiences, how can it come back into the brain and deliver the experiences in the form of memory. You know? It is the brain that holds memory."

"I know that," I told him. He thought I didn't know about my brains. "But your mind does whatever the hell it wants."

"No. Your mind emerges from your brain." Like I said, he's a writer so he was a genius with words and he had a different way of telling about things. Not different, unique. He told me that my brain isn't what I think it is, like it's not a lump of memories and commands. He said it was a casserole of individual organs, each evolved for a billion years to do different things. One organ balances you when you walk, one keeps your heart beating. One organ writes your speech, another scans for danger. This organ feels the blister on your foot, and that one makes you want to beat up some pussy. He told me each brain organ plays a note and all the organs are connected by a trillion wires. Then he told me that my mind, all it is, he said, is the *sound* the organs make resonating on wires.

"Brains exist without a mind," he said. "But minds do not exist without a brain."

Theo's knife handle was a rusty gold color and curved like a Tiger's tooth. The short blade was thin and dark against the raw branch. Pink slivers curled away from its edge. I sat quietly for a while just watching Theo carve the branch. I felt very strange. Demaris sat next to me and rubbed my back.

Every time I turned my head the scenery, like the rocks, the glowing logs, the faces around the fire, came unstuck. No matter how far I turned, the rocks and things would follow for a quarter second then dart back where they belonged.

Everyone started laughing. I didn't though. Nothing was funny. First of all, my mouth didn't fit on my face. If I tried to talk, about god or whatever, my mouth liked to fall off. My tongue felt like a banana. It stuck to my lips and my lips stuck to my teeth. Oil dripped out of my skin. I wiped at my forehead to sponge it up with my sleeve. I was leaking or melting or something, I was oozing out of my pulp. I wanted to run into the darkness.

The whole time we talked Pasqual rolled cigarettes. He had two sandwich bags filled with tobacco, one big one with shredded wheat looking tobacco and another smaller one with clumpy, green tobacco. "Is that paper," I asked while he was rolling. You know when a newspaper is in the wet street and it's been run over by a thousand cars? The next day when it's dry it gets clumpy. That's how the tobacco in the smaller bag looked, like clumps of old paper. He mixed the tobaccos together. We kept passing the cigarettes around instead of smoking one apiece. It was a Canadian thing, I guess.

"What is interesting from your story," Pasqual said, "is that Joey gets convinced about god through personal experience. Revelation is, to me, not a convincing argument. If someone was telling me they saw ... what's the elephant with the big ears? He can fly?"

"Dumbo," Adam said.

"If someone tells me they see Dumbo," Pasqual said, "not in a cartoon but flying in the air, I would think the same as when they tell me god revealed himself. They are insane."

Adam laughed. Hard. He laughed so hard he choked. Man, that pissed me off.

"But your friend's revelation did not come from god, but from the devil. In the *mall*!" Pasqual said more to Adam than to me. "This is at least entertaining, no?"

"I didn't say anything about god," I said.

"The devil does not imply him?" Pasqual asked.

I didn't care if they believed in god. But if they didn't believe what happened to Joey, what I saw with my own eyes, that bothered me. I mean if it happened it happened. Why would I lie?

Theo finished carving the branch. He held it over the fire, turning it slowly, taking it out and spinning it around, grabbing the hot end and whispering "hothothot" then roasting the other side.

"Well anyway, you're right, Pasqual," I finally said. "The Dumbo people are insane. The bag men did it."

They all laughed again. Assholes!

The fire whistled and popped. Heat flew at my face. All around us clumps of darkness clung to the trees. Pasqual kept talking about god with Adam. They called the bible fairy tales and said the words naïve and gullible about fifty times, taking turns describing the world in a very ugly way. Everyone was an idiot except for them. And it was all god's fault.

"What about Joey's mom," I interrupted. It was rude but I was angry and there was something I remembered about the story I had to tell them.

"What about what," Adam asked.

"That time Joey went to the cave in the mall and all that and saw his mother in the Footlocker."

"Okay."

"We were in his house watching TV. Joey's mother left us alone. She was always getting her nails polished or buying groceries. Soon as she was gone me and Joey went to our fort." I didn't tell them we went there to whack off. That part didn't matter. We did that first. Then we passed each other out.

"He told me he saw his mom in the Footlocker and all the doors and brown bags, like I told you about. He passed me out after that but he didn't want to play it himself anymore. He passed me out twice before I got the headache and stopped.

"We went back to playing video games and a little later his mom came home. She made us stop playing because she'd been gone for a long time and she figured that's all we'd been doing. Joey told her no, we oiled his bike chain and pedals. We had oiled them, too, but the day before. Then he goes, 'All you did was get your nails done. That's no better than playing video games.' Mrs. Nailati, she's Joey's mother, she goes, 'I went to Macintosh Farm to get tomatoes for your dinner tonight, Joseph. They were terrible. But I got some nice basil. And I brought your brother's jacket to the cleaners. *Then* I got my nails done if it's any business of *yours*.' They kidded around with each other that way. She walked out of the room and then, listen to this, she goes, 'And I stopped at Footlocker for a pair of sandals.'"

"…"

Nobody said shit. They stared. I hate when people stare at me. Joey told me you can kill a cat by staring at it. It dies from embarrassment.

I felt funny as hell. Everyone was quiet and looking mostly at me but a little at the fire and each other. They finally shut the fuck up about god.

I don't know why I said it but I asked, "You think it's possible to die from embarrassment? Like to get embarrassed to death?"

Holy shit, did they laugh! My stomach turned to jelly.

"You're a weird little dude," Adam said.

"Oh, don't say that. I like weird," Demaris said. "Weird is good."

"Nah. Weird is good. You're a good little dude, Larry," Adam said.

"Good little dude," Pasqual said.

They all kind of chanted it. "Good little dude. Good little dude," and laughed about it. Even Theo did.

Gnats whipped around our faces. Pasqual reckoned they should've set up the screen tent like last year but Adam disagreed. It was early in the season and he said, "I don't think that gnat'll need a net." So then they all started chanting that, too. "Gnat'll need a net, gnat'll need a net," and laughing until they fell off their seats. It was okay, though. All a sudden it was okay, them laughing about that.

Pasqual tried to bring the conversation back to god but nobody wanted to talk about him anymore. It's annoying when someone wants to talk about serious stuff for too long, trying to get you to think differently. Me and Joey never talked about anything serious. We didn't give a crap about making people think. I don't know what Pasqual would have called us. Nothing nice.

It got quiet for a bit, then Demaris told them about the talent show and that my group was a winner. She told them I'd worn her bra. When she said that Adam asked a thousand questions. I was worried they'd ask me to play my part, the girl part, to entertain them. They didn't, though. They just congratulated me.

The fire crackled, the leaves clapped, and the night seemed bigger, heavier. Pasqual and Adam, their conversation really got to me. It never occurred to me that god wasn't a real and active person. He just was, like one of Mr. Brush's constants. Without him, nothing. All a sudden, just for now, he was gone. But the sky didn't fall. And my heart beat on its own. We'd talked a lot about god that night but none of us were gathered in his name. We were regular animals, like Adam said, with a particular order of bones, the will to live, and supercharged brains. As the night squeezed in I felt closer to the counselors and Demaris than I ever had to anyone in church. Bonfires are better than sermons.

# An Untrue Story

And then everyone was tired and hungry. Adam dumped a bucket of water on the fire and stirred the ashes with a stick. I learned how put out fires during camping trips with the firehouse so I helped. I put my hand in the wet ashes to make sure it was cool underneath and wouldn't smolder and catch roots on fire. Adam told me I did a good job and we shook on it. My ashes got all over his hands. He laughed about it and wiped the ashes on our faces.

"Oh, look at our mineral masks, Demaris," Adam said in this real girly voice.

"You look like animals, not girls," Demaris said.

With the fire out it was dark, but the moon was pretty high and the short trees spread apart enough for light to come through, goopy and soft.

I'd never been so hungry in my life. All I wanted was ice cream. Usually when I get very hungry I want macaroni and cheese with peas and black beans and cayenne pepper in it. All I could think about now was a banana split with whipped cream and hot fudge and maybe Reese's Pieces on top. Theo said he'd go down to the Center. They never locked the doors. He'd bring back food and we all thought that was the best idea anybody ever had, ever. I told Demaris how badly I wanted ice cream. She said they had some in the counselor's cabin.

We walked that skinny trail again. Each of us fell at least twice. Demaris held my hand at the spot where the roots and rocks and darkness were thickest. Then we came to the fork in the path. The moon was a little lower in the sky but still bright. We could see everything. Theo started towards the Center. The rest of us walked as quietly as we could to the cabin where the counselors stayed.

The cabin had nothing in common with our breadboxes. The counselors' cabin was stone and wood. Lacquered beams crossed the ceiling and there was a fireplace big enough to stand in. The mullioned windows had a hundred pains in them, some with cracked glass, some with a funny texture, and there were curved iron bars outside them. The wood floors were creaky wide planks. There were double doors way in the back near the bedrooms where the rest of the counselors slept.

"This used to be the servants' quarters. The big house got destroyed in a fire about eighty years ago. How does a brick and stone mansion get destroyed by a fire?" Adam couldn't believe it. He didn't know how quickly curtains and bed sheets and furniture go up, or how much wood there is in an old house, even if it's brick, to hold up the walls and the floors, and especially the roof. Once a roof caves, forget it, the house is gone. "The foundation's still there, near the bonfire," Adam told me. "We were sitting on it. The guy that owned it—he owned all of Springkill's property—was a copper baron. He kept his race horses in the Center. It used to be stables."

Demaris went to the kitchen. There was a big cutout in the wall with a counter top in it and you could see into the kitchen. Demaris opened the fridge and put her face in its light. "We have only vanilla, Larry," she said.

"That's okay," I said.

"And you would like whipped cream?"

"Yes."

"The story is," Adam said, "the government was paying for thousands of miles of electrical wires, all copper. Two rich fucks, both copper barons, bid on the contract. Everybody *knew* one of'm was connected to the Mafia. This is just after the Capone days. No politician wanted to look like they had any tolerance for the mob. Who do you think got the job?"

Demaris came into the room and handed me a bowl of what was *supposed* to be ice cream. It was frozen rice milk. There wasn't real whipped cream on it either, just soy cream oozing all over the bowl. I ate it, though. It wasn't too bad in the first place, plus I didn't want to hurt her feelings.

"The Springkill baron was the mafia guy," I said. "And he got the job."

"That's what you think? Even though I told you politicians were fucked if they were soft on the mob."

"The obvious answer would be the other guy got the job because he wasn't connected or whatever. But you wouldn't've asked me who I thought got it. It sounded too tricky."

"You're right. But that's not the twisted part. The copper baron with mob ties, who owned Springkill *and* got the contract for the wires, he was a senator's son. That's America. Always will be."

Demaris sat next to me on this small couch. After every bite of rice cream she asked if it was okay and told me I didn't have to eat it if I didn't want. We were sort of ignoring Adam.

"When did your father work for Grumman," Adam asked.

"For what?" I never heard of Grumman.

"Demaris said your dad built A10's. He must have worked for Grumman."

"You don't have to talk about your father anymore tonight if you don't want to," Demaris said.

I forgot I told her my dad built friggin airplanes. It was lie. See, I lie all the time! But it wasn't an untrue story. I didn't spend ten hours making it up.

I shoveled in the watery rice cream.

"My Grandfather worked for Grumman," Adam said. "They laid him off a long time ago. Before he could retire, of course, so he got almost nothing. But Demaris told me your father was still building them."

"Used to," I lied.

"But when?"

Pasqual was practically asleep. There was this big windowsill with a cushion on it and Pasqual was laying on it.

"Adam, why do you want to ask," Demaris said.

Then, all a sudden, I started this story. "My dad's pretty old," I told Adam. "Probably like your grandfather's age. I got one of those old fathers who have kids when they're around fifty. My mom's way younger. She was a beauty queen, Miss Long Island, actually. She's my dad's third wife. Married him after she graduated high school. My dad used to own a car repair garage and he only fixed Porsches and cars like that, and he worked at Grumman, too, because he was such a good mechanic. They laid him off I don't even know when because he's always so busy I didn't really see him." Not a word of it was true. But it felt like I'd told Adam to go fuck himself.

And *that* was the truth.

I wished Joey was with me. I mean, Demaris was comforting. She rubbed my back and held my hand, and my pin bent against my zipper. But I kept feeling very, very nervous. I tried to think up excuses to leave while everyone waited for Theo to come back with the food.

When Theo finally banged his way into the cabin, all he had was vegetables and a bowl of hummus that looked like mud. I ate it anyway. I was very hungry.

I kept checking the wall clock. It felt like an hour passed but when I looked it was two minutes later. My head felt funny as hell, like when I passed out too many times. I wanted a cigarette badly.

Me and Demaris sat on this chair that was really for one person, cracking jokes only we understood. Demaris said, "This chair is so small. Should we pull the couches together?" And I said, "I might drop my tit on the floor." We kept making jokes and laughing. We didn't tell anyone what we saw, about Mrs. Ackerly. Adam pretended to ignore us, but he watched, I could tell.

"Oh, I forgot. I was telling you a story," Adam quit being a creepster to finish his story. "The copper baron's supply trucks kept getting held up. His drivers were dragged from their trucks and beaten. The trucks were burned or they just, what, disappeared. Then the baron starts getting threatening letters in the mail. Obviously from the other baron's goons."

Goons. What a cornball.

"He's in the mountains. Up here in the woods. There's no one around. No cops. He has a wife and children. The letters don't just threaten him, but his staff, too, everybody. His drivers got beat up, remember, so he had to take it seriously. And yeah so that's why we have these bars on the windows. But guess what?"

"What," I said, pretty disinterested, though. I wished he'd stop talking and give me a smoke.

"Those bars trapped him inside when arsonists burned his house down."

"Jesus," I said. "He died?"

"Yep." Adam leaned back in his chair and stared at me. "Him and his whole family."

"Holy shit," I said. Adam creeped me out completely.

"Stop it, Adam," Theo said. "Don't joke with him like that. He'll tell the whole camp and they'll start rumors the place is haunted."

"Paper bag men," Adam said, and screamed with laughter. Asshole!

"Well, perhaps some rumors are better than others," Theo said.

"So he didn't get killed?" I asked.

"No," Theo's face got all painful looking. "This was only one of his homes. He wasn't here when it burned down. He willed the estate I think to his daughter on condition that if she left it, it would go to the state. She lived where Demaris's father is, in the cottage over there. She died in the 80's. Now it's a nature preserve. It's Springkill."

The vegetables crunched in my teeth. I know you can always hear your food being chewed but you don't notice it because you're used to it. You stop listening, and watch TV or talk. Nobody was saying anything. There wasn't any music playing. Other counselors were sleeping. It was dead silent. All you heard were four mouths chomping. They made other noises too, groaning, saying, "Uh, so good," and soon I wasn't eating anymore just listening instead.

We learned about the digestive system in class, how the alimentary canal is basically a long tube curling through your body, squeezed by muscles, with glands hanging off it squirting enzymes. Food goes into your mouth opening and gets mashed into soft, shapeless mush. Then it goes through your tubes and gets squirted by glands until it comes to another opening, your asshole.

Whatever was wrong with my mind that night, my brain organs or whatever, started mixing things up. There was no difference between my mouth and my asshole, as far as my alimentary canal was concerned. They were two ends of the same tube. And I felt as uncomfortable eating broccoli as if I was shitting on the floor in front of them.

"Adam. Hey, can I get a cigarette," I finally asked. I had to get out of that room. "A real one, from your pack?"

He took his time answering me. He was in love with the vegetables. Finally he said, "Sure bud," with a mouthful of cauliflower. He slipped a smoke from its box. "You haf'ta smoke outside. Be careful. Don't let anyone see you. And don't burn the forest down."

# Haunted Tongue

Outside, I started feeling better. Actually, I felt so good I couldn't go back into the cabin. It's like when you get out of a cold pool and warm up in the hot sun. I had that bullet in my breast pocket. I slipped the cigarette next to it and walked down the path some. I wasn't sure what to do next, so I stood there watching the moon. What I wanted to do was lie down in the dirt and close my eyes. I got all the way down on my hands and one knee.

"Boo!" Demaris poked me and startled the hell out of me. That's something Ashley would've done.

"Fuck," I sort of shouted.

"Shush, that's my dad's cabin," she pointed. "Where are you going?"

"I was thinking I'd go back. I'm sorta tired. I feel weird, too. I might'a caught Ben's cold or something." I was kneeling in the dirt looking up at her. Then I wondered, "Why do you stay in the cabin with us instead of here, with your dad?"

There's something girls do that drives me nuts. It makes almost any girl look pretty. They cross their legs at the ankles and stand up on their toes. Demaris did it. She put her hands behind her back, too, and stuck her neck out. She stretched out all long and the moonlight turned her skin white and her hair black-red. I'd never seen anyone so beautiful. I've forgotten many things from that night because of how strange I felt. My dad had a paper bag, he was hunting down my door, and I didn't know it yet. But I can still see Demaris standing against the yellow and black sky. It's like a picture pinned to a wall.

I remember Demaris telling me, after I got up from my knees and brushed my pants off, that she'd been staying in her father's cabin since she moved from Colombia two years earlier, when she was fifteen. "Two years ago," I said, too loud. I'm no math whiz but that made her seventeen years old. "Why'd you tell me you were my age?"

"I never said that. You assumed."

Then I figured her father was an alcoholic, was why she didn't sleep in his cabin. Maybe he abused her. Maybe he touched her. Jesus. I didn't want to know anymore and I was sorry I asked. She saw I was upset. You can always tell with me.

"My father caught me sneaking out of the cabin last month, that's all." She explained.

"So he makes you stay with the students?"

"Yes. When I snuck out, he caught me with Adam. Do you understand?"

I understood, the Springkill rumors were true.

"He wanted to keep me far from the counselor's cabin so he put me with the children as punishment." Then she did the thing again with her crossed ankles and her body stretched long. She was way up on her toes and I noticed for the first time that, even when she got off her toes, she was taller than me. Her face was two inches from mine. Her chin was level with my nose. She kissed my forehead. "You're not a child anymore, though."

"I don't know what I am," I said. Dumb, I know. I wish I hadn't said it but what can you do?

She rubbed my cheek. "You have ashes on your face," she said. I forgot about that. I must have looked deranged. She kissed me anyway, mouth open.

Usually when I kissed a girl, like Ashley for example, I put my tongue in her mouth. That's what a boy does. He puts it in. Demaris stuck her tongue in *my* mouth, which was dry and hot. Her tongue was wet and cool.

Every July, Huntington Manor Fire Department has a fair. There's a cascade slide, a pony carrousel, and a Ferris wheel for little kids. For older kids there's a Gravitron. I can only ride the Gravitron twice before I want to puke. There's a roller coaster, too. It doesn't go upside down or corkscrew, or even go very fast. But it goes backwards, that's the thrill. There's a slingshot they strap you in and launch you about a hundred miles an hour. It's scary as hell. The girls scream like they're being murdered.

There are game booths, too, skill tests. You can shoot water guns into a plastic clown's mouth until a balloon growing out of its head pops. Whoever pops a clown's head first wins a prize, like a pom-poms or vampire fangs. There're two machines to test your strength, the High Striker sledge hammer game, and the Big Punch boxing arcade. There's always a group of guys at those machines wearing tight shirts, and they have tattoos and clean sneakers, and their heads are shaved up the sides. It's pretty much like any other fair; cotton candy, fried dough, sausage and peppers, the sounds of games and rides, and some asshole making fun of people from the Dunk Tank. Cops and firemen are everywhere. I know them all.

All the adults do is play cards and roulette, or sit in the beer tent all friggin day. I got on the rides for free because the woman selling tickets from the little hut was Elsa Lundgren, the Fire Chief's wife. She worked the books at Don's office with my mom.

There's this one game called The Pyramid. Goldfish bowls are piled about ten feet high. You paid a dollar for three ping-pong balls. The game was tossing balls into the bowls. The ground was muddy from the booth man walking around the pyramid in his rubber boots picking up ping-pong balls and mixing the splashed water and spilled beer with the dirt. If you landed a ball inside a bowl you won a goldfish. The booth man handed you a long plastic bag, like what your newspaper delivers in, with a fish darting around the water inside. They didn't give you a bowl. You had to buy one at the pet store. You'd see people walking around the fair with their water bags, going on rides with them, whisking down the humpy slide on a burlap sack. Someone always broke one open. Nearby people got down on their knees to scoop up the fish and run to the pyramid booth with their hands cupped over one another, or sometimes with the fish still inside the torn dripping bag.

There were a hundred goldfish leftover when the fair ended. I took a couple home every year. They never lived longer than a week. I tried them in sunlight, in shade, feeding them more or less. They always died.

The firemen kept the fish in a copper tank. Fair mornings they'd scoop out a few dozen and plop them in bags, then pile them inside a beer cooler and wheel it out to the game booth.

There were EMTs at the fair waiting for someone to fall off a ride, or to drink too much, which was more likely. I stayed morning to night, riding, eating, and bringing my dad and other firemen Coors Light in red cups. I was the only kid allowed in the beer tent. I got dollar tips. At the end of the day I was tired. One of the EMT's, Gil, let me sleep in the back of the ambulance while the rides shut down and the firemen swept and cleaned the grills and shuttered the booths. The only time I ever could fall asleep quickly was in the back of an ambulance in the firehouse garage.

One fair night, I woke up in the back of an ambulance. There was no one around but I could hear noises coming from the big hall where they had holiday parties and weddings. I kept following the noise until I came to the game room. My dad and some firemen were in there. The room was white with smoke. There was a bar on one side with Coors Light on tap. I'd been in that game room about a thousand times with my sister and Steven Lundgren Jr. when the firemen got together for birthday parties, or for the 4th of July or something, and with a million other kids, too. But it never looked like this. I used to think the game room was ours, like it was made for the firemen's children because parents were never in there, just kids.

Now they were smoking cigars and cigarettes and drinking beer from glass mugs. I stood in the doorway.

"Where'd the Doritos go? We got'ny more chips?" Andy was a rookie then. Now he's the best player on Manor's softball team. We call him Awesome Andy.

Chief Lundgren goes, "Otis, show Andy where the snacks are at."

Then Otis, my dad I mean, he went over to this antique copper cistern they used to carry water back in the horse and carriage days. A hunk of ash dropped from his cigarette into the water. He pulled out a goldfish with a net. "Ya hungry, hah? Here," and he shoved the goldfish at Andy. Hazing doesn't stop in eighth grade, I can tell you that. You can be a grown man and get hazed if you join the fire department. "What's'amatta, Andy? I thought you were hungry."

"You fuckin kidding me? C'mon, I just got done stackin the chairs and puttin'm away and now you're gonna pull this shit?"

"You don't like sushi?"

"I don't eat eyes and assholes," Andy said.

My dad pinched the fish's tail. It didn't shake or wiggle. You expect a fish to wiggle like crazy when you grab it by the tail but goldfish just dangle, mostly. He dropped it into his mouth and swallowed it whole. "They're not too filling. You gotta eat about twenty of'm."

"Otis, you dumb bastard," Steven said. "You're supposed to make *him* eat it."

"Why waste good food on this prick? Let him eat Doritos, ha ha ha. Hey Lou. Lou, how many'd I eat last year? Twenty-five?"

"I think it was more like twelve, Otis."

"You fat son of a bitch. It was twenty at least." He scooped another fish out of the tank. He dropped it in his beer and drank it all down. Then he put his fist on his pin. "They keep ya like a rock," he said.

"No wonder Fran looks miserable the rest of the year," someone said from the corner. I couldn't see.

"Doesn't matter, Sutkevik. When it don't get hard I turn her upside down and dip it in."

"The keg's finished," one of the men said from behind the bar.

"Hey An," Chief Lundgren called. "Ah, Andy boy. Looks like we got another job for ya, kid. The keg."

"Yes, Chief."

"Take it any way you can get it, Otis," said a red and grey fireman from a hundred years ago. He bit a cigar with his flat teeth. "I haven't had it with the wife in thirty years. Her cunt's healed over." Man they laughed, and repeated it, too. *Her cunt's healed over hahaha.* They laughed like madmen.

That's when my dad saw me. "What'a you doing here? Hah? Downstairs. Where's your mother? Tell her to take you home and come back'n get me later."

There were two goldfish in a bowl on my bedroom windowsill I got the day before. Tricky and Goldie. It was hard to choose which one to eat and whether I should chew or just swallow it. In the end I chose Goldie. First of all, it was the smaller fish, and, second, it was easier to catch than Tricky. When you eat a goldfish you can forget about chewing it. They don't shake much when you hold them by the tail, but put one in your mouth and they go crazy. They're wet and cold but not slimy. They're easy to swallow with a little water. They shoot straight down. You don't feel them swimming around in your guts, though. I thought I'd feel them swim.

All those things, those memories, lived in my mind, inside their own room.

When Demaris pushed her tongue into my mouth it was cool and wet. It flicked and turned, rough on one side, smooth on the other. It felt like old Goldie the goldfish. My father was in the room. He had his brown bag and now Demaris's tongue was a goldfish. It didn't matter that it must be a tongue. It wasn't a tongue but a little fish struggling past my lips.

I pulled away from her. I did it rude as hell, too, with a push. The night before, I'd whacked off thinking about Demaris, but on that moonlit path her kiss nearly sent me screaming into the night. She grabbed me as I turned. "Where are you going? I'm sorry," she said.

"It's alright. Seriously. I have to go."

"You have to go," she repeated. "You have to go?" I was ten feet from her and walking fast. "Larry," she called out as I turned the first corner towards camp. "Wait." Her voice flew down the trail. I saw it go like a shock wave. I ran. The path was narrow as your shoelace, and up ahead, ten feet, it disappeared beneath the heel of an enormous night that had suddenly crouched upon me.

# Shot Dog Music

And then I didn't know which way to go. The path forked and turned. There were no colored arrows. No bent branches pointing back. The moon was low. The forest was a black, furry mass. I could almost feel it on my skin. When I looked it was there! Not the furry mass but sapling leaves, or a China jute's velvet on my arm. And I jumped as if was my father's hand.

I walked slowly so I wouldn't trip. My eyes were so wide open they stung. I wouldn't call it seeing, it was more like feeling my way through the darkness with my eyes. My feet crunched on the path. I couldn't hear anything else. I stopped to listen. No wind, just my breath, which I held because it scared me. I walked a few steps and tripped on a rock. "Motherfucker," I said. That was my father. He found the organ that made me speak. He was getting the hang of haunting, or hunting as Pasqual would say, and I wondered if he could turn me crazy.

I sat on a boulder and took the cigarette from my shirt pocket. Then I struck a match. The leaves above me swirled into darkness. I lit the cigarette and had a long drag and started to feel better. I took the bullet out of my pocket and drew on my thigh with it. Nothing specific, just patterns. I lit matches and looked up at the leaves and pretended I was under water and that the leaves were fish or something. I kept lighting matches and standing up and spinning around under the leaves. What happened though, from spinning, I forgot which direction I was going.

The cigarette really calmed me down. Even though I was lost and all, I didn't feel very scared anymore. That's something, at least, not being afraid for a while.

I couldn't stop thinking about my dad. What worried me though, I knew he was looking for me. He was in the cave, opening doors, testing the organs. Then I figured out what it was, like why I'd been feeling so strange all night and how my dad found the right door. It was the bullet. He cursed it in the kitchen the day he put it on top of the fridge. He marked it with his death.

I was nearly finished with the cigarette and wished for another. I didn't want to smoke, really, I just didn't want to be finished with one. There's something sad about the end of a cigarette.

I sipped the last drag, dropped the filter and stamped it with my toe. Then what I did, I threw the bullet as hard as I could. "Fuck you!" I screamed. I nearly chucked my arm off my shoulder.

The bullet hit a rock I guess, because there was a tremendous bang and a flash so quick and bright it was like lightning through the trees. I felt a shock, then the noise echoed around the mountain. All a sudden I thought of Ashley and Steven. I could smell horse shit and I felt horribly impatient.

He was close to something.

A drop of light flicked around in the trees up the path, then it steadied. It shined bright onto the path. I kept still and quiet, trying to shrink into the darkness. "Larry," I heard, and then the branches opened.

I don't expect anyone to believe this. I don't even believe it anymore, I guess, even though I saw it, even though I *know* it happened. Maybe Pasqual was right, personal experiences are a losing argument. But when those hellish looking dogs crept onto the trail, a dozen at least, twice the size of Fat City's, sniffing around then one by one spotting me, staring down their snouts with recognition burning in their eyes, their lips curling over their teeth, nostrils flared, it was as real to me as the pack in my own driveway.

I bolted! Full speed in three steps.

It was all downhill. My legs couldn't keep up with my fear. My eyes singed. My heart thumped in my throat. The forest was dense and blurred, and the harder I ran the more dense it became, until the trees were solid rock, oily, and lined with doors. Men in suits. Women in skirts, hair pulled back into buns. A paper bag in every hand. "Outta the way!" I barreled through them. Hot breath on my neck. I saw a hole in the rock wall. A hundred feet ahead. A pale light gushing.

The trail, curled like a flame, opened into the field. The Center's peak leaned my way. I sprinted for it.

"You can't touch me now," I yelled. "You got no belts. No dogs. No bullets. Motherfucking motherfucker! Motherfucking motherFUCK-ER!" I screamed like a wild man.

# And Then The End

It wasn't morning yet but the night was over. My stomach hurt. I snuck up to the cabin with my hand on my gut. I don't remember anything hard or unordinary there, just pain. A few stars pricked the sky. It was very quiet. The birds weren't even awake.

I went into the cabin as quietly as I could. I wasn't worried about waking anyone, or about Brush and Ackerly catching me, I was just quiet and out of breath. I figured I'd go to my room and lie on the bunk until everyone woke up. My problem was the ashes on my face.

Then I remembered the toilet paper the girls used to stuff my bra. I tore into a block of Marcol Standard 2-Ply Toilet Paper in the closet. When I pulled out a roll he was there! Not really there, like in the closet, but my father was in a room with Ashley, Megan, Alicia and Demaris, picking at the remembered make up, holding the bra I wore, examining the silk blouse I'd unbuttoned all sexy and I tried hard not to think about it. I forced the firehouse up front, and Ashley too, my fight with Joey, that sad eagle over the cliff, anything I wanted to forget and didn't need to care about, whatever would fill his bag and make him leave me alone because I did not want him to see it. But when you dress up, those memories share a room and he saw: I am seven years old, wearing red lipstick, hair in a French braid, scalp burning under barrettes. My sister and Sexy Lexy, and my mother, too, are smiling. I could cry from embarrassment, but I do not. He watches me massage my bent and hairless pin. My mother calls me a lovely little girl. He turns his face to me.

I pushed my fist into my belly. Pressed on the pain. My fingers got wet and sticky. The pain was so strong it made my ears ring. The shirt's fabric was squishy and soft, like a fruit too ripe, even rotten, with a hard pit that slipped into my hand.

I'd been shot! Not shot, it was just a ricochet. But the empty shell sat in my palm. Some skin flapped open and red blotches formed around the hole where blood trickled from.

I opened the skin flap and pinned it with a finger. Blood poured from the wound. I scraped the shell against the trickle to fill it and splattered blood against the wall. Over and over, I filled the shell and splattered the walls. The blood ran faster. It hit the plastic toilet paper wrapping. I made X's on the door.

The bleeding slowed. Just a drop rose to the surface, all shiny, balancing on a black glob of jelly at the wound's edge.

I cleaned the casing with my shirt and put it on the shelf beside the starter fluid bottles.

If you could only imagine the firemen's bonfires when we went camping! You couldn't see over it. It's taller than a tool shed if the shed were burning, and so big around, after dinner in the darkness, I can't find Steven or Ashley. I walk around, tripping over people laid out on towels, on beach chairs and benches. I slip between coolers, around piles of logs ready to get thrown onto the fire along with platefuls of chicken bones and cheese wrappers and dirty napkins.

A person reaches out. Grabs my arm. "Where you running to, slick? C'mon over here." Firelight changes a person's face. It's hard to recognize. A face looks punched-in, knotty, and shiny as Parade Boots. "You run like a green grasshopper. Ya know that?" Elsa Lundgren, I can tell by her breath. She's been drinking screwdrivers. She pulls me onto her lap. She's wearing shorts. Her legs are sweating. "Who taught you to throw a Frisbee, huh? Who?"

"You did," I tell her.

"That's *right* I did, didn't I?"

"That's why I throw a Frisbee with my left hand even though I'm righty," I say.

"That's right. Because I taught you and I'm lefty! And you're gonna teach your kids to throw a Frisbee left handed. Ah ha ha ha!" I can see her black fillings and her throat squeezing with laughter.

The fire's best when the old couples go to bed. The radio's turned down. You hear the fire crackling and whistling and steam hissing. You lie around watching the yellow tracers wiggle into the sky.

I don't sleep in late on camping trips. I wake up earlier than almost anyone because I have to pee. I crawl over my sister if she's there and past my mother and unzip the tent flap a little and crawl out from under it while the stones and pieces of sticks under the tent stab my knees. The ground is cold on my bare feet and the chilly air seeps through my clothes. The wet grass and weeds stick between my toes as I walk behind a tree. The only person who's up before me is my dad. After you pee against a tree in the cool morning and you've crawled over the hard ground and got your feet all dirty, you can't go back to sleep.

The fire's heart glows in the pit, crusted with charcoal. A breeze twists in the heat and breathes ash. Me and dad sit on beach chairs near the warm pit, adding wood wedges and working up the flames.

He always brought a coffee maker with him. He fills the bottom cone with water and the top cone with coffee grinds then screws the parts together and sticks it in with the hot clinkers. In five minutes the coffee maker hisses and spits. My dad grabs the coffee maker from the flames with his bare hands. He drinks his black. Mine has a ton of milk and sugar in it. We don't say a word, we just sit and look at the fire.

That's all we did together on camping trips, drink coffee in the morning.

I remembered those fires. And I really missed them. Like I knew we wouldn't go camping with the firehouse on Labor Day that year, and maybe never again. It doesn't explain what happened after I closed the closet door and snuck out of the cabin again, and ran around it, the cabin, until I was winded. I was out of my mind. Maybe it was grief, like my counselor said. I told you I'd talk about everything. But I can't explain what happened.

How often do you think of traveling? The actual movement, I mean, like switching gears, and your foot going from the gas to the brakes, and all the miles passing under the wheels? It all folds into one sleepy trance, or maybe it fills the space around the things you actually experienced and remember: the cherry Slurpy, the deer on the side of the road, dead. Or your hat catching wind and flying through the window.

That's how lighting those matches feels to me now, a dreamy memory lost in motion. I don't recall striking them, and tossing them, as I must have done, against the Striklight fluid absorbed in the cabin walls, trying to get the cabin started. I think about it hard, trying to remember. One moment I was in the closet flinging blood, then a bubble pops, and I'm facing the cabin's back wall, smelling lighter fluid fumes and burnt sulfur.

I've thought about those matches a thousand times, probably. I know I lit them, but how many? How long did I stand there, trying to get a fire started? That's miles on the road to what happened. I'll never stop trying to remember. What was I thinking, or if I was thinking anything. Was I just a passenger driven along, dozing, dreaming?

What was my intention?

Maybe it's like I said, some things just happen and it's not your decision. Nobody knows how your brain organs work, how they can make you do things. Maybe it was my father, he'd made me crazy, like Joey said, and maybe I'd trapped him in the closet with the bullet case and blood, and saw a chance to escape.

It's complicated.

"There you are!" I don't know how Demaris found me behind the cabin. She saw the wet arches on the wall and my hand working the matches near my zipper. She thought I was taking a piss I guess, and she turned around. It was still a bit dark. I pretended to zip myself up and kicked the empty Strikelite bottle under the cabin.

"We looked all over for you, me and Adam," she said over her shoulder. "We saw you on the trails and called to you but you ran. We heard you screaming." She whispered but with a lot of force.

"Shh" I told her. She seemed loud as hell.

What else is complicated is punishment.

"Are you okay?"

"I'm okay," I said. "Be quiet!" All a sudden I wanted everything to be quiet.

"I have to text Adam," she said, pulling out her phone. "I have to tell him I found you. And that you are in *bed* in your *room*."

"I'm sorry. Serious. I don't know what happened."

"What time is it? You're dirty with ashes. You have to clean up. There's a shower in the Center."

"I know it," I said.

"There are towels in the cabin closet. I'll get them."

"No," I said. The closet looked like a friggin murder scene. "I'll get a towel from my room."

"You will wake your roommates?" I loved the way she said things like a question.

"Ben's cold medicine puts him to sleep hard. Joey'll pretend to be dead rather than talk to me."

She didn't understand. She thought I was still acting funny.

"It's alright. I feel alright again, like I just woke up or something. Wait here a second."

When I went into my room Joey woke up. He sat on his bed with his back against the wall, squinting all over the place.

"Where the hell you been," he asked.

"Bathroom," I said, sitting on the bunk. My duffle bag was at my feet.

"I woke up all night," he said. "I looked for you in the bathroom, bro. You weren't there. Fuck's all over your face?"

"I'll tell you later. You mind if I tell you about it later?"

"Later's cool. What's all over your face?"

I sat on the edge of the bed. Joey leaned on his elbow. He said, "Hey man. The show was funny. You looked like a fag but it was funny."

"Thanks," I said.

"You aright," he asked again.

"Yeh. You aright," I asked.

"Yeah man."

"I'm going to take a shower."

Like in the bible it says if you take someone's eye, they can put out yours as punishment. But what if you take three eyes?

"You're gonna wake up Brush," Joey warned me.

"He won't wake up. He slept through some crazy shit last night. I'll tell you about it later. About Mrs. Ackerly. You'll see."

"What'a you been doing?"

"I'm going to the Center. Going with Demaris."

"The redhead?"

"The redhead."

"That's who you been with? Oh shit, tell me you beat that!"

"I'll tell you later."

"Are you fucking retarded? Tell me now. D'you beat that?"

"No. Jesus. It's something else. I'll tell you later."

"Aright aright, tell me later." He sort of calmed down when he heard I didn't beat it up. He pulled the covers over his head. I grabbed my duffle and left.

There was no smoke. No orange light waving. I remember clearly. It was calm, and nearly morning.

The sun hadn't risen above the mountains yet but its light had, layered in colors like some wild birthday cake. We went to the Center, around back, through a door on squeaky springs that slammed shut behind us. We were in the room with the mullioned windows and wood paneling.

"Theo's office," I said.

"No, my father's office," Demaris corrected me. "He stays here very late sometimes. He does consulting work for a company in Colombia."

"There's a bar over there."

"Are you asking for a drink?"

"No. I mean, I don't know. Sure, I guess."

I put my bag on the floor and sat on the cot. Glasses clinked.

The colors in the office looked wet, like if you touched anything it would leave a mark. Demaris's voice, coming from the corner, was deep. Not deep, saturated or something. She said, "My father will go back to Colombia after next year. I will maybe go with him. I don't know. Oops," she spilled something. "I haven't seen my mother for two years."

"Is that where she is? Colombia?"

"Yes."

"Why'd you come here? I mean, your dad works here, okay. But why'd you come here?"

"My mother. She was working for the same company as my dad, in Colombia. Making chemicals for the government to put in the cacao fields. My parents were always with bodyguards but my mother, she has a very strong head, like me. She felt like she's a prisoner. Sometimes she sneaked away to go to the market by herself, or to just walk free in the streets."

Demaris came with a glass in each hand and sat on the cot beside me. "One day, a taxi drove beside her. And the driver asked, "Do you need a ride?" The *motoristas* pay the police so they can drive foreigners around the city and charge them too much. And sometimes they pick up another man who robs the tourists. My mother she knew this, and she told the driver, in Spanish, to fuck off."

"Nice."

"Nice, well. There was another man in the car. With a machete. They took her. It's called *el paseo millionario.* They drove her to every ATM machine and forced her to take money."

"Holy shit."

"My father found her at our house, at the gate, unconscious from scopolamine, the drug kidnappers use. They cut off her finger to take her wedding ring. In her pocket, a note. 'We know you. We know your daughter,' it said. So we came to Springkill. My father will stay until I am eighteen, when I can go to University. Maybe become a citizen. But I want to go back."

"Why doesn't your mom come to America? I mean, your dad's here and maybe she could come, too."

"My parents hate this country. No offense."

No offense. I don't understand it. People from other countries, horrible places where everyone is poor and the cab drivers will kill you. They hate America, it's the worst country in the world, they say. They're jealous, I guess, but they should admit it, there are worse countries. Like with dictators killing a million people, or where you're allowed to chuck acid in a woman's face if she won't marry her cousin or something.

"You want to go back to Colombia?"

"Yes. I have no friends here. No family after my father leaves. Do you think I want to sleep with school children the rest of my life?"

"What if they kidnap you?"

She didn't answer me. "A drink," she said.

I gulped what was in the glass. Pure fire. My chest exploded. I couldn't breathe through my nose. It burned. I pretended to yawn and turned away from her to dry heave a little bit.

"Do you have your clothes to change," she asked.

I kicked my duffle bag. "Right there," I could barely say it without puking.

"This is a nice bag. I love old canvas and worn leather. It is a beautiful bag, covered with paint," Demaris said.

It was my dad's, the bag he used to carry dust masks and boots and a change of pants when he went to work. I'd never gone anywhere alone. I didn't have my own duffle. My mom packed it for me.

"You have paint on your shirt, too?" I loved the way she said things like a question. "God. Larry, you are bleeding." Her fingers fluttered around the bottom of my shirt. It was stuck to the wound. I tried not to, but I cringed. It didn't hurt really, but the sound it made tearing loose, it was just like pain. "What happened?"

I told her about the bullet. She said they heard it and wondered about the noise. They'd never heard a gunshot before. They thought it was a friggin firecracker. "Wash this carefully in the shower. After, I will bandage you."

If I took too long in the shower, my father would turn on the kitchen sink's hot water to make the shower's water cold. He tried to freeze me out. It didn't make sense though because, what I'd do, I'd turn down the cold water and the trickle coming out of the showerhead was warm again. It just made the shower last longer is all. Then he'd stand outside the bathroom door and yell at me.

All a sudden it was funny, dad thinking about me the whole time I was in the shower. That crazy old bastard Otis, thinking about me all day. What did it cost to feed me, was I making trouble in school, and what time should he go to the firehouse if he wanted to bring me along? All those miles you don't see.

Demaris found a first aid kit under the bathroom sink. She was very gentle when she cleaned me. I flexed and grunted anyway. Gentle or not it hurt like ten motherfuckers. I was only wearing a towel and I sort of shivered, sitting on the edge of the sink. I got a boner. It bulged from the towel. I didn't hide it.

"Why did you run away from me? When I kissed you? A boy never ran from me before."

"Nowhere to run, now," I said.

"Do you think I would kiss you after that?" She screwed a cap onto a bottle.

"You followed me all the way through the woods."

"Only because Adam was worried. I didn't care if you got lost forever," she said, bratty.

"Now's different. I won't run now."

"In one hour you are different? This is not possible."

I gave her this real movie style look.

"You're done," she said, kneeling, picking up band aid wrappers.

I grabbed her face, like I put both my hands on her face and pulled her fat red lips to mine. Her tongue came out cool and wet. I sucked it in. Felt the roughness on one side, the smoothness on the other. Then she pulled away, smiling, but her eyes looked wicked.

We practically ran to the cot. Jumped on it, buckled it. It slid sideways halfway across the room.

We kissed a little more. Then Demaris sat up, Indian style, and pulled off her dress. She glowed in the early sunlight oozing through the windows. Her underwear was pink cotton. Her bra was black but I could see through it. She popped it loose and leaned back on her hands. Her nipples were the same puffy color as her lips, and stuck straight out and a little upwards, like two fingertips pointing in victory.

"What," she said. I must've been looking at her funny. I'd never seen a girl naked before. Everything felt like the first time and the last time.

She uncrossed her legs, wrapped them around my waist. I started rubbing up her legs. But Demaris, she grabbed my wrists and put my hands on her tits, both of them. She pulled my towel off. Rubbed herself on my thigh. We were kissing like crazy, it must have looked like a dog fight. My hands were on her chest like I was set for pushups.

I could feel where she was wet. She left spots on my skin that cooled in the air. I wanted to see it, her pussy. So I sat up, sort've pushed her knees apart, and took a good look. The first one I'd seen for real. Up close it looked like a mouse's ear, hidden in a little lock of red hair. "Use your tongue," she said. She was salty, and tasted like the inside of my mouth when I bit my cheek, like blood's aftertaste.

Demaris pushed me onto my back, and mopped her hair down my body. Kissed around the bandage. My pin lay beside it, she could probably hear it pulse. She picked it up. I thought, "Is she going to? Is she going to!" It'd never been inside anything but my fist. And then her mouth was on it, smooth and warm and empty. I wasn't nervous. I didn't have to pull any bullshit, like rubbing her thigh for an hour. I didn't care about my pubes or anything. My pin was where it'd never been before. That changed it somehow. Made it, I don't know, its own person or something, separate from me.

Demaris sat on her knees, bounced up and down. "Hmm, hm," she giggled. Then she jumped on me. Like she pounced. Held my pin up straight, between her thighs like two fresh loaves of bread. "Should we," she said.

"Yes." I practically yelled it.

"I really want to," she said.

"Me too."

There was a sound like when she peeled the shirt off my wound. A sticky, wet sound as it went inside her.

Her hair tickled my face. She drooled into my mouth. I swallowed her spit. I sucked at her mouth, drank from the end of her tongue while she bounced on my lap.

I thought about Adam, out there looking for me while I was here, where he'd been. I thought about Joey, laying in the cabin, waiting for a story, which story was happening now and never again. I thought about my father, who I'd been told was dead, but who with every thought I gave new life, better life, like more meaningful, immortal life. And then, as I was fucking Demaris, my father seemed, I don't know, not dead but reimagined. He was a memory. He was always just a memory. He will always be a memory.

This crazy chant repeated.

Then Demaris said, "Don't cum in me."

I wasn't wearing a condom or anything. Dumb, I know. But I didn't care. I pushed her off before it happened. I rolled her onto her back and sat on my knees. My pin pointed into the cool air, all wet and drooly. I was ready to shoot my batch. What happened though, I didn't want her to know I whacked off. Seriously. If she saw me whack off, if she saw how naturally it came, how practiced it was, she'd know. I was a pro. Still, the awkwardness was there. Like a third person in the room.

It stung, same as when you hold back a piss. I grabbed it with my whole hand. No teacup. No fucking around. If nothing is shame free, if embarrassment and guilt is the price of new pleasure, I've paid. I grabbed my cock with something like anger. Not anger, pride. As if it were a slaughtered animal, a bear I'd killed and dragged home for breakfast. I whacked off furiously.

My batch spurted across the sheets. Demaris watched, curious as hell. She put her fingers in the stringy jets. She played with it a little more. Helped me finish. "It's warm," she said, pumping away. "Oh, I love it. Men are so beautiful."

She said it first. I was a man. Then a million other people said so at the funeral.

We laid on the cot awhile. It got brighter outside. I felt very good. I felt strong, clean.

Then I got up and put on my jeans. I'd never felt so good before, or even since. So it was weird when I found the belt at the bottom of the duffle bag. My mother had folded outfits. Jeans, shirts, socks and underwear, in a sequence and piled up like sandwiches. Underneath the outfit sandwiches was my dad's belt.

I didn't put it on right away, the belt. I folded it and snapped the sides together. Over and over, smack, smack. I walked around the room, snapping. Behind the desk, near the coat rack. "What are you doing," Demaris said. She had a sheet wrapped around her. "Come over here to me." She took the belt from my hands and threaded it through my jeans loops. It almost went around me twice. "To the first hole it goes, Larry," she said. "But you will grow into it."

My nose burned and my eyes stung. I didn't sob, didn't cry hard or anything. I didn't *want* to cry but that was it, the end, and there was nothing to distract me from it. The room blurred and sat inside the tears. Demaris held her arms out but those were not the kind of arms I wanted around me.

There was a pack of cigarettes on the desk. I slipped a few smokes from it, put two in my shirt pocket then lit one with a Zippo beside the pack. I sat on the desk's edge and smoked while Demaris dressed and straightened up.

"We should go back," I suggested. "They'll be up soon."

"You go," she said. "I want to cook here in the kitchen. I want to bring my father breakfast in bed."

That was the last I saw of her. We never spoke again. Never wrote or anything. I wonder about her, like if she's American now or was she kidnapped. Far as I know, she never said a word to anyone about what happened. I wonder if she hates me.

I left the Center, a cigarette in my mouth, just as they started scrambling out of the cabin. I saw them across the field. The sun was way up, and so bright you almost couldn't see the flames. All you saw was smoke, rolling black.

It sounded like some of the kids were laughing. Like it was a big joke, even fun. Others looked confused and still half asleep. Windows broke and kids spilled out, dragging the curtains with them.

What else I try to remember is if I saw anything in the smoke, a clear spot or something. Just three unordinary things.

No, it was four that died.

They promised us, the counselors we had to see, over and over all summer, that we were young and, though we'd never forget, we'd recover, like psychologically, with time.

You got used to the scars. The one's who got burned. Plastic surgery fixed them up pretty good. Like Megan, she had a balloon under her skin for a year, to stretch it, so they could cut the scar off. You almost can't see it anymore. A pale line on her jaw, that's all there is.

I talk to Rusty pretty frequent, Ashley's dad, at the deli or when I ride my bike to Station One. Last week he gave me a Huntington Manor Fire

Department hat when we were in the firehouse kitchen eating cookies and drinking coffee.

My birthday is next week. I'll be seventeen.

It's been over three years since Springkill. I think about it every day. And I wonder about those matches. Did I intend to burn the cabin down? Maybe I did, in one psychotic moment. Should I have made sure the leaves weren't smoldering after Demaris found me and snapped the world back into my head? Of course, any fireman would. So I think I'm sorry about that. But a fire was bound to break out. Even the investigators said so. "Inevitable," was the word they used in court. Inevitable. The wood was practically kindling. A tinderbox! And Springkill would've been liable anyway, like the jury decided, finally, this week. And that's the only opinion that matters.

But still I see those scars, like wax, nearly invisible. Maybe I'm the only one who notices. I think about Ashley, the three others, too. But mostly Ashley. And then I feel sorry. But it wasn't my decision. I keep saying that.

Yes, I'm sorry. Dear god, I killed them.

God forgive me please.

It wasn't my decision.

Please Lord, forgive me.

I'm sorry!

I'm so sorry!

# Acknowledgements

There are many people I would like to thank for inciting this book, which, after it was written, sat on a shelf for six years, and now I've forgotten how it started. Then Marley Rizzuti found a dusty manuscript lodged pathetically between great books, read it without permission, and convinced me that she loved it. LOVED IT! And that I had to DO something with it, and stop talking. Marley, here it is, as you insisted. Chris Campanioni, thank you, too. I've trusted your feedback and relied on your encouragement since the first short story I sent you, for the most part because you generously compared its voice to Selby and Sartre, and I've continued to chase that inordinate praise ever since. And, of course, if we're talking integral individuals who are materially responsible for bringing this book to bare, I offer my sincerest thanks and praise to my publishers, John Gosslee and Andrew Sullivan. Without their madness and dedication to written English, *A Diet of Worms* would remain lodged and dusty. Rockwell Harwood, thank you for your vision, for letting me see surprising things. And to my friends. I don't have many, but if we've spoken over the past year something you've said embedded in these pages. You'll see.

# About the Author

Erik Rasmussen is the Editor-In-Chief of *At Large* magazine, and the former Deputy Editor at *Man Of The World.* His articles, essays, interviews and photographs have appeared in numerous magazines and websites. He's written for Lexus, J.Crew, Hermes, Glenfiddich, Santoni, Zegna, and other brands. His only literary award was a grant to Long Island's prestigious Lutheran High School for an essay about his father, "My Unsung Hero" — a true story with a false premise, and how he learned fiction's meaning and value. *A Diet Of Worms* is his first novel.

CPSIA information can be obtained
at www.ICGtesting.com
Printed in the USA
FFOW04n0526200218
45145858-45629FF